DEADLY NATURE

Deadly Nature

HARDIMAN SCOTT

THE BODLEY HEAD
LONDON

DEDICATION
For Jimmie and Mary

British Library Cataloguing
in Publication Data
Scott, Hardiman
Deadly Nature
I. Title
823'.914[F]   PR6037.C925
ISBN 0 370 30853 0

© Hardiman Scott 1985
Printed in Great Britain for
The Bodley Head Ltd
9 Bow Street, London, WC2E 7AL
by
St Edmundsbury Press
Bury St Edmunds, Suffolk

Set in Linotron Plantin by
Rowland Phototypesetting Ltd
Bury St Edmunds, Suffolk
First published 1985

No matter how high the aims predicated by terrorists
(and often there are no such justifications) their activities
are always criminal, always destructive, throwing human
kind back to a time of lawlessness and chaos, provoking
(perhaps with the help of the secret services of foreign
governments) internal and international complications,
contradicting the goals of peace and progress . . . I hope
that people all over the world will understand the deadly
nature of terrorism whatever its goals and will deprive
them of any kind of support, even the most passive, and
surround them with a wall of condemnation.

— ANDREI SAKHAROV,
Washington Post, 9 March 1980

Acknowledgements

Many people have helped the author with information and advice, and he would like especially to thank John Barnett, Leslie Bear, Squadron-Leader John Bloomfield, Jimmie, Mary and Annie Bullen, John Cryer, Roy Farndon and colleagues, Captain Barry Hawgood, Richard Jackson, Walter C. Patterson, H. Russell Ross, the Chief Constable and officers of Suffolk County Constabulary, and alphabetically last but by no means least, Christopher Wain.

1

The man crouched in the shelter of the hedge. He stared at the point where the road crossed the culvert almost a quarter of a mile ahead. He could see clearly through a gap in the foliage, but binoculars were slung round his neck, just to make sure there was no mistake. He did not make mistakes. That was why his price was high. On the grass beside him was a small keyboard the size of a pocket calculator.

He felt neither excitement nor tension; only pride in his professionalism. It was a job, an assignment, and he'd been picked for it because he was the best, and had been paid accordingly, in advance.

Beneath the boiler suit his clothing was expensive and well cut. He couldn't abide sloppiness or untidiness. He must be as smart in his appearance as in his work. Those groups and brigades, and so-called armies, sincere but slovenly, earned only his contempt. He partly shared their idealism, but even that was wearing a bit thin. He had found instead his own justification.

He looked around, quickly but calmly checking the landscape. His practised eyes immediately took in the whole stretch of parkland. A large copse suggested that perhaps once the whole area had been woodland. Otherwise it had probably changed very little in several centuries. It remained dotted with trees and, taller than anything else in the whole landscape and dominating the entire pasture, was one majestic Wellingtonia. In the distance were the smudged black-and-white shapes of grazing Friesians.

On the far side of the park were a few large houses, but with the thickness of summer foliage there was really no chance that he would be seen, not even if someone was wandering along the far boundary with binoculars.

He glanced at his watch. It was twenty-five minutes past

7

twelve. The car carrying Hans von Erbacher, one of West Germany's leading industrialists, was due within the next five minutes.

Andover has a number of industrial estates, and the advanced electronics factory which the industrialist was visiting was fortunately on one of the smaller of these. It was approached along a road that, on one side, was conveniently bounded by hedgerows and rolling parkland.

Even if the Mercedes had tinted glass, obscuring a sight of the passenger in the back seat, the man in the hedgerow would still be able to use his binoculars to confirm the number plate.

He had fixed the device beneath the culvert the previous night, and had checked its position only half an hour ago. There were unlikely to be police cars or any form of escort for von Erbacher. It was an informal occasion. The man knew that much, but he had no idea of the real purpose of the visit. Had he known this he might even have declined the job and the substantial fee he had been paid. He might have. On the other hand, he enjoyed the luxuries that money brought him. Life was too short to be troubled by an uneasy conscience.

The throaty noise of a motor cycle cut through the persistent sound of blackbirds and thrushes which filled the hedgerows around him. A couple of cars followed. A magpie flapped up from the grass twenty yards ahead. 'One for sorrow,' he muttered to himself. It was another three minutes before he saw a large dark blue Mercedes approaching. Keeping himself hidden, he focused his binoculars on the number plate of the car. It was von Erbacher all right.

The man turned, aiming the glasses through the gap in the hedge to command a view of the culvert ahead. His right hand was poised over the miniature transmitter on the grass. Immediately the Mercedes reached the culvert, his forefinger pressed a key. There was an instantaneous explosion. Bits of the car flew in all directions. The main passenger compartment was wrenched into a twist of metal and hurled to the side of the road.

The man took from the pocket of his boiler suit a piece of paper. On it was printed the image of a large, brightly coloured eye, and he had cut it from a magazine a few days previously. Carefully he skewered it to a thorn in the hedge-row. Then, without a trace of nerves, he slipped out of his overalls and tucked them under his arm, pocketed the transmitter, and began walking back along the hedge to the other side of the park. In the adjacent lane he had left a blue Vauxhall Astra which he had hired the previous day from Munro's in the Newbury Road.

Hammond Acton was thirty-two, and had opened his electronics factory no more than five years ago. Admittedly, his father, the distinguished architect Geoffrey Acton—whose love of cricket explained his son's first name—had provided some financial backing, and there had been substantial help from a shrewd bank, but it was Hammond's own drive and enthusiasm which, within three years, had seen the loans paid off and the firm heading for phenomenal success. From the start, Hammond had offered high rewards for the best design brains in the business. That, too, had paid off. His company's success, particularly in the export market, was the reason for today's visit by the government's Trade Minister, the Right Honourable Brian Thomason. It was also why they were now both awaiting the arrival for lunch of the West German industrialist, Hans von Erbacher.

The Minister had toured the factory accompanied by Hammond and his personal assistant, Gillian Ward—a tall, willowy young woman of striking appearance, her dark hair contrasting with bright blue eyes that Mr Thomason found both attractive and disconcerting. He had listened while Hammond and Miss Ward had together explained to him the advanced computerized guidance system which was one of the firm's latest achievements. Hammond claimed that it was well ahead of any other guidance system produced anywhere, including the United States.

'And it can be used for—?' The Minister raised his eyebrows questioningly.

'For almost anything,' said Hammond, 'from transport for a disabled person to the guidance mechanism of a nuclear missile. It is simpler, smaller, more reliable and infinitely more accurate than any existing system.'

'And I suppose von Erbacher is interested in it?'

'I hope so. If he's interested, the German government might be. The more N A T O countries that show an interest the better.'

Thomason nodded. 'Of course, of course—I think,' he said, more by way of conversation than anything else, 'we've also given you a licence for certain exports to East Germany.'

'That's right—nothing important, obviously—well inside your own guidelines, and nothing that would interest CoCom. Just some minor electronic components that are available on the world market. The East Germans make them themselves, or they could get them from the Soviet Union. Ours just happen to be better, more reliable. In fact, I've one or two useful contacts in the GDR for that kind of stuff. Indeed, I need to go to East Germany again any time now. It's not a lot of business, Minister, but it's worth it.'

Thomason nodded thoughtfully. He saw Miss Ward watching him, almost, he thought, suspiciously. The woman's total self-possession disturbed him. Hammond Acton, on the other hand, was more easy-going—bright, alert. The Minister liked him; the fellow deserved his success.

They were sitting in Hammond's office. It was spacious and well designed, the furniture modern but not extravagant. Gillian Ward had brought them each a gin and tonic before being called from the room. They were talking about economic prospects and the role of new industries when she returned and asked if Mr Acton could possibly take a telephone call in her office.

Hammond looked surprised. This was not a moment when he should be interrupted, and she knew that. So it must be something of exceptional importance. He made his excuses and left Gillian with the Minister.

'Hammond? It's David.'

'Yes, but—'

'I know, you've got Brian Thomason with you. And you're expecting Hans von Erbacher. I'm sorry to interrupt you, old man, but this is important.'

'I'm sure, but what—?'

'Will von Erbacher be seeing the guidance system?'

'Of course—but how did you know about it?'

'My job—remember?'

'Well, I'm hoping von Erbacher will be so impressed that he'll persuade the Germans to buy it.'

'That's a hope. But don't let him even see it. He's not to see it at all, Hammond.'

'Now, look here, David—'

'Well, even if he was in a position to offer you a contract—and he isn't—you wouldn't be able to export the thing. We'd see to that.'

Hammond paused. 'O K. So it's that important?'

'H'm, 'fraid so. Just keep him away from the damn thing, will you?'

'And are you going to say the same thing about the Americans? They could be itching to buy it.'

'I thought as much. No, that's all right.'

'Obliged, I'm sure.'

At the other end of the line David Rackham chuckled. 'There was a young man of Andover, Who lived with his chips in the clover . . .'

'Oh, shut up,' said Hammond, in good humour, and put down the receiver.

He paused, standing by Gillian's desk, puzzled. He looked at his watch. The German should be there within a few minutes. Why was David Rackham so concerned? Hammond had first met him when they were at Cambridge together. Rackham, no more than average height, was freckle-faced, slender, wiry, and hard to beat on the athletic track. Even in those days he had a light-hearted approach to life that could sometimes be irritating, but Hammond had recognized that this concealed a thoughtful and shrewd intelligence. He never inquired too closely about what Rackham did. Had he done so, he would not have been told. He would have been left to assume that it was something in the Foreign Office. In fact, Hammond supposed that his friend worked either for MI5 or MI6. On reflection, he favoured 6, because he had occasionally been asked to do one or two small, quite unimportant, jobs when he had been in East Germany. Really, it had been no more than information which might have been available to any visitor with a little perseverance. But why this ban on von Erbacher? The man came from West Germany, for heaven's sake.

Hammond still looked pensive when he returned to his office. Gillian was talking animatedly to the Minister, but stopped immediately her boss entered, and Hammond apologized for his absence. Meanwhile, his brain was rapidly inventing excuses to make von Erbacher unsuspicious, and he was also wondering how he would get away with it without explaining to Thomason. He was quite certain Rackham wouldn't want that.

He had only just resumed his seat and taken a grateful swig of his gin and tonic when they heard the explosion.

They looked at each other apprehensively. Thomason got up and went to the wide expanse of window.

'Sounded like a bomb,' he said. He could see nothing, and returned to his chair, his drink still in his hand.

It was half an hour later before a police sergeant was shown in. 'You were expecting a Mr Hans von Erbacher, sir?'

'Yes,' Hammond nodded.

'I'm sorry, gentlemen. He's been blown up in his car —with his driver.' Then, seeing their unspoken question, he added, 'Oh, both killed, sir. It was a big explosion. We don't know anything yet, sir. Could be an IRA job.'

From the lane where the Vauxhall Astra was parked the man could hear the shrill wailing of police and ambulance sirens. Within minutes uniformed figures would be fanning out over the nearby roads and stopping every car in sight. That was the automatic police reflex. So it was important to get back to the centre of Andover as quickly as possible, especially if, as he assumed, the police would be concentrating their immediate attention on the Andover by-pass leading to the main A303 road to London.

He reached the first roundabout on the 303 before road blocks had been set up and then, avoiding the bypass, he turned into the Weyhill road and off into side streets. By a circuitous route he made his way into the town centre and out along the Winchester road until he came to the golf course on the left.

The parking area was an expanse of rough, cindered

ground immediately before the club house—a brown, wooden structure with green corrugated-iron roof and windows that looked mainly on to the rising land of the course rather than on to the car park. There was no gate, nothing to prevent him driving straight in and parking on the right, in a space between other cars. He reckoned it could be some time before anyone concluded that his car did not belong to a club member. As it happened, golf had never interested him, and he was far fitter than most for his thirty years.

He stared back at himself in the rear-view mirror. He saw steady brown eyes and regular features covered by a full but well-trimmed beard and moustache. Once he was back in London, both would come off.

He adjusted his tie in the mirror. It was a bright red—his favourite colour. It looked good, too, with his light grey suit. He enjoyed his good looks and his well-groomed appearance. He caught his stare, as though his eyes were independently assessing himself. Well, the mission had been completed efficiently. That was no more than he would have expected. He never recognized the possibility of failure. Now he would spend another night at the White Hart. Then he would drive himself back to London in the other car he had hired. This was a two-litre Ford Sierra, which now bore false number plates and was in the car park at the back of the hotel.

He left the keys in the glove box of the Astra. There was nothing to link this car with the explosion, and there was no reason to be unhelpful. Then he walked back about a mile to the White Hart hotel in Bridge Street. It was really too warm to be so formally suited, so he chose a leisurely pace, but was unable to avoid a certain spring in his step. After all it had, so far, been a satisfying day.

A board above the swing doors of the hotel entrance told him that the inn had been founded in the fifteenth century, and that Charles I had stayed there on several occasions. He, too, the man reflected, had lost his head.

'It's a lovely afternoon, Mr Lane,' the girl smiled from the reception desk immediately on his left, as she reached for his key. She looked at him with more than polite interest.

'It is,' he said. 'Too good to be sitting at a reception desk, h'm?'

Only the very perceptive would have noticed the merest suggestion of an accent colouring the otherwise perfect English.

'I'd rather be watching the tennis at Wimbledon,' the girl confessed.

'And I'd rather be watching with you,' he answered, as he turned away and walked up the stairs to his room. She was quite attractive. If he'd been staying much longer he might have done something about it. It was time he had another woman.

The road that fringed the parkland on one side and the industrial estate on the other had been closed within three minutes of the arrival of the Andover police. Stakes were driven into the soft verges and white tapes stretched across as a temporary measure, but within fifteen minutes portable steel barriers had been put in position. Immediate radio communication with headquarters ensured that road blocks were set up at the exits of the town and the entrances to the motorway. It was possible that whoever was responsible for this mess might just be caught before he got away from the area.

The CID inspector took one look at the scene of mangled car wreckage and bits of human bodies, and decided instantly to call in the Anti-Terrorist Squad. Apart from the bodies that were collected and borne away by ambulance, he ordered that nothing should be touched at the scene of the explosion until C13 arrived. That didn't stop squads of his men going over the remaining area in a methodical and practised routine.

The inspector himself found the place on the field side of the hedgerow where he concluded the terrorist had been. The grass was slightly more flattened, and there was even a suggestion of the earth having been disturbed. It was hardly noticeable, because there hadn't been any rain for several days, but he was sure that shoes had recently trodden there. No traces of footprints, however, were found. Nevertheless, he ordered a constable to scrape together some of the earth. Like many other bits and pieces it found its way into a polythene bag.

The inspector peered at the ground carefully. He began slowly to walk along the field side of the hedgerow. The grass was slightly laid. It had been recently walked over. He followed the pattern until he reached the other side of the park. There, at a gap in the hedgerow, the flattened grasses ended. The impression was only very light. He might even have been mistaken. But when he saw that the grass beyond the gap was much more upright, he was sure he wasn't. The fellow had come to this spot—to what? A waiting car?

He emerged through the gap cautiously. The metalled surface would show nothing. But if the car had been drawn close off the road—? Yes—there it was, in the loose dust, a distinct impression of a tyre tread. With his personal radio he summoned a photographer.

The inspector retraced his steps to the scene of the explosion. As he approached, one of his constables called out, 'Here, sir, come and look at this—in the hedgerow.'

The man the hotel receptionist had called Mr Lane had a half-bottle of champagne sent to his room to celebrate his feeling of professional satisfaction. The task having been completed so successfully, he was now very much aware of the need for another kind of satisfaction. If only there were time, he was sure the receptionist would have been amenable. She might have been quite interesting, too.

Early that evening, however, when he was studying the menu outside the dining room, he saw the kind of woman who really would have been worth staying for. She was at the reception desk, and seemed a little disturbed by whatever it was the receptionist was saying to her. She was tall and slender, with dark hair and very bright blue eyes. But it was her poise that attracted him. Although he could detect her disappointment, even dissatisfaction, with what the receptionist was saying, there remained about her a self-possession to match his own. He stared, willing her to look at him. She half turned. Briefly their eyes met. He tried to prolong the encounter, smiling faintly, but she turned to go. Quickly he was by her side.

'Is there anything I can do to help?' he asked.

She turned to face him. 'I don't think so,' she said.

'I thought perhaps, if there wasn't a room for you—well, you might have mine. I could just as easily go tonight instead of in the morning.'

He was aware of the very blue eyes weighing him up. She said, 'That's very kind,' and then added dismissively, 'but I was not asking for a room.'

She walked briskly through the swing doors, and he wished he did not have to return to London the next day.

Gillian Ward hurried to the pair of phone boxes by the river. She picked up the receiver of 52045, dialled a number and waited for it to ring four times; then she rang off, lifted the receiver and dialled again. She let it go on ringing for three minutes before deciding that there was no reply. She was curious more than irritated. Something was happening that she didn't know about. She even wondered if, after the unexplained killing of von Erbacher, her own life might be in danger. Someone must have known what was planned, and had interfered. That troubled her, but she refused to be panicked.

Modern phone boxes are vulnerable places. She was uncomfortably aware that she could be seen through the small glass panes from several angles. There did not, however, seem to be anyone or anything suspicious. She dialled the number again. There was still no reply. There was nothing for it then. It would have to be the master control. She dialled a different number. She let it ring three times before redialling. There was an immediate response.

The voice said, 'Goethe.'

She identified herself simply as 'Ann Dover'.

Then she said, 'You know what has happened, I suppose?'

'Yes.'

'Who did it?'

There was a momentary silence before the voice said, 'I'm not sure.'

'What should I do?'

'Carry on.'

Gillian was puzzled. She wasn't to know that Goethe was equally perplexed, and was playing for time.

'You know Stoebel has left?' she said.

'No.'

'I've tried to contact him. There was no reply. Perhaps he's not back yet. But, in view of what has happened—von Erbacher, I mean—what should I do with the drawings? You know I was letting von Erbacher have them—'

There was a quick interrupted, 'Yes.'

'Well, I assumed in the circumstances I should pass them to Stoebel. But I can't get him. I don't like to hold on to them any longer.'

'Can you bring them to me—tonight?'

'I can drive up in an hour and a half, hour and three-quarters.'

'I'll meet you in the foyer at the Savoy, riverside entrance. I'll buy you a late dinner.'

Hammond Acton lived only a few miles from his factory in the Hampshire–Wiltshire border village of Penton Mewsey, occupying a self-contained wing of his parents' large neo-Georgian house. It commanded a view over the very parkland where Andrew Lane had hidden in a distant hedgerow. The arrangement suited Hammond well enough until such time as he married. Up to the present he had been too busy establishing his company to settle for anything more than occasional and casual relationships. They were never really very satisfactory, and he was beginning to feel that it was time he looked for something more settled and permanent.

Thus it was, with his business an established success, he had begun to become aware of Gillian Ward as rather more than his attractive and very efficient personal assistant. She had, after all, shared with him much of the effort and many of the difficulties that had preceded the company's present success, and recently her behaviour had suggested that she might be ready to share much more. So he was disappointed that after such a traumatic day she had been unable to return with him and share a simple meal which, he had hoped, they might have prepared together. Her excuses had not carried conviction.

'I'm sure,' she had said, 'I wouldn't be very entertaining company. You must admit, it's been a hell of a day. I think I just feel tired.'

17

But she hadn't looked tired. Puzzled, perhaps—and that mystified him a little—but not tired. It was an expression he had noticed several times recently, and it made him realize that perhaps he didn't know her as well as he thought. And yet—oh well, he'd had to settle for dinner with his parents instead.

Hammond admired his father. Geoffrey Acton's brilliance as an architect had earned him an international reputation. But it wasn't only the success that Hammond admired. His father had seemed always to like the same things; had taught him to play cricket and, more important, to appreciate it. He had taught Hammond other things as well—like thinking his way through problems tolerantly, but solving them decisively. He'd never been aware of it at the time, but now he realized how closely he had tried to follow his father's example. Yes, there was no doubt the old man combined tolerance with decisiveness.

His mother, Margaret, was quite different. Well-meaning, certainly, and undoubtedly kind, but excessively cautious and never quite sure what she thought. Her husband must have been a great consolation to her. She was most at home in the garden, which Geoffrey had designed.

Hammond's sister was, he supposed, an interesting combination of the two. Six years younger than himself, she taught in a primary school in London and invariably turned up at weekends, except whenever she felt her commitment demanded her presence at Greenham Common or some other CND rendezvous. She had her mother's endearing muddle-headedness, as well as her father's decisiveness, and this led, in Hammond's view, to some sincere but irrationally held opinions. She'd been christened Cassandra. Hammond was never sure why, but presumed it arose from his father's admiration for Jane Austen rather than from any notion that the child was going to grow into a great beauty with a gift for prophecy. For a long time her father had been the only one to call her Cassandra. Sometimes, to her annoyance, he still did. The rest of them had settled for Cass, until she was old enough to protest. Since then she'd become Sandra.

He'd expected a phone call from her, but perhaps she hadn't read the papers or seen or heard the news. His mother, who had done both, looked horrified when he came in.

'Hammond, it might have been you,' she exclaimed illogically.

'Oh, Mother, it *might* have been anybody. But obviously, whoever it was, was after Mr von Erbacher.'

'Yes,' she muttered distractedly. 'Terrible.'

His father, after he'd remarked on the mindlessness of modern terrorism, had been more interested in motives.

'Have the police any idea?' he asked.

'I don't know. All they said was it might be the IRA.'

'What the hell would the IRA want with a West German industrialist?'

Hammond shrugged. 'Just the first thing the police thought of, I suppose.'

'Much more likely to be the Baader-Meinhof, or whoever's succeeded them.'

They continued the discussion while they had a pre-dinner drink. Hammond settled for a gin and tonic, his father for one of his favourite finos. As Geoffrey savoured the pale, straw-coloured liquid, his son was aware of a kind of silent interrogation.

At last he took a mouthful of his drink and said, 'Oh, I might as well tell you. I had a phone call just before von Erbacher was due to arrive. I won't tell you from whom, if you don't mind. But I was told not to let him see our new guidance system. That's what he'd come for.'

Geoffrey Acton raised his eyebrows. 'I wonder why? Do we keep secrets from NATO partners?'

'Well, he didn't represent the West German government —but I still found it puzzling.'

'But in the end,' said his father, 'you didn't have to bother.'

Hammond was considering the implication of this remark when there was another telephone call. His mother poked her head round the door. 'It's for you,' she said to her son.

Hammond followed her into the hall. He waited until she had disappeared before he spoke. At the other end, the voice said, 'It's David. The problem solved itself.'

'Not a very elegant solution. The police say it might have been the IRA.'

There was the mildest snort of contempt down the line. 'They won't hold that view for long.'

'Well, it doesn't seem all that logical,' Hammond conceded, 'but do you know who it was?'

'Perhaps.'

'It wasn't your lot?'

'Come, Hammond, you know we don't go in for that kind of thing. Not allowed.'

'But I don't understand why an industrialist from a NATO ally could not be allowed to see—'

'Hans von Erbacher was not all that he seemed.'

'So, who was his killer?'

'I said *perhaps* I knew. I'm not sure. If you discover anything, let me know. But—' Rackham stopped.

Hammond waited. The silence lengthened. At last he said, 'But what, for god's sake?'

'The CIA might have been. They're less squeamish.'

2

David Rackham didn't know who had killed von Erbacher, but he suspected, as he had told Hammond Acton, that it was a professional assassin employed by the CIA. He hadn't the slightest evidence to support this view; it was only that he could not imagine who else it could be. Unless the whole thing was a coincidence, and it was an ordinary murder committed for some personal reason. Possible, but improbable.

Apart from this unfortunate lacuna in his knowledge, he felt mildly pleased with himself. He hadn't known that it was intended to pass a copy of the drawings of the guidance system to von Erbacher during his visit. He had only assumed that the man was going there, under the guise of his reputation as a West German industrialist, to have a look at the system, and generally spy out the land before devising some plan of action. That was why he had warned Hammond not to let the fellow near the system. Now, by happy chance, he was preventing the drawings from getting to their original destination—the East Germans.

The West German authorities had suspected for some time that von Erbacher had been working for the Soviet bloc, and were only waiting for the right opportunity to arrest him. Erich Stoebel had a minor post in the embassy of the German Democratic Republic in London. Rackham had discovered, only by chance, about a year previously that he was Gillian Ward's control. It was then that he had decided on a distinctly dangerous game in the hope of ultimately unmasking a pretty little nest of spies—with Gillian Ward among them, he had reflected with amusement, it would certainly be pretty. Thus it was, speaking fluent German, he had decided to set himself up as her master-control, under the code name 'Goethe'.

Fortunately, although his old friend Hammond Acton had often spoken warmly of his able personal assistant, Rackham had never met Gillian Ward, perhaps because he had never had occasion to see Hammond during working hours. So, posing as Stoebel on the telephone, he had set up a meeting with her in Kew Gardens.

He recalled the occasion, wryly, as he waited for her now in the foyer of the Savoy. They had met beneath the great arching glass roof of the tropical house. He had spoken in German, saying that he was glad she was punctual, because he just could not stand this humidity. She had replied stumblingly in the same language. So then he had spoken to her in English. He had avoided an obvious German accent because, as he told her, the reason for his presence in Britain was his excellent English. Instead he conveyed an impression of German origins by the selective thickening of certain sounds.

She had been surprised and instantly suspicious. Where was Stoebel? Rackham had flattered her, told her how pleased they were with her work, was able to show that he had some knowledge of what she had previously done, and assured her that she was valuably contributing to what, in the end, would benefit all mankind. It was just because of the value and potential importance of what she was doing that he had been asked to become her master-control. He had emphasized that not even Stoebel would know about it—at least for the time being. There would come a time when it would be necessary, even advantageous, that he should be informed, but until then Goethe's role must remain secret. He'd had a little difficulty in convincing her. So he had gone on to extol the virtues of Erich Stoebel. Everyone, Rackham had stressed, had the greatest confidence in Stoebel, and he would remain her normal control; she was to follow his instructions implicitly. Just occasionally, and very rarely, there would be a special instruction from Goethe and that would take priority. Stoebel would not know about it because it would not be necessary for him to know. The service always operated on the need-to-know principle.

Gradually, as they walked over the endless green acres, not even seeing the trees they walked between, Gillian had come

22

to accept the situation. Moreover, she rather liked Rackham himself. He ended the briefing convincingly by telling her that she could always have direct access to him at any time. In an emergency, or if there was something she wanted to tell him or wanted to know herself, she could telephone him direct. He gave her a special and safe number. She was always to let the phone ring three times and then redial.

Since then there had been no more than three contacts, each time initiated by Rackham himself. The system had worked well, but now the time was rapidly approaching when it would have to be brought to an end.

As the commissionaire swung the door for her, Gillian came through looking cool and immaculate. Rackham marvelled at how she managed it after a fast drive from Hampshire.

'This is rather splendid, isn't it?' she said, as she sank down beside him, and Rackham summoned a waiter. She ordered a Campari and soda.

'Well, it's a rather special day.'

Gillian sighed, gave him a penetrating blue stare. 'You can say that again.' She lowered her voice, although there was no one remotely within earshot. 'Von Erbacher must be a serious loss.'

Rackham nodded, thinking to himself that it would have been much better if the Metropolitan Police, or the West Germans, had been able to arrest him. Now a lot of evidence that would undoubtedly have incriminated other people had been removed from them. That could only be the CIA. He was almost sure of it.

The waiter brought her Campari and a gin and tonic for Rackham. She drank a grateful draught and then smiled at him. 'Well, I've got the drawings anyway,' she said, tapping the slim, black leather document-case that she still hugged under one arm.

Rackham insisted that they consult the menu and order before discussing anything. They each settled for fresh salmon and salad, and Rackham told the waiter they would be at his table in fifteen minutes.

Then he said, 'The drawings, my dear—you have done very well.'

She unzipped the black leather case and extracted a large unsealed envelope which she handed to Rackham.

He looked inside and removed the contents no more than three or four inches, sufficient to satisfy himself that they were indeed the drawings of Hammond's advanced guidance system.

'You won't be suspected?' he asked, thickening his voice slightly.

'They won't be missed. I deposited all copies of the drawings in Mr Acton's bank. I kept back this set.'

Rackham gave her a congratulatory smile.

Only when they had moved to their table in an isolated corner of the riverside restaurant did she refer to what he realized must be uppermost in her mind—the killing of von Erbacher. 'It must mean,' she said quietly, 'that someone is on to us.'

'I don't think so,' Rackham lied. 'On to von Erbacher, not on to you.'

She retained her cool self-possession, but Rackham thought her eyes disclosed an underlying anxiety.

'I don't quite understand,' she said, 'why he had to be killed.'

'To prevent him receiving the plans or seeing the guidance system.'

'Then someone else must know about me.'

'Not necessarily. They might only have known it was going to happen—not how or by whom—something picked up from von Erbacher himself in Germany.'

She looked only marginally reassured and Rackham wondered, as he had before, why she was doing this. Eventually it was going to be one hell of a blow for Hammond. He watched her eating. She was very desirable, and he considered the prospect of taking her to bed. It wasn't really stealing his friend's girl, he rationalized. She was quite simply a spy, and he didn't see why he should have any conscience about it. That's if she were agreeable. He suspected she might be.

The wine waiter materialized from the background, extracted the Puligny-Montrachet from the ice bucket and poured her another glass.

She looked up at Rackham. 'I mustn't drink too much, I've got to drive back tonight.'

The waiter had disappeared again. 'You needn't if you don't want to. You could drive back first thing in the morning. It wouldn't take long, against the traffic.'

Her blue eyes softened. Rackham wondered if she might welcome the chance of giving herself to him as a way of relaxing, of giving in, disowning responsibility, shifting the burden. In the silence, as she looked at him, he felt he could even guess her thoughts. Why not? Life was a dangerous business. Von Erbacher had been killed today. She had rushed up to London with the plans. What was going to happen next, how could she know? Why shouldn't she have some pleasure? Hammond? Yes, there was Hammond, but he would always represent the inevitable conflict of loyalties. Her lips twitched into a diminutive and knowing smile.

'The road going out of London,' she said, 'would certainly be empty in the morning. And I don't really like driving in the dark.'

'Much safer in the morning,' he smiled, 'after a satisfying night's sleep.'

'Oh, yes,' she murmured. 'That sounds nice. Here?'

'No. I'll drive your car back to my flat which, as far as you are concerned, doesn't exist.'

'Of course not—just like you.'

Rackham's flat was small, part of an expensive block overlooking the Thames between Westminster and Vauxhall. While he would never have described himself as sybaritic, he nevertheless appreciated what he called 'sensible comfort', and if he could afford it—and he could—he saw no reason why he should not modestly indulge himself. When he held open the door for Gillian, her eyes widened in surprise.

'What's the matter?'

'I didn't imagine the comrades would be so generous.'

Rackham chuckled. 'It depends on one's position. It's because I'm almost as English as the English. It's hoped —expected—that I shall be here a long time—to the continuing benefit of our comrades.'

She smiled. She was relaxing, her eyes soft and liquid. For

a night she was able to escape. He thought he detected gratitude.

She stood by the picture window and looked down on the Thames. It was almost dark. Lights reflected in the water, which shimmered with the night's early luminous sheen.

'It's lovely,' she said.

He took the drawings out of the envelope, unfolded them and spread them over the teak table. There were several separate sheets, each minutely detailed.

Still staring out of the window, she said, 'Don't tell me you can understand them, or is there no end to your talents?'

'For all I know,' he said, 'it might be Linear B.'

'H'm.' She smiled.

He refolded the plans and crossed to the Danish-designed sideboard to pour each of them a cognac. Then he came up behind her, passed his right arm in front of her and put the drink in her hand. At the same time he bent and kissed her long neck. She lifted her head and breathed deeply. He kissed her neck again, and then she turned towards him. They held aloft their glasses, each took a sip, linked arms and kissed. They laughed together. Then, as they stood looking into each other's eyes, they kissed repeatedly and passionately. They progressed naturally, but unhurriedly, towards the bedroom.

She was as lovely naked as he had imagined she would be, and her slim body was strong. She made love urgently, searchingly, and in one brief moment of self-conscious detachment, Rackham hoped that his friend Hammond was taking advantage of the situation while he could. That, he told himself, was cynical, and immediately resubmerged himself in the tide of passion that was sweeping them both towards mutual fulfilment.

Afterwards she lay with her head on his chest, her fingers idling with the sandy-coloured hairs there. 'Do I have to go on calling you Goethe?' she murmured.

The incongruity of the whole situation made Rackham laugh. 'You were managing quite well with darling,' he teased. She didn't answer, her finger tips still moving lightly on his chest. So he added, 'It's better, isn't it? Safer for all of us.'

'If that's what you want.' She lifted her head and looked at him. 'I suppose it is dangerous, isn't it—what I'm doing? A man has been killed.'

For a moment Rackham was desperately sorry for her, almost angry with himself. The light-hearted attitude with which he disposed of most difficulties was cruelly inappropriate. He stroked her hair. He wished he could comfort her, provide her with a more permanent escape from her anxieties than that offered by a night of sexual abandonment.

'Why do you do it?' he asked. 'Me, I'm different. A German, a member of the Party and a professional. It's my way of life. But you—you're not a professional.'

Her head relaxed on to his chest again. 'I don't know. It became inevitable.'

'You weren't blackmailed?'

'Oh, no. I mean my life made it inevitable.'

'Do you want to tell me?'

She sighed. 'I clawed myself up. A slum in Bradford. My father died too early of byssinosis. My mother worked in the mill, but drank herself to death. I wouldn't give in. I don't know why. But I fought my way through school, won a scholarship to a grammar school. I did well, but not well enough to go to university. I had elocution lessons instead. It was the best thing I ever did—getting rid of that accent. If I had any relatives left, I didn't know them. I was fostered for several years. With my determination to escape from it all, I suppose there grew up a kind of hatred for those who were responsible for the conditions into which I'd been born.' She lifted her head, and he saw her eyes were now a bright, burning blue. 'I was going to revenge myself—by god I was. Yes, I did join the Party. No, I'm not still a member. But I did believe in it—I believed in sweeping away all those inequalities that divided society into the haves and have-nots. It was wrong, it was immoral, it was unjust. And if working for the Party would get rid of it—I'd work for the Party anyhow, anyway. Oh Christ, do I have to go on?'

Again he stroked her forehead, and then ran his hand through her hair and down over her shoulders. 'No—but that isn't the reason now, is it?'

'I don't know. Partly, I suppose, it must still be. It's in the blood. But as I got on—made my way in the world, as the cliché has it—I suppose I rationalized it differently. I began to believe that what I was doing was for all mankind. Patriotism was something for one nation, but I imagined that by making sure the Communist states had all that we had, knew all that we knew—well, it was a kind of international sharing that I was involved in. No one would have an advantage over anyone else. Everything was for everyone. Oh hell, I'm not putting this very well. And to you—you of all people. Why am I saying it to you? That can't do me any good.'

'It's all right,' he soothed. 'And now you're beginning to have doubts about that—your new rationalization?'

'Yes, I suppose so. Perhaps, when this is all over, I shall stop. These years with Hammond Acton have perhaps begun to change me again. I don't know. Hammond sees me as a very self-possessed, self-assured person. I suppose, by appearance, I am. It's my shell.'

They were quiet for a few moments. Rackham was sorry for her. It was a reaction encouraged by feeling such a swine himself. Yet it was what she had wanted—to escape.

While he was still thinking, she said, 'You could really screw me now, couldn't you? Pouring my heart out to the top man. I must be mad.'

'No,' he said. 'It was right to tell me. It has helped you.'

'Well, I certainly couldn't tell Hammond, could I? God knows I've needed to talk to somebody.' She sat up and looked down at him. 'You must think me a bloody inept kind of informer.'

He reached up, pulled her down to him and kissed her. He felt her relaxing again.

'I don't think that,' he said seriously. 'But don't ever spill your heart out like this to Stoebel. He won't be so understanding.'

She shook her head, stroked his face. 'And I still have to call you Goethe?'

He laughed. 'And you still have to call me Goethe. Why don't you escape—get out of the country?'

Again she lifted herself up and looked at him. 'You're a

28

strange man. Surely you've got too much compassion for your job, haven't you?'

'It's my job to keep our agents safe,' he said. 'If you were in danger, I should try to get you away.'

'What, to the Soviet Union, to East Germany? I'm not sure that I want to go any more.'

'No. I was thinking that if you wanted to give it up, get out altogether, there's nothing stopping you. I'd see nobody stopped you.'

She sank back on to his chest and curled into his arm. 'I'll remember,' she said quietly.

He went on intermittently stroking her hair until she fell asleep. It was some time before he did; he was too uneasy in his mind, even found himself admitting that he was worried about her.

In the morning, he slipped quietly out of bed without disturbing her, poured out some orange juice, and made some toast and coffee. He took it all to her on a tray, just as she stirred and sat upright. She looked lovely. He smiled. 'Good morning. It's six-fifteen. You can be away in half an hour, in Andover by nine o'clock easily.'

She nodded. She was looking at him, he thought, in a strange, almost incredulous way.

At length she said, 'I don't think I feel any different with the dawn.'

'Good,' he answered before he realized that he had uttered the word.

They ate breakfast with the tray resting on the bed. Then he left her. Within fifteen minutes she had bathed and dressed and joined him in his living room. Sunlight was flooding through the large riverside windows. Rackham could understand why Hammond thought of her as such a self-possessed person. Her poise had returned, and she looked at him confidently.

'Thank you,' she said. 'For everything. I shan't forget.'

He kissed her, and for a brief moment she clung to him, and then she hurried to the lift. Rackham followed, and watched her drive out of the forecourt into Millbank and along Grosvenor Road.

When he returned to his flat he looked at the plans again. Well, at least he'd saved them from reaching the Eastern bloc.

Such self-justification, however, didn't satisfy Rackham on this particular morning. He was uncomfortably conscious that the original justification—that the woman was a spy anyway—had been displaced by the night's events, by the realization that she wasn't just a one-night stand. He was a little surprised at his own feelings.

From his wardrobe he took out the jacket he had been wearing the previous evening, and from the inside pocket retrieved a miniature tape recorder. He pressed a button on the side, the tape rewound rapidly, and then reproduced their conversation at the Savoy. He listened to Gillian's voice saying, 'They won't be missed. I deposited all copies of the drawings in Mr Acton's bank. I kept back this set.'

When she was charged, his own evidence would help to convict her. For a moment Rackham was tempted to destroy the recording, but his training took over. He removed the cassette, sealed it in an envelope and locked it in his desk.

But there was nothing, he reasoned, to prevent Gillian flying off to wherever she wanted to go. He would, he told himself, be prepared to advise her about countries that had not signed an extradition agreement. Hell, what was he thinking about? That would remove her from him as well. No—she had been systematically supplying information to the Eastern bloc for years, and that carried its own penalties. But she had her reasons; she'd had a hell of a time. He could understand. Perhaps there would be some way of helping her . . .

He cursed himself. This was no way to behave. But then last night had been no way to behave either. He should not have got himself involved. He had broken the first rule. For the only time in his life, he had broken the first rule.

'Now, Rackham,' he muttered aloud, 'also for the first time, if you're not careful, you'll pay for it.'

3

Some of the early roses were already in flower in Queen Mary's rose garden in Regent's Park, London. Philip Strang scarcely noticed them. He made his way urgently to one of the seats that encircled the fountain. He was tall and gangling, sharp-faced, with an untidy mop of fair hair. He wore faded blue jeans topped by a blouson. He drummed his long fingers impatiently on the seat, looked round nervously. His impatience arose as much from his innate anger as from his nervousness.

He had convinced himself that he was nearly always under surveillance, ever since the occasion when he had seen a policeman snapping off a 35mm camera at him at a CND demonstration. Well, sod the pigs. He didn't care. He had more important things to do than any of them. That's why, as an active Party member, he was in the CND. He lit a cigarette, puffed at it quickly for three minutes, and then ground it beneath his heel.

The water of the fountain made a seething, chuckling sound as it slipped over the smooth green bodies of girls and dolphins, and then fell back like rain into the great bowl of the fountain. He stared, but didn't see. The fountain was an irrelevance. And the girl on the seat forty-five degrees opposite? She didn't matter. He bit at the flesh by the quick of his forefinger. He felt the excitement straining in him. If only they would agree. He felt he'd smash the bastard's face in if the man only listened politely and then disdainfully invented reasons why it would not work. It would. He was convinced of it. He was surprised at his own daring. The idea had been such a leap of the imagination. Yet, like so many such ideas before, it was so obvious, once it had been thought. Even for the complacent British people it could be the last straw. Then even they might stir themselves into forcing the government to get rid of its nuclear weapons. He had thought about it for days until he had convinced himself.

'It's usually good weather for Wimbledon.'

Strang looked at the figure seated beside him. The man was conventionally dressed but wore no hat to cover the crisply cut and deeply waved grey hair. There was a greyness about the square features too.

'That's because it's June,' said Strang. How the Soviets liked these ridiculous code phrases.

The man's acknowledging smile could only be called wintry. Strang was disappointed. He refused to show it, but did manage to curb his enthusiasm. Coolly and precisely, he outlined his plan. The sound of his own voice encouraged him.

For some moments the thickset figure beside him said nothing. For the first time Strang became conscious of the sound of the water, and the pattering back of the fountain's rain was suddenly irritating. The man began to nod, slowly, and uttered a staccato humming sound.

Strang said, 'Well, not even those massive demonstrations stopped cruise or Pershing. And radioactive seaweed at Sellafield did little more than cause a local row and a government inquiry. A few people need to be killed. But if we tried for one of their own cruise missiles that would be too bloody horrible, wouldn't it? It might even cause a war, and—' He left the sentence unfinished, and turned anxiously towards the man beside him.

'It would have to be done by—"terrorists". Not by you. They know you.'

The man's English had the slightest of guttural accents. He saw the look of angry disappointment in the younger man's eyes.

'You mustn't mind,' he said. 'You have very useful work to do for us. No sense in getting yourself put away. It's a job for a professional terrorist. We must not be seen to bear any responsibility.' He smiled again coldly.

'What do you want me to do?'

'About this? Nothing. You have had the idea. Leave it to us. We'll be in touch.'

The man got up, and stepped briskly down the central

walk. Strang waited some minutes. He fought his irritation. Of course he couldn't do it. He'd *thought* of it, hadn't he? That was enough. Now it was up to others. He supposed it was the Politburo itself that would take the decision.

It was only a few hours later that, in his office high in New Scotland Yard, Superintendent Arthur Whitaker of the Special Branch studied the photograph taken in Queen Mary's rose garden. He had a file on Philip Strang, and he recognized the other figure as the new cultural attaché at the Soviet Embassy, Dmitri Shokolov.

He hunched his bulky shoulders and reached for the pipe that rested in the huge glass ashtray his wife had given him on their twentieth wedding anniversary. With his other hand he felt for his tobacco pouch, and then methodically charged his pipe, applied the match and watched the smoke drift upwards in blue spirals.

Whitaker's immediate reaction to the photograph was that it was just another one for the record—something that helped to fill out their picture of the activities of young Strang and which might, on some future occasion, provide another strand in the evidence needed to declare the Russian diplomat *persona non grata*. He didn't see that it had a special significance. Just the Russians up to their familiar tricks again. In any event he had something more important to occupy his mind—the murder by terrorist bomb of a West German industrialist in Andover.

Arthur Whitaker, slightly overweight, fiftyish, was the Special Branch's expert on terrorism. His speciality was I R A terrorism, but he was expected to know everything there was to know about terrorism in general. Although he was a rational and kindly man, his attitude to I R A terrorists was one of dedicated enmity. It was him against them, and he was determined to win. About other terrorism he was more detached, dealing with it, when he had to, in a rational and painstaking way. He had no doubts about the primary aim of all terrorism—to destabilize the Western democracies. As far as he was concerned every terrorist was the enemy of all that was good and decent in humankind. There were no justifications.

33

His immediate colleagues knew him affectionately as Art, an abbreviation that owed its origin to his favourite hobby of painting portraits in what could only be described as a curious, lumpy style. They surrounded him on the walls of his office, and although his wife had with a kindly tolerance frequently urged him to hang some at home, he always resisted the temptation.

'You might actually get to like them then,' he'd said wryly. Meanwhile, he put aside the photograph and buzzed for Sergeant Colin Cawston. He, too, had a hobby that had given him the name by which he was generally known—'Snap'. The sergeant, however, had managed to avoid being pushed into the photographic department. He had, he said, no interest in photographing dead bodies and crashed cars and the paraphernalia of evidence. For him, his photography was an art, and the superintendent had admired the excellent collection Snap had made of famous London buildings.

The sergeant stood on the opposite side of the desk, one eyebrow cocked questioningly. He was young and bright with a distinctly dour appearance, but Whitaker quite took to the man's dry manner.

'I've had all the relevant information typed out, sir,' Cawston said as he passed a buff folder to his boss.

Whitaker sent another spiral of smoke into the air, and thumbed over the typewritten sheets.

'I don't believe it,' he said emphatically. 'It's not the IRA.'

'C13 only says the device was similar to that recently used by the IRA, sir. Radio-controlled bomb set off by a signal from a miniature transmitter, perhaps no more than a few hundred yards away.'

'Ah, just so. Don't like these things that pull in MI5 and MI6. They expect all the help but they don't tell you everything in return. Keep things to themselves.'

'I'm getting out all the stuff we've got on West German gangs, sir.'

'Yes, and get photographs of any of those we know pushed round to Immigration.'

'That's already in hand, sir. And we've had a call from Mr

Rackham. Wants to be kept in touch. Everything we get, sir.'

Whitaker sighed, rested his pipe in the ashtray and stroked his chin thoughtfully. 'Who would want to go for a West German industrialist?' he muttered more to himself than to Cawston. He shifted uneasily. He was recognized in the Force for his hunches, and at present he had a hunch that this one was going to be messy. For the moment though he merely added, 'I think we can leave it to the anti-terrorist boys and the local cops. Any clues are going to come from that end.'

He leant over and picked up the photograph of Strang and Shokolov, and then handed it to Cawston. 'Come to think of it,' he said, 'you might as well copy this one to the Friends. I suppose one of these days we shall pull young Strang in for something or other—breaking into Greenham Common, I shouldn't wonder. He's a member of the Party, isn't he?'

Snap nodded. 'He's an unpleasant character,' he said.

It was the next day before David Rackham saw the photograph. He had it now beside him on the settee in the living room of his flat. He was waiting for Hammond Acton to arrive, and meanwhile amused himself scribbling thoughts on a pad that he might turn into a humorous piece for *Punch* or the *New Yorker*. Of course he wrote under a pseudonym, and his department had no idea that he was the author of these occasional tilts at the Establishment's foibles.

He'd had his first success with *Punch* when he was at Winchester, continued at Corpus Christi, Cambridge, and had become a frequent contributor when he was briefly running an office for the British Council in the Middle East. His father, who had been given a life peerage after long service to the Conservative Party, and had been let into the secret when irritatedly complaining about the boy's dilet-tantism, grudgingly conceded that it was probably the only thing the fellow would ever do well. This, in fact, overlooked a better than average academic record and an undeniable prowess on the athletic track, the more remarkable because the speed came from his slender strength rather than length of stride. He was smiling to himself at a nice turn of phrase when the door alarm buzzed, and he got up to let in his friend.

'You know, I wouldn't mind a flat here myself,' said Hammond as he appreciated afresh the furnishings and the view over the river. 'I've always envied you this.'

'Envy? Not you. You could probably buy the block.'

'It's on my shopping list. If the Americans buy my new guidance system, I might even become a neighbour. By the way, why didn't you want von Erbacher to have a look at it? What's wrong with West Germany? Part of the NATO alliance.'

'But I told you, von Erbacher was not all that he seemed. He may have been a West German industrialist, but he was working for the East.'

'The Russians?'

'Got it in one. Pour yourself a drink. Me too.'

Hammond went over to the sideboard and mixed gins and tonics in two cut-glass tumblers. He turned round with the drinks in time to see Rackham take a large envelope from his desk.

'Here, you might like these. I think they belong to you.'

Hammond looked puzzled, put his drink down, then lifted the flap of the envelope and withdrew the plans of his guidance system. He stared at them, temporarily speechless. 'But—where the hell did you get them?'

'A little birdie,' Rackham grinned.

'Don't be a fool, David. This is damned serious. The only copies of these drawings are in my bank in Andover.'

'Except that set.'

'So how did you get them?'

'I can't tell you. Just be grateful they didn't reach the people they were meant for.'

'The Russians again?'

'The East Germans. Same thing.'

'But—' Hammond shook his head despairingly. 'No, this is appalling, David. For pity's sake tell me. You can trust me.'

'Of course I can trust you. But I can't tell you at the moment. You will know soon enough.'

'Are there any more floating around?'

'No.'

'I don't understand. It's impossible, short of a bank raid.'

Rackham smiled faintly. 'They're clever,' he said. 'Spies have to be.'

Hammond picked up his drink and took a long draught. 'What more can I do?'

'Nothing, I imagine. Make sure you put these in your bank—yourself. And don't discuss it with anybody. I mean anybody,' Rackham emphasized. 'Not even your parents, your personal assistant, your solicitor, your bank manager, the police. With nobody. Is that clear?'

Hammond nodded. 'I wish I understood.'

'You will. But at the moment things are too difficult, delicate, to permit of explanation. Here, take a look at these.' Rackham produced a photograph. 'Not a very handsome couple. Do you know them by any chance?'

Hammond shook his head.

'The thickset one with the square head and grey hair is Dmitri Shokolov. He came here about six months ago —cultural attaché at the Soviet Embassy. Keen on football. Goes to watch Arsenal at Highbury. And a regular attender at concerts at the Royal Fesitval Hall. But, er—' Rackham paused and looked up with a freckly smile, 'he's busy doing other things as well. And that long thin creature with the unbrushed hair, who is not quite as young as he appears, is Philip Strang, at present unemployed, but formerly a surveyor, card-carrying member of the Communist Party, and also active in the rather more extreme Socialist Workers Party. Fanatical member of CND, and always to be seen at their big demonstrations.'

'Where were they?'

'Queen Mary's rose garden in Regent's Park.'

'And what have they got to do with it?'

'Don't know. Most likely nothing at all. Although Shokolov, of course, could be interested. There may be no connection. I just wondered if you'd seen them.'

Hammond shook his head. He considered. 'Perhaps my sister knows the boy. She used to go to Greenham Common quite a bit. Still goes to CND things from time to time.'

Rackham looked surprised.

'Oh, she's very emotional about it,' Hammond continued. 'It's the one thing big brother and kid sister don't agree about.'

'Kid?'

'She's twenty-six. Teaches.'

'Would she tell you?'

'Of course.'

'Just ask her. Not that there's much we don't know about young Strang. He's more fanatical than clever. Not really likely to be given anything important to do. But—you never can tell.'

David Rackham got up, stretched himself and poured out two more drinks. He changed the subject.

'D'you know, I was thinking the other day, you've never introduced me to that personal assistant of yours. What's her name? Gillian Ward? Why are you keeping her to yourself? Tell me about her.' Rackham was enjoying himself, and disliking himself for doing so.

Hammond smiled. 'Come to think of it, there's not a lot to tell. I really know surprisingly little about her. Oh, she's quite stunning, I can tell you that. But she's never really talked about her background, where she comes from, and so on. In fact, she's always avoided it, as though she just didn't want to talk about it. I've respected that, content to accept her for what she is. After all, she's been with me from the very beginning, almost like a partner. And yet—' He looked puzzled. 'Sometimes there's something strangely detached about her. As well as being attractive, she's incredibly efficient, but recently I've begun to wonder if I really understand her at all.'

Before Rackham could reply the telephone shrilled.

Superintendent Whitaker had been preoccupied by the discovery that one of the most wanted men of the Irish National Liberation Army, the extremist offshoot of the Provisionals, had slipped into Britain. It was bloody obvious that something was being planned on the mainland, and somehow the bastard had got in. They were clever, but he was damned if they'd be too clever for him.

It was Cawston's knock that interrupted him.

'It's Andover, sir.'

Whitaker tapped out his pipe irritatedly. 'Oh—yes?' he muttered wearily.

'The local boys have done a good job, sir. It's only twenty-four hours. They've come up with the car, and—'

'What car? Let's have it simply, Snap.'

'The one the killer used.'

Whitaker was interested.

'They've found a blue Vauxhall Astra,' Cawston continued, 'abandoned at Andover Golf Club. It was hired by a tall, well-bearded man, around thirty.'

'How do they know he bombed von Erbacher?'

'It was the boiler suit—found in the boot. The trouser ends have dried mud on them. Hasn't been analysed yet, but it seems to be the same as that in the ditch alongside the road. Then tyre-tread marks matched those found on the far side of the park. All slightly careless, sir—yes?' said the sergeant eagerly.

'Yes. Either that, or he's so well covered he *knows* it doesn't matter. I think I prefer the second explanation.'

Whitaker fiddled with his tobacco pouch, and then thoughtfully refilled his pipe.

'The car was hired locally,' Cawston continued, 'by a bearded man named Andrew Lane. Someone answering that description stayed at the White Hart, Andover, also under the name of Andrew Lane.'

Whitaker's stubby forefinger tapped the tobacco into place. He held the match flame just above it, as he drew on the pipe. 'As soon as we can get it from Andover let's get an artist's drawing of Lane distributed—press and television —and get it shown around.'

'They're working on it down there, sir.'

'How did Lane get to Andover?' Whitaker went on, thinking aloud. 'Did he go by train or by car? If he went by car, then he hired another somewhere. It's a fair assumption, I suppose, that he came from London. So get the picture shown round all the railway stations and the car-hire firms.' He sighed. 'Why can't C13 handle all this?' Whitaker knew the answer. The Commissioner had given his instructions.

39

He wanted Whitaker in overall charge. Perhaps the Commissioner knew something he didn't. Whitaker peered at his sergeant through the haze of smoke.

Cawston concealed his disapproval behind his dour professional manner. 'There's one other thing, sir.'

Whitaker wafted the smoke away.

Cawston handed him a photograph.

The superintendent stared in astonishment. 'Good god, what the hell is this? Don't say it's bloody witchcraft, Cawston?'

He thought for a moment, and then dialled the private number of David Rackham.

Rackham respected Superintendent Whitaker. He knew his stuff. He was professional. That suited Rackham very well. He knew that the superintendent was never greatly pleased at having to work closely with MI5 or the Secret Intelligence Service, and Rackham could understand why. There were always some things that couldn't be told, and the Special Branch understandably resented it. Rackham didn't much like it himself, but he persuaded himself that there was really no alternative.

He listened intently to what Whitaker had to say. There was no need to interrupt. The superintendent's account was as full as it could be. Only at the very end did Rackham mutter, 'Hell!' Then he added, 'No, it's not witchcraft, Arthur. That eye's been used before. Check your terrorist files. Code name, Argus.'

After he'd put the receiver down, Rackham turned to his friend, and relayed most of what Whitaker had told him.

Hammond's own reaction was, 'Careless bugger—leaving the boiler suit in the car. Then hiring the thing in Andover. Must have known he'd be recognized. Surely, given efficient police action, it's easy now?'

'You'd think so. I doubt whether Superintendent Whitaker does. I think you'll find our Mr Lane has disappeared off the face of the earth. He was a real professional.' Rackham paused, looked up, an almost amused expression in his eyes. 'Yes,' he repeated, 'I think I can promise you, he was a real professional. Mind you, that doesn't necessarily mean that he wasn't also pretty vain. Most of them are when it comes to it.'

Hammond swilled the colourless liquid in his glass reflectively. 'I haven't minded doing little jobs occasionally, David, but I've got an uneasy feeling now that I'm being dragged into something rather unpleasant.'

The freckled face grinned. 'Can't help it, old man, if you will manufacture something everyone wants.'

'Like toilet rolls? That's what I should have gone in for.'

Rackham grimaced. He went over to a small desk in the corner, and returned holding out another photograph.

Hammond stared at it. It was a blown-up picture of a wooden door, the outside door of a house or flat, but occupying almost all the frame was a big coloured eye.

'What is it?'

'It's the drawing of a large eye. Four months ago Herr Martin Lange, a minister in the West German Government, was shot in his flat in Bonn. That drawing was on the door of his apartment. At Andover, about three hundred and fifty yards from where the bomb exploded, the police have found a large coloured eye, cut from a magazine. It was pierced into the hedgerow.'

4

Dzerzhinsky Square in Moscow is more of a circle than a square, with nine roads feeding into it. In the centre, atop a grass mound and on a column plinth, stands the bronze figure of the man who gave the square its name—Feliks Edmundovich Dzerzhinsky, a Polish aristocrat, whose burning passion to become a Roman Catholic priest he managed to redirect into the formation of the Revolution's first security service, the Cheka. He might be said to have masterminded the deaths of hundreds of thousands of people described as enemies of the new Soviet state.

On this foundation the KGB was built, and on the north-east side of the square, behind the statue of Dzerzhinsky, stands the present-day headquarters of the KGB. It is a mustard-coloured building that still has a turn-of-the-century air about it. Alongside, and now part of the whole complex, is a nine-storey extension built by German prisoners of war. There are neat white curtains at the windows of the vaguely rococo façade. Those at the window on the third floor, just to one side of the main entrance, were drawn close. They hung behind the bullet-proof glass of the office of the Chairman of the KGB and a member of the Politburo, Mikhail Kalinsky.

Kalinsky was a comparatively slight figure, but what he lacked in stature he made up for in cunning and determination. None of his colleagues was foolish enough to underrate him. They knew that his cold grey eyes were set on the Soviet leadership itself. He had a sharp and, he liked to think, Lenin-like face.

This afternoon he had reason to be well satisfied. A few hours previously a black Zil saloon had carried him through wrought-iron gates to the old arsenal building in the Kremlin. The Politburo always met there in a salon on the third floor, overlooking an inner courtyard. The room, about fifty feet long and half as wide, had its eighteenth-century decorations picked out in white and gold. The Soviet leader sat at the head of the table, and on the wall facing him was an oil painting of Lenin. Kalinsky's eyes frequently strayed towards it. He could see himself in that picture.

The Minister of Defence, sitting next but one from the Party Secretary, had been very helpful in persuading the Politburo to agree with the KGB chairman that the plan was worth trying. Public opinion, as an instrument of policy, was not something the Politburo had to bother with in the Soviet Union itself, but in the West it could be exploited to the advantage of Soviet policy. Thus the leadership had first been encouraged but, more recently, disappointed by the peace movement. Admittedly, it had never stood much of a chance in the United States, but that didn't matter if it was sufficiently disruptive to be influential in Europe. It could then increasingly create dissension and ultimately drive a wedge between the continental NATO countries and the United States.

The European peace movement, however, had not come up to expectations in spite of the huge demonstrations in West Germany and the splendid efforts of the women at Greenham Common. One had to admit, as Kalinsky emphasized to his colleagues, that at the end of the day it had failed. The cruise and Pershing missiles had been deployed, and the Soviet Union had been forced into negotiating positions it would rather have avoided.

The Defence Minister had argued that the Soviet Union's greater superiority in conventional arms had, prior to the cruise and Pershing deployment, given them a considerable advantage in Europe. The only way NATO could have prevented the Soviet forces sweeping through to the Channel ports would have been by the use of tactical nuclear weapons, and that was something which could have been contained within Europe. The Americans would not willingly precipitate a nuclear holocaust for the sake of the Germans and the French, and the Minister's own opinion was that NATO would, in any event, hesitate to use tactical nuclear weapons. So all the advantage lay with the forces of the USSR—until, that was, cruise and Pershing. Now they were back to nuclear war on an international scale, and that was unthinkable.

It was at this point that Kalinsky argued that their efforts to promote the work of the peace movement should be intensified. After all, it still existed; it was still increasing in numbers. Moreover, anything that exacerbated public opinion in the Western democracies was to be exploited. People needed to be frightened by the full horror of nuclear radiation. If that could be achieved in reality, as distinct from articles in newspapers, programmes on television and demonstrations by the CND, then some progress might be made. People needed to be shocked into the horror of the thing. The problem was: how to do it without the wholesale slaughter that a nuclear weapon would cause? They needed something that would cause a comparatively small loss of life and, because of its own frightening nature, would incite panic. It was at this point that he outlined the plan he had received from Dmitri Shokolov in London.

The comrades listened intently, they argued, and the Defence Minister and the Foreign Minister together maintained that it might be a useful complement to the deliberate stalling of the international discussions on various aspects of nuclear weapons and arms control. At worst, there was nothing to lose, and there might be much to gain. If public opinion in Britain was so outraged that it forced the government into action, then the result could be of lasting benefit to the Soviet Union. After all, in Britain, governments could be made to change policies by the people. That fortunately could not happen in the Soviet republics. But in the United Kingdom, if the people were so angered—

Kalinsky had been pleased with himself, and with the response of his Foreign and Defence colleagues. Thus it was that the Politburo agreed that the plan should be implemented.

Back in his office, Kalinsky permitted himself the slightest of smiles, and turned to study again the papers that Shokolov had provided. It was important to choose the right man. He leant across his large and ornate desk and pulled towards him a tray that held half a dozen files. One of them especially interested him.

It bore the code name *Argus*. There were two photographs inside—one taken several years ago of an earnest but handsome youth; the other was recent and showed a still good-looking man with regular features, dark hair and brown eyes of about thirty. He was six feet and, in this photograph, clean-shaven. Not even Kalinsky was sure of his real name, although the one by which he preferred to be known when he was 'resting' was Karl Heinze. He was born in Bonn. He had attended the university there, the Lumumba University in Moscow, and then the London School of Economics. He was bilingual in German and English, and had a reasonable knowledge of Russian.

Lumumba was used mostly for students from the Third World, to see that they had a good university education, a thorough grounding in Marxism-Leninism, and a proper loyalty to their benefactors, the USSR. This, however, was not the exclusive use of the university. Occasionally a student who showed exceptional ability was found a place, irrespective of his origins. Such a student was likely not merely to train for the KGB, but also to have the special training required by Department V of the First Chief Directorate. That was the department concerned with assassination and sabotage. Only a tiny number of the third-world students ever became members of the KGB; the majority returned to the better-educated professions in their own country and became useful to the Soviet Union in subtler ways.

Argus, whatever his name might be, was one of the exceptional students. He had received the full KGB training. He had not only been to the school on the corner where Metrostroevskaya Street and Turnaninski Pereulok meet, but had gone on to the country establishment at Kuchino to be taught how to use those special poisons and drugs that defied the pathologist. He had even been to the special camp at Finsterwald in East Germany, where Arab guerrillas were trained, although, Kalinsky reflected, by the time the KGB had finished with him, he knew a great deal more than the instructors at Finsterwald. Kalinsky turned over the pages. Heinze's parents—but no, he wasn't much concerned with that kind of biographical background. He was more interested in the record of achievement. And that had been

45

quite remarkable, and of consistent value to the Soviet government.

Some of the operating groups in Europe—the West called them international terrorists—had become too large. Carried away by the enthusiasm of their success, they had expanded, brought in new people and new groups distinguished more by their fanaticism than by their training or ability. So the police in Germany, Italy, France, even Britain, had penetrated them, and several of the good operators, as well as the others, had been caught. It had been embarrassing and a nuisance for the KGB.

Argus, however, had always insisted on working with the smallest and most highly qualified groups and, if possible, he preferred to work alone. The result, as Kalinsky discovered, thumbing over the latest reports, was that the identity of Argus was quite unsuspected. There was even the occasional operation that the KGB knew nothing about, but for which they suspected Argus was responsible. The proof, Kalinsky noted with a grim smile, was never forthcoming.

The last operation was in his own home town of Bonn. It was about four months ago, and Herr Martin Lange, the West German minister, had been assassinated in his own flat. Argus had worked alone on that one. Most efficient. Now he was in London, apparently 'resting' again, and Kalinsky noted several addresses, at one of which he was sure to be found.

The KGB chief looked up at the portraits on the opposite wall—one of Lenin, the other of Dzerzhinsky. He thought they would have approved of Argus. The grey eyes narrowed as he read on through the typewritten pages. Argus enjoyed serious music. He also seemed to have one weakness. Carlos had had the same. Women. But Carlos had been a bit of a playboy. Not Argus. He just had to have a woman. Innocent women, after all, were frequently useful as a cover. There was no sign that a woman had ever interfered with an operation. Argus needed them for sex. On two occasions, when evidently the woman had not been content to end the relationship, Argus had simply disposed of her. Quite painlessly, of course. Then, as always, he disappeared. He was paid highly. Reading closely, there seemed no reason to doubt his loyalty, but he wasn't a simple terrorist who acted purely from idealistic motives. He demanded a high price. On the whole, Kalinsky reflected, he deserved it.

The K G B chairman closed the file. He leant back from the huge expanse of desk before him, his hands gripped tightly together, his eyes squinting. He had decided. He would send a coded signal to Shokolov.

5

Sandra Acton stood naked before a full-length bedroom mirror in a small flat in a side street off the Bayswater Road in London. In the background on her stereo system Itzhak Perlman was playing the Beethoven violin concerto with the Philharmonia under Giulini. She stared at herself, cupped her breasts in her hands. She wasn't bad-looking. There was nothing wrong with her figure. All right, she wasn't stunningly attractive, but her hazel eyes—almost green—were large enough to be expressive, the mouth was well-shaped, perhaps, she thought, even sensuous, the nose slightly up-tilted. Her hair was light brown and soft—mouse-coloured, if she was feeling depressed. On the whole, though, she was quite pretty. Pretty? Really? She looked back at herself, disbelieving. She stared at the triangle of pubic hair. It was a darker brown.

'For Christ's sake,' she shouted accusingly at her reflection.

She was twenty-six and a virgin, and was beginning to resent it. It was this resentment, and a growing impatience with her own inexperience, which, more than a month ago now, had nervously but deliberately led her to begin taking the pill. It was almost a gesture of defiance. Now, suddenly, she was sexually aware. They called it frustration, she supposed. She resented that description too. It didn't fit—not her, she told herself. After all, she was passionate enough, passionate about what she believed in. What was the matter with her? Her brother was thirty-two, and he wasn't married, but she bet he'd screwed lots of girls. Had he? She wondered. What about Gillian Ward? Why was she thinking about her brother, anyway? The fact was, she supposed, she really rather loved him. No, not like that—not sexually.

'I don't, do I?' she muttered aloud.

She was confused. She knew he disagreed with her about nuclear disarmament. That was about the only thing though, wasn't it? But she didn't ever feel the hostility for him that she sometimes felt for her father. Hammond had always been understanding; she had always been able to talk to him. He was good-looking and successful as well. How would she describe herself?

Primary school teacher. It was a cynical comment rather than a description. The children in the school a quarter of a mile away liked her, loved her perhaps as a kind of surrogate mother. She'd begun by feeling she had a mission to start children on their life in the world. She was laying the foundations. Now she was not so sure. She was sincere enough in her objectives but perhaps, in a way, she was using them. This troubled her. The Beethoven had reached the agonizing, breathless end of the slow movement before it uninterruptedly burst into the finale.

She couldn't go on like this. Something had to happen. She thought of the two men teachers on the staff, both recently out of teacher training. They weren't for her, they were too young. Who was? For heaven's sake, who was? She ran her hands over her body. Hell, she was becoming aroused again. She got dressed quickly, flung a few things into a weekend case, switched off the stereo, and hurried down to the white Ford Fiesta in the residents' parking bay outside. She headed out along the Bayswater Road towards Kew, and south to the M3.

She drove impatiently. Yet there was no particular reason why she needed to be at home. Of course she wanted to hear from Hammond what had really happened. Sandra always suspected the press. But curiosity didn't explain her impetuousness. The London traffic on a Saturday morning— housewives scurrying across the road, shopping—irritated her. She was glad to be out on the M3, where she ignored the speed limit. In less than an hour and a half she turned in briskly between the shining boles of two great beech trees, and swung the car round the circle of gravel to crunch to a stop by the columned porch of her parents' home.

Her mother greeted her warmly, her father was playing golf, but Hammond was there, in his own wing of the house.

'Oh, good,' he said, as she came in, not minding about being disturbed. 'Come to hear the full story from the horse's mouth, have you?'

She was instantly at ease. He was a good deal taller than she was, and she still felt protected by him. For his part he was aware of the admiration, and liked it. They talked about the murder of von Erbacher, and Hammond, walking to the window and looking out over the expanse of parkland, said, 'You know, it might even have been possible to see it all from here. But I suppose those trees would be in the way. In the winter, yes; but in the summer leaf—no, I reckon the bastard was safely out of sight.'

'Why should anyone want to kill him?'

'I don't know. Unless it's got something to do with my new electronic guidance system.'

'Guidance system? What does it guide?' she asked. 'For god's sake, you're not guiding nuclear bombs?'

'I'm not guiding anything, poppet. But it's so advanced it could be used for all sorts of purposes.' He saw her look of puzzled apprehension. 'It could guide a motor car, a disabled person's wheel-chair, and—yes, of course, it could guide a missile, with no danger of interference and far more accurately than any existing system.'

Sandra put her head in her hands, ran her fingers through her hair, then she looked up, dismayed and disappointed. 'But if you hadn't made it, it couldn't be used for missiles.'

'No—or for guiding a motor car safely in fog.'

'Oh, Hammond, you're sheltering behind the scientist's old excuse, aren't you? You only invent the thing. You're not responsible for its use.'

Again he smiled, tolerantly. It didn't irritate her, as it would have done had it been her father.

'I don't have a moral dilemma,' he said quietly. 'We've designed something that has infinite applications. I should think countless more good ones than bad. Are people to be denied those benefits?'

She made a small gesture of despair. 'And if you hadn't made it, someone else would.'

'Eventually—yes. But we're a long way ahead.'

'You're proud of it, aren't you?'

'Yes, I am. And not just because it's going to make me a lot of money. It's going to make money for Britain, too. It's nice to be ahead of the Yanks and the Japs for once.'

'Oh, my god, Hammond, what a bloody mess.'

'I don't see what's messy about it.'

'Somebody's been killed, haven't they?'

'Well, that was hardly my fault.'

'Except if you hadn't started work on military projects—'

'It's not a military project.'

She looked at him, disbelieving. 'What does Gillian think?'

He looked mildly embarrassed. 'D'you know, I'm not sure. She's been so upset by the whole thing that, for once, she seems to have lost her self-possession.'

'Are you going to marry her, Hammond?'

He laughed. 'I'm sure that's what Mother expects—'

'Well, it hasn't just been a boss/PA relationship, has it?'

'Stop being inquisitive, Sandra. But no, it hasn't, not entirely. And I'm not sure I know what I expect. Oh, well—'

She took his hand, patted it. She felt comfortingly close to him, a feeling that wasn't even disturbed when he suddenly asked, 'By the way, do you know Philip Strang?'

She looked at him, surprised. 'Yes, I've met him at demonstrations and things. But I don't know him well. He's not a mate. Why?'

'Just wondered. I'd heard his name mentioned somewhere —something to do with CND. Only he's a Communist.'

'How do you know?'

'I just heard that too,' he smiled.

She shrugged. 'Well, I'm not involved with him. You needn't worry.'

He nodded, and again she felt reassured by his presence. It wasn't a feeling she any longer experienced with her father. She was made acutely aware of this when they were talking together after lunch.

Geoffrey Acton had returned from golf in good spirits. He'd gone round the whole course in only four over par—his best for a very long time, and he was quite elated. Looking at him, Sandra could understand from whom Hammond got his good looks. Geoffrey Acton was just as tall and, in spite of the full head of grey hair, looked a good ten years short of his fifty-seven. His eyes were bright blue, his complexion fresh, and he appeared to be in abundant good health. The scene arose only because Sandra, desiring to keep the atmosphere good-humoured, determined on a natural filial interest and asked what was the architect's latest commission.

'I expect,' she said, teasing, 'you're designing a yacht marina in the Bahamas.'

Geoffrey smiled indulgently. 'Good try. The firm is working on one in Portugal. But my latest project is designing a nuclear power station. I've got plans of all the existing ones in my study,' he went on enthusiastically, 'but mine is going to be quite different. It will sit in the landscape as if it had been there for ever.' Then he noticed how Sandra's face had clouded over.

'Good god,' she said. 'I don't believe it—as though that defence thing up in Scotland wasn't enough. I—'

'Oh come, Sandra,' he interrupted calmly, 'I know what you feel about us having nuclear weapons, but you can't be against nuclear power as well, surely?'

Sandra felt a mixture of despair, anger, frustration. She noted what she thought was an understanding glance from her brother. Her mother sighed and, muttering that she had so much to do in the kitchen, gratefully left the room. 'Bomb factories,' Sandra said. 'That's all they are.'

Her father was infuriatingly calm, tolerant. 'I thought,' he said gently, 'they generated electricity for the national grid.'

Sandra made an exasperated sound. 'They also produce plutonium. That's to say the spent fuel is reprocessed to extract the plutonium. It's plutonium that's used in nuclear weapons—Oh god, there's no end to the bloody madness, is there?'

Geoffrey decided a few seconds of silence might have a healing effect. But before he could reply, Sandra went on, 'I know, if you don't design it, someone else will. That's the way to salve your conscience, isn't it?'

'About this,' said her father equably, 'I don't have a conscience. I'm not designing the nuclear side of the business, obviously. That's not a job for an architect. I design the building it goes into.' He spoke with a decisiveness that implied that was the end of the matter.

Sandra felt like screaming. His urbanity infuriated her. So did her feeling of impotence. It was Hammond who interrupted the silence.

'We've got nuclear power stations,' he said, 'and we're going to have some more. The important thing is that they should be safe. All right, Sandra,' he added, 'I know about plutonium. Well, it's up to people to ensure that the recovered plutonium is not used in nuclear weapons, isn't it? Meanwhile, let's make the power stations safe. That's why you employ the best architect, h'm?'

The tone was soothing. She didn't any longer know whether she agreed or disagreed with her brother, but at least she wasn't angered by him. She sighed, slumped down in a chair, and then, seeing her father's understanding smile, she jumped up and said, 'I'll go and give Mum a hand in the kitchen.'

As the door closed, Hammond looked at his father.

Geoffrey Acton shook his head and sighed. 'I'm worried about that girl,' he said. 'I really am.'

6

After the Ford Sierra had been returned to Godfrey Davis, Andrew Lane ceased to exist. Every piece of paper bearing his name was burned and the ashes flushed down the toilet of a pub in Baker Street, where the moustache and beard were also quickly shaved off. He preferred a clean-shaven appearance, and so did most of the women he'd known. After that, in the name of Karl Heinze, he booked into a suite of three rooms—sitting room, bedroom, and bathroom—in the Bromsgrove Hotel, a small but extremely comfortable establishment in Knightsbridge. Since he had only one suitcase with him, he then went out and bought himself another suit, several shirts, ties, underclothes, a pair of slacks and other leisure wear.

When he returned to the hotel, he ordered a bottle of champagne, stretched full-length on his settee, and scanned *The Times* for forthcoming concerts at the Royal Festival Hall. He also noted with a certain detachment that the police had failed to discover where the blue boiler suit had been purchased. It was the most common type, and widely available throughout the country. It wouldn't matter very much even if they did trace it to the large Tesco hypermarket where he'd bought it. It had been one of a number of purchases, and it was very unlikely that the assistant at the check-out would have remembered what the purchaser looked like. In any event, that person no longer existed. He smiled with satisfaction, and took a long draught of champagne. It would be nice to settle in London for a while, enjoy some music, and find a woman to share some pleasurable nights with. But he wasn't put out when, the next day, it looked as though his services were going to be required again. That, after all, was as essential to his satisfaction as was a woman.

The indication came in a note left with the reception desk.

It directed him to a telephone kiosk two streets away, from where, the following morning, he was instructed to ring what he guessed was another kiosk number. After he had committed this to memory, he held the note over an ashtray in his sitting room and set light to it. He crumpled the blackened paper to ashes, and then blew them out of the window.

The note was headed *Argus*. That was enough to tell him it had come from the KGB, and not from his most recent employers. He'd been puzzled by that assignment. Why should they want a *West* German industrialist disposed of? Not that it really concerned him. The bastard had come from the West. That was a good enough reason.

After he had made the telephone call the next day he had another twenty-four hours in which to do a lot of thinking and come up with a solution. In the meantime a parcel was delivered to his hotel. It contained overalls, a plumber's bag and tools, and a cap with a long peak that he could pull well down over his eyes. The next morning he put the lot into a small case, and left the hotel to summon a taxi. He asked to be taken to Euston station. There, in a toilet, he changed into his plumber's clothes, and then secured the suitcase in a left-luggage locker.

The Russian Embassy in Kensington Palace Gardens in London stands behind an arched stone wall. This is topped with iron railings and an even higher privet hedge. The embassy is built of those bricks usually known as 'whites', but which are in fact a dull yellowy grey. They give the place a dour appearance. It is quite unlike any other building in that exclusive, tree-lined road. The centre section protrudes almost like a tower, and is buttressed. It rises one storey higher than the two-storey wings on each side. These are surmounted by a looped balustrade. Behind the glass of the windows are steel grilles.

There is a yellow-and-black striped barrier arm barring access to the road, and this is operated by a man in a dark-green tail coat and topper. But there is ready access to the adjacent footpath. Karl Heinze loped along as he imagined a plumber would, clutching the loops of his triangular tool-bag. He walked through the lofty tunnel of foliage formed by the plane trees planted on each side until he came to No. 13.

The two black iron gates were firmly closed, but Heinze found the side gate yielded to a push. On the grass immediately before the building three slender silver birches added the only light touch to a sombre façade. His shoulders slightly hunched, and the cap pulled well down, he mounted the steps beneath the black glass canopy to the oak double doors. He was immediately admitted after a single tap on the knocker. He was shown into a sparsely but functionally furnished room that had a tall window laced by a steel grille overlooking the front shrubbery.

Dmitri Shokolov, square-faced, his grey hair cut short and crisp, got up from his desk as Heinze entered. They shook hands without speaking, and the Russian indicated one of the two easy chairs in the room. It stood aslant beneath a portrait of Lenin.

'You have considered?' Shokolov queried.

Heinze nodded, as he studied the thickset figure that ambled to a similar chair placed a few yards opposite.

'It has the blessing of the Politburo,' said Shokolov.

'I thought as much.'

'The weakness of the West is as important as the strength of the Soviet Union. The role of the peace movements is to induce that weakness. Napoleon used them very effectively against the Austrians, the Germans made good use of them before both world wars. We have not been unsuccessful in promoting the peace movements ourselves. They've grown considerably in Britain and Europe. But they haven't yet defeated their governments. It is so much slower in democracies.' He smiled coldly. 'This operation would give the movement a big impetus—an outburst of public opinion. It could do more than—'

'You can spare me the propaganda,' Heinze cut in.

Even the cold impassivity of Shokolov's expression gave way to a modicum of surprise. It was the first time that he had met Argus. Already he was aware of the man's cool detachment and his authority.

'You should be acquainted with objectives,' the Russian said.

'I am. Who is Strang?'

'He works for us—politically. He's in C N D. He also got himself elected to a local council.' The Russian smiled frostily. 'He's qualified as a surveyor, but he's conveniently unemployed.'

'He's known then?'

Shokolov nodded.

'I shan't want him on the operation.'

'No. The idea was his. But it's much too big for him. We have considered the vulnerability of spent fuel during its journey to Sellafield, but there's not enough radioactivity. It has to be a power station. But there's more than four inches of steel and twelve feet of reinforced concrete protecting the core. Can you get sufficient explosive there?'

'I've thought of that,' said Heinze. 'It will have to be a missile fired from a ship outside territorial waters.'

Shokolov concealed his surprise.

'The Styx 2C is a reliable weapon. Would it be up to the job? There will, of course, need to be laser target-designation on the bridge of the ship.'

This time Shokolov did raise his eyebrows. 'I'm not sure about the Styx. I'll check,' he said.

Heinze smiled faintly. 'I suggest we conceal the missile,' he said, 'by fitting it inside a container. There must be enough room for the container to swivel round and its sides collapse, leaving the missile ready for firing. So the deck will need a turntable. And, of course, the master and crew will have to be carefully selected. I can't have any trouble with them. Immediately after the firing I shall need to be lifted off by helicopter and taken to East Germany. Is all that possible?'

'If the K G B consider the operation important enough —yes. And they do. You will have to work on the detail.'

Heinze nodded. 'There's one other thing,' he said.

'Which is?'

'What am I paid?'

'That will have to be discussed too,' said Shokolov remotely.

'I want a quarter of a million. Pounds, I mean. That's the minimum. If the comrades are not prepared for that, it's off.'

He looked down at his overalls with distaste. 'I will produce an operational plan in detail within twenty-four hours. Work will need to begin on the ship immediately. It ought not to take more than ten days.'

Shokolov returned to his desk, made some notes and calculations. Then they discussed communications, and set up a system for passing messages and arranging meetings. Heinze was anxious that the whole operation should proceed as quickly as possible. The longer it took, the more opportunity there was for the enemy to find out.

The two men shook hands. As Shokolov opened the door for him, Heinze stared steadily at the thickset Russian and added, almost menacingly, 'No messing over the money. I want immediate confirmation of the fee. Or forget it.'

By the time he reached the front door, he remembered to adopt his plumber's lope and stoop. He went by tube back to Euston station, recovered his suit, changed in the toilet, and returned to his hotel. Fleetingly, he remembered the tall dark girl he had seen in the White Hart at Andover. He wished there had been time to get to know her.

7

It was a Brahms evening at the Royal Festival Hall—the Academic Festival overture, and then two works representing the young Brahms and the mature Brahms: the First Piano Concerto and the Fourth Symphony. Sandra was looking forward to it. She'd bought two tickets, and impulsively offered one of them to a fellow teacher. She suspected he was younger than she was, but—oh well, it was only for an evening. Then, at the end of school, he had suddenly said that he was very sorry, but he wouldn't be able to come after all. He offered a pathetic excuse about some parents who wanted to see him, and it was the only night they could manage. He was terribly disappointed, he said unconvincingly. Sandra took back the ticket, and despised him for the transparency of his lie. In a moment of irrational anger she almost tore up both tickets, but quickly came to her senses and decided that she would arrive very early at the Festival Hall, so that she could hand in her spare ticket and give someone else a chance.

She bought herself a gin and dry martini at the bar in the centre of the main concourse. She needed the little fillip of alcohol to counter her feeling of isolation, sitting there alone at a small table in the wide spaces among the chatteringly enthusiastic concert-goers. She went early to her seat, up the stairs on the green side to doorway 4, and then to row G, almost in the centre of the hall, just under the grand tier. Seat number 22 was the third in from the gangway. She settled down, again aware of spaciousness, as few people had yet entered the hall. Ahead of her, in a wide rectangular panel, the organ pipes looked like an abstract sculpture. She shifted in her seat, opened her programme and began to read the notes.

The seat on her right, which should have been occupied by

59

her teacher colleague, remained empty until about two minutes before the concert was due to begin. Then a tall man, looking immaculate in a light-weight grey suit with a red tie, moved swiftly in front of the elderly couple seated to her left, and she got up to let him pass. He looked about her brother's age, and had dark brown hair and strong features. His eyes were dark brown too, and even momentarily, as he sat down and glanced in her direction, she was aware of them. They didn't look right through her; the glance was too brief for that. But they disturbed her, so that she gave him a quick, nervous smile. He had scarcely sat down and opened his programme before the London Symphony Orchestra filed on to the platform, and applause erupted all round them. It was renewed almost immediately for the conductor, Claudio Abbado, but the loudest outburst of all came after the overture, when Maurizio Pollini came on to the platform for the piano concerto.

From the thunder-roar of the timpani's opening chord and the rolling crescendos of the symphonic beginning, Sandra found herself being borne along excitedly by the music and yet at the same time—perhaps just because of the music —being aware of the man beside her. It was as though the awareness of one heightened the awareness of the other. After the enormously long first movement, the entire audience was ready with fidgets and coughs for their brief release from the intricate abundance of Brahms's interwoven themes. Sandra breathed deeply, a kind of satisfied relief. The man turned his head towards her with a slight, quizzical smile. She acknowledged it rather more nervously. As she shifted in her seat she could feel him watching her. Her breath quickened; she tried to control it. The hall was suddenly silent. The music crept into the hushed opening of the adagio. Sandra luxuriated in the sublime lyricism of the movement, and all the time was aware of the man beside her, sharing the experience. So she wasn't surprised when, at the end of the movement, he turned to her and whispered, 'Beautiful.'

'Oh yes,' she said, feeling her breath catch in her throat.

Then the piano had launched into the monumental finale. Now she was listening to the music with a fresh intensity, and yet was all the time physically conscious of him. After the four final exuberant chords, she turned towards him, as their hands clapped. The audience re-called both soloist and conductor several times, before Sandra collapsed back in her seat with pleasurable exhaustion. She and the man were now smiling openly at each other.

'I'm so glad you were able to get a seat,' she said, almost before she was aware of the thought.

'I was lucky. It was a returned ticket.'

'I know. It was mine.'

'Then,' he said, 'I am extremely grateful.'

She thought his voice was velvety and warm, and there was something a little unusual about the tone, not exactly an accent, but the merest suggestion of something different. She was excited by it.

'Don't you think,' he continued, 'that deserves my buying you a drink?' He was already standing, straightening his jacket, and reaching a hand towards her.

He led her confidently down the flight of stairs to the wine bar that overlooked the main concourse. He seated her in the right-angled corner, and returned with a half-bottle of champagne. She watched as he expertly removed the cork with the faintest of pops, and the light honey-coloured liquid frothed into their glasses.

He raised his glass. 'With thanks,' he said.

She smiled. 'You obviously like Brahms.'

'I think he's my favourite. That last movement of the concerto, full of little hints—did you notice?—of Beethoven's Ninth.'

She nodded, but all she could think of to say was a ridiculous, 'Do you come often?'

He smiled, but she noticed how his brown eyes were watching her intently as though they were summing her up and coming to a judgement. 'I go to concerts as often as I can,' he answered.

He momentarily looked away. She felt released, and chatted on animatedly about the music. Then she was aware that he was watching her again; aware, too, of his physical presence, as she began to feel a gradual arousal within herself.

Suddenly she said, 'Isn't this silly? We don't know each other. I'm Sandra Acton.'

'Karl Heinze,' he said.

She felt elated. 'Like the fifty-seven varieties?'

'I'm the fifty-eighth. There's an *e* at the end.'

They laughed together.

By the time they returned to the concert hall for Brahms's fourth symphony she was feeling light-hearted and happy, and—thank heaven—sexually aroused. She was sure he knew this. She sensed it in the way he touched her arm, and then let his body brush against hers as they moved into their seats.

Heinze, for his part, was aware of it all right. He could always sense sex in a woman. Between movements he studied her, as dispassionately as his own aroused feelings allowed. What would she be like? Would she be worth it? He doubted if she would be as good in bed as that German girl. But she looked as though she needed it. She was really quite nice. If her hair hadn't got much colour at least it was soft and feminine. Her eyes were interesting, almost green, and he liked her tilted nose. Her mouth was especially promising. In her light summer dress she seemed to have a good figure, too—not large breasts, but a handful, and, after all, who wanted more? Yes, he thought, she might be all right. As the last movement began, he reached out and took her hand. She returned a grateful smile.

After the performance they went out on to the terrace. Beneath them was a wider terrace with clumps of tubbed evergreens and, beneath that, a green bank, promenade and trees. Lights looped between the lamp-posts on the river bank, flickering through the leaves, and reflecting in the water in orange sequins. To their right were the slim white spans of Waterloo Bridge. They began to talk of the music—the massive architecture of the Fourth Symphony, the profound consummation of Brahms's symphonic achievement and even, Heinze said, the end of a musical era.

They wandered down to the river level and strolled towards Westminster Bridge and the orange-floodlit towers of the Houses of Parliament. Soon they were talking of themselves. Or, at least, Sandra was talking about herself, telling him of her job, how she had idealistically seen herself as helping children to put down their educational roots, helping them to develop their own personalities. Then she told him of her parents, and her brother, Hammond, whom, she confessed, she had always adored. Heinze listened intently, at no time showing surprise, but watching her closely. It was only when they were about to part, and he suggested she should have a meal with him on Friday, two nights later, that she realized he had spoken very little about himself. Not that it mattered; that would do next time.

He told her he had been lucky that her friend—whoever he or she was—had been unable to come to the concert. But for that he might never have met her. Think, he said, how life was built up from a series of chances, over which none of us had any control. She remembered how she had nearly torn up the tickets. They exchanged telephone numbers, and arranged to meet at seven-thirty at Odin's restaurant in Devonshire Street.

She arrived five minutes late, and he was already seated at their table, waiting for her. At such an early hour the restaurant was almost empty. She had never been there before. It had a sumptuous and expensive air, and the walls were thronged with oil paintings like an art gallery. Heinze told her that he only very occasionally came to this place, but he liked it because it was off the beaten track. He assumed it was used more at lunch time than in the evening, but he promised her the food would be good. She noticed that the menu reproduced a crayon illustration of portly gentlemen whom she imagined might be the owners.

She had taken care to look her best. Her dress was close-fitting and showed her figure. She had been sparing with her make-up, but had accentuated her eyes, so that they really looked green. She saw his glance of approval, and was pleased.

They each had a fino while they studied the menu. She chose a mushroom paté and a veal dish cooked in marsala. He decided he would have the same, because, he said, having shared her seats at the Royal Festival Hall, it would be appropriate to share the meal. She laughed, nervous and excited at the same time.

'What do you do?' she asked.

'I listen to music and go to concerts.'

'No, seriously.'

Heinze was ready for this. 'I'm an economist and a political scientist. I act as a consultant to anyone who requires my services. So I travel a good deal. Usually I do work for large companies or even government departments.'

'And who're you working for now?'

'At the moment I'm what an actor would describe as resting.' He smiled. 'But there'll be another commission shortly,' he added confidently.

'Isn't it all a little precarious?'

'Not at all. My fees are large.'

She admired his assurance. She was very aware of his physical presence. She desperately wanted him to like her.

'That's good,' she said, 'but how actually do you earn them?'

'I write reports of studies I have made of political situations, economic prospects—perhaps about a specific industry, or a country. Oh, I can afford to pay for your meal, don't worry.'

She thought he was charming. By the time they had finished eating, and stimulated by the wine, she was wanting him. There was no point in pretending she felt anything else. So it seemed natural and right that they should get a taxi back to her flat. She would make some more coffee, and they could listen to music on her stereo, she said.

Heinze had also made up his mind. Throughout the meal he had been studying her as objectively as he could against the awareness of his own unsatisfied desire. It had been several weeks since he had a woman. Now there was this girl who was obviously asking for it. She would do nicely while he was in England. He hoped her flat was not untidy, like those of so many girls. He couldn't abide slovenliness. That was another, if minor, reason why he preferred to work alone. So many groups were careless of their appearance and indifferent to their surroundings. Heinze enjoyed comfort, and was meticulous about his own appearance.

He wasn't disappointed with Sandra's flat. If not excessively neat, it wasn't a mess. It had a lived-in feeling, and although the furnishing was simple, it was attractive. He stretched on a divan near the wall, while Sandra put on a cassette of Pollini and the Quartetto Italiano playing the Brahms Piano Quintet, while she busied herself making coffee. He was glad she didn't smoke. He thought it was a filthy habit, and he didn't like the breath of a woman who had been smoking.

Sandra returned with the coffee and a bottle of white wine, an Italian Soave she had found in her small rack in the kitchen. They talked—about the music, which she had put on very quietly—about him going to university in Bonn, where he was born, and then to the London School of Economics. He didn't mention Moscow. She told him about her life and her family, and how upset she was that her father was going to design a nuclear power station.

'Are *you* against the bomb?' she asked him earnestly.

'Who isn't?' he responded cautiously.

'At weekends I often used to go to the women's camp at Greenham Common. It was like a fortress—great rolls of barbed wire, searchlights and watchtowers, and even helicopters. They woke us up in the morning. The policemen weren't so bad, though. But the women—they were wonderful. It was a marvellous feeling at night, sharing a bender with them, straw on the ground, thick sleeping bags and blankets, trying to keep out the damp, even hearing the rain on the polythene. Sometimes, from the other side of the wire, soldiers would hurl stones at the tents. But it was the feeling of solidarity, of unity in one aim—the compassion, the love, the humanity. Yet we couldn't keep out those bloody cruise missiles.' She was surprised at her own passion, and looked at him anxiously.

He smiled, and gently stroked her arm. 'You're active in CND?'

She nodded. 'I go to most of the big demonstrations. I've organized a group from the parent–teacher association. Couples with young children are the keenest, I think.'

'I've worked for it too,' he said, 'in Germany.'

She looked up at him fondly. 'What *are* we going to do? It's

65

just incredible—isn't it?—how they can have these terrible weapons. They don't seem to care that they can wipe out the whole of life. It's madness. It's a wonder the people don't rise up. We need a Cromwell. Oh god, I don't know—'

'The British people,' he said, 'won't do anything until they're shocked or frightened into it.'

'How? God knows we've demonstrated enough—thousands and thousands of us, and what's happened? Nothing. We live in more danger than ever.'

'That's because,' he said, 'they don't really feel threatened. Life goes on comfortably. There's no real threat. But supposing they were *really* threatened—with a release of radioactivity—enough to kill some people?'

'You don't mean the bomb, Karl? You can't mean that?'

'No, of course not. But supposing there was an escape of radioactive materials from a nuclear power station, sufficient to kill a number of people in the neighbourhood? Oh, I know there have been deaths from cancer attributed to radiation from power stations, but that's long delayed. But if there were a leak, and people died instantly. That might shock the nation into action, force the government's hand.'

She stared at him with a mixture of admiration and perplexity.

He responded to her anxiety. 'It would probably be enough just to threaten. Only it would have to be a well-organized threat, so well-organized that the government believed it was going to happen.'

'You mean, sort of hold them to ransom?'

'Sort of.'

She poured out two more glasses of wine, looked thoughtful. He leant over, took a glass from her. They each took a sip of wine, and then he kissed her gently.

'Would it work?' she asked.

'If it was well enough organized.'

'But how could you threaten an escape of radiation from a power station?'

'How about a missile attack?'

She felt tremendously stimulated—by the wine, by him,

66

by what he was saying. She even chuckled. 'Oh, I've got lots of missiles,' she teased. 'My father was paid in them when he designed that secret defence place up in Scotland.'

'No, I'm serious. Threaten them with a missile attack on a specific power station.'

'But who could do that?'

'Well, I suppose the British government would call them terrorists. We might call them peace workers.' He looked at her determinedly. 'It could be done, you know.'

She warmed to his self-confidence, his authority. 'You mean a C N D group?'

He was tempted to laugh, but all he said was, 'Could be—in theory. But they'd be known to the authorities, wouldn't they? It would have to be a group that no one knew.'

She took his hand, squeezed it. 'Oh, we're just talking. None of it's possible, Karl.'

'Anything's possible if you want it enough—'

'But where's a group like that coming from?'

'Us.'

She looked into his eyes, bemused. 'Us?' she repeated, preoccupied. Yet, with him there, she felt anything *was* possible.

'I've met a lot of people in my work. I've contacts. I could organize it.'

She believed him. 'It would only be a threat?'

'Of course. But we'd have to have the means, the capability, otherwise the threat would be meaningless.'

'But how could we?'

'I think I could.'

'A missile?'

He nodded.

She looked up at him, wondering. It could be. She was sure it could be. Workers for peace, she thought. They might actually achieve something. They might really be able to force the government to get rid of those weapons. She believed it. Suddenly, impulsively, she hugged him.

He drew away from her slightly, and then kissed her passionately. When, fifteen minutes later, they moved into her bedroom, he undressed her slowly, and looked at

67

her body appreciatively. He touched her gently, and she shivered with delight.

As he began to make love to her, he discovered her inexperience. She was passionate and desperate, but very naïve. Then, as he went on, he saw the sudden grimace of pain on her face.

'My god, you're a virgin,' he breathed, disbelieving.

She nodded, made a soft confirmatory sound.

For one moment he wanted to hurt her, to brutalize her. But he checked himself. He saw the adoration and submissiveness in her face. If he were considerate, he would be able to get her to do anything for him. So he was careful and tender, and saw the gratitude in her eyes. And afterwards she murmured, 'Thank you. Oh, Karl, thank you.'

He stayed the night with her. That was what she wanted. All the time he was sensitive and caring. In the morning she felt she had never been so happy in her life.

Heinze didn't like being unable to shave, but Sandra found him a razor her brother had left on a previous occasion. She also had a spare toothbrush, and this pleased him. He disliked not being able to look and feel clean.

She had muesli and cornflakes, orange juice, and she made toast and coffee. She sat at right angles to him at her small dining table and looked at him with unabashed adoration.

'Did you say last night that your father was designing a nuclear power station?' he asked suddenly.

'Yes. I think it's horrible.'

'Has he designed one before?'

'No—why?'

'Well, if he had, he might still have the plans.'

'Oh, he's got plans of the others. He told me.'

'Sizewell?'

'I should think so.'

'Could you get them for me?'

'You mean, steal them?'

'No, borrow them. He can have them back.'

She knew she would do anything for him.

'Yes,' she murmured. 'Yes, darling, I'll get them.'

'If we're going to threaten a nuclear power station,' he said, 'it's just as well to know what it's like in detail.'

'But is it really possible? Can we really do that?'

'I told you so last night.' The tone was unequivocal.

'Then, when do you want them?'

'Why not go down today? Bring them back tomorrow. I'll come round tomorrow night. Then you can take them back next weekend. I'll get them photocopied. Will he miss them?'

'I shouldn't think so—not if he's got lots of others. Anyway, I imagine he's already studied those—probably won't look at them again.'

An hour later he watched her drive her Ford Fiesta out into the Bayswater Road and head west. Well, that settled it. She was part of the operation, providing essential information. She would be reliable enough. Her passionate endorsement of the CND, combined with her infatuation, would see to that. She might have remained a virgin for twenty-six years, he thought to himself, but, by heaven, she was going to learn about sex now. He stepped across the road into Hyde Park, enjoying the warm touch of the sunlight on his face, and feeling very pleased with himself.

8

Gillian Ward had slept badly. When at last she had drifted into sleep, she was muttering to herself, 'This is the last time—last time.' Saturday morning, and she was tired.

Her flat was in a small three-storey block, faced with brick and green tiles, called Wellesley Court. It had picture windows and balconies that overlooked Andover golf course. She pulled aside the net curtain and peered out. The day looked tired too—uncertain of itself. Would the haze lift and sunlight break through, or would it stay a gauzy, overcast day? She couldn't see anyone playing golf yet; it was too early.

'This must be the end,' she said to herself, and thought of what Goethe had said, about getting away—escaping. She thought of Goethe, and she thought of Hammond, and if she had been the weeping kind of woman, she would have wept. There was a time when she would have been totally convinced of the rightness of what she had done. Part of her—a smaller part than ever before—still was convinced, but mostly she was troubled by doubt. She had been trapped by her own actions rooted in earlier convictions, and now she was worried about their validity. Yes, this must be the end—just one more thing to do.

It was two nights ago that Stoebel had telephoned. He had uttered one word only, and she had then gone out to a public phone box and followed her normal routine.

'I'm booking into the White Hart tomorrow, Friday,' Stoebel had said. 'Saturday, you bring it to me—the thing itself.'

'Aren't the drawings enough?' she had asked. 'Surely the drawings are enough?'

'We need the system,' Stoebel commanded.

'I can't—I can't get that.'

'Only you can.'

'But—'

'We've looked at it. Impossible. Has to be done from inside.'

Gillian knew that well enough. There was no possibility of breaking into the premises. 'I—I didn't think this would be necessary. I thought the drawings would be enough.'

'We need the system. What else did you think you were doing, eh? You don't have an alternative—understand?'

'I suppose so.'

'Saturday, then!'

Gillian had mumbled her assent and put down the phone. Now Saturday had come, and she had the damn thing to deliver. When she saw Stoebel she would tell him that this was the last time. What would happen then? Would they consider her a danger? She would be able to name names. She would be putting her own life at risk. But all this had got to come to an end. Somehow she had to finish it. Would Goethe help her—against Stoebel? Would he protect her from one of his own staff?

She helped herself to some orange juice from the fridge, and decided that breakfast wasn't possible.

The telephone rang. She stared at it. Of course, it was bound to ring—inevitable. At first she thought she'd just let it ring until it stopped. But then, automatically, she picked it up. 'Yes?' she said wearily.

'Gillian?' It was Hammond. 'The factory—it's been broken into. The guidance system has been stolen.'

She was silent, not knowing what to say. Fortunately, Hammond assumed that she was shocked.

'I've been with the police for the last couple of hours,' he said.

'Oh god, how terrible.' She hoped she sounded convincing. 'How awful, Hammond. But who? Who on earth would want to steal that?'

'Oh, a lot of people. I'm going up to town. I've given the police your address. They'll be round shortly, I guess.'

'Yes,' she said. 'Yes, of course.' She felt she was being inadequate. 'Oh god,' she muttered.

'I—I'll see you this evening—as arranged.'

'Yes,' she said.

The door bell shrilled.

David Rackham was in his office, a floor below his chief in the steel, concrete and glass building that rose twenty storeys above the Thames, when he received the report from the agent in Leningrad. He stared out towards the towers of Parliament, and wondered if there was any significance at all in it, or whether it contained no more than further scraps of information that were collected and collated lest, at some time in the future, they should be of use. He looked at the decoded notes. A Russian container ship of about 25,000 gross tonnes, the red flags removed, the hammer and sickle painted out of the stack, the name changed to *Argus Viktor*, and men building what looked like a turntable on the main deck amidships. What do you want a turntable on a container ship for? And why remove the Soviet insignia? Well, if he *would* come into the office on a Saturday, he must expect these little irritations.

The other item on his desk was of more immediate concern. It was a photo-fit picture, provided by the West German authorities, of the terrorist whom they believed had assassinated Martin Lange in Bonn. It showed strong, regular features, piercing eyes, and the lower part of the face moustached and heavily bearded. Rackham mentally removed the beard and concluded that it was, perhaps, not a bad likeness of the man that he knew was code-named Argus. He doubted whether it would be of any great help to the police who, so far as the murder of von Erbacher was concerned, had still got no further than the abandoned car at Andover Golf Club. That, doubtless, was as far as they were intended to get, and Rackham saw not the slightest likelihood of further progress.

An hour later the whole affair was suddenly complicated. Rackham had scarcely been five minutes back in his flat, a little further westward along the Thames, before the buzzer at the front door was repeating impatiently. There, facing him, was a distraught Hammond Acton.

'I've driven up here like a bloody maniac,' he said. 'Tried to get you a lot earlier on the phone—'

'I was at the office,' Rackham told him as he ushered his friend into the lounge overlooking the river.

'Have you heard from the police?'

Rackham shook his head.

'They've broken in. No, not the police. Someone broke into the factory last night. They've stolen the guidance system.'

'You've got—?'

'Oh, of course I've got another. We're manufacturing the bloody thing. They've only taken one.'

'That's all they need.'

Rackham looked thoughtful. He picked up the phone, turned his back on his friend and punched out one brief number.

'Arthur? David Rackham. Yes, fine, thanks. Last night the factory of Digitalia at Andover was broken into and some electronic equipment was stolen—'

He heard the superintendent grunt, 'I know. Just had the reports read over to me.'

'Well, keep in touch, Arthur, please. Every single detail of the investigation.'

The policeman responded warily. 'You think it's connected?'

'I don't think, Arthur. I know. So the closest co-operation, please.' He put down the receiver, and took the glass that Hammond held out to him.

'So, who was it? One of von Erbacher's lot?' Hammond asked.

'I should think so. And we know the Americans are interested, don't we? What's so special about it?'

'Its total accuracy. It can guide anything to—well, a pin's head in the Sahara Desert. And so far nothing can divert it. It can't be confused or jammed. And it's small.'

Rackham sighed. 'Just the thing for the bloody Ruskies. The Cousins are going to be mighty mad. After all, it was important enough for someone to take out von Erbacher.'

'The Americans wouldn't—?' Hammond began.

'Von Erbacher? Yes, sure, if they thought it important enough. The theft though is hardly necessary, is it? When they can have all they want to know quite freely. You can

73

discount the Americans. There's no doubt about it, it's the Eastern bloc, in one form or another.'

Hammond looked mystified. 'But if it's the Russians how do they get it out?'

Rackham smiled, tolerantly. 'The diplomatic bag, Hammond. Easy.'

'So it's probably already on its way to Moscow.'

'Not necessarily. Two possibilities. One, the police pin it on someone quickly—before the Russians have time to do anything about it. Or two, we manage to intercept it. One, I think, is frankly unlikely. Two is not impossible. Anyway, the destination is more likely to be East Berlin than Moscow.'

Hammond looked surprised. Rackham went back to the settee.

'Their best expert on weapons guidance systems is in East Germany. That might make it a little easier for us.'

Hammond had gone over to the window. A solitary barge was moving down river. The water was crinkled like silk.

'There's one odd thing, David,' he said. 'The police are not sure how they broke in. It looks like the front door, but that's a bit too obvious.'

'What kind of alarms have you got?'

'Oh, they're electronic too, and quite sophisticated. The system is, of course, connected direct to Andover police station, and at the most sensitive places we've got video cameras that will record a picture of any intruder.'

'And none of it worked?'

'No. Because the master control had been switched off. But to do that you have to get into the building. The locks on the main front doors had been broken. Which shouldn't have been possible. The alarms would have been activated and the break-in would have been recorded by video cameras—even in the dark.'

'So we're looking for an expert.'

'That's what the police said,' Hammond muttered, as he came back from the window and lowered himself, exhausted, into a comfortable chair opposite his friend. 'Isn't there anything else we can do?'

'Yes, there's quite a lot I can do. The best thing you can

do, though, is to go back to Andover. Why don't you take your personal assistant out for a meal, keep her out of mischief. Leave the rest to us—and the police.'

'I was going to tonight, anyway—take Gillian out, I mean.'

'You should introduce me sometime—Meanwhile, make sure your place is well guarded. If the police are not mounting a twenty-four-hour watch, get in a local security firm.'

Hammond nodded. 'It's all being done,' he said.

When his friend had gone, David Rackham made a series of telephone calls. Then he decided to get back to the office. There were some signals to be sent. He couldn't understand why the Cousins were not being more helpful. By the end of the day, however, his American counterpart, somewhat embarrassed, conceded that the guidance system had been nicked by a foreign power, and they didn't know who'd got it. They believed, however, that it was an inside job, but had failed to confirm it. That was something the police should be able to manage without too much difficulty. Rackham had muttered his agreement. He was tolerably sure that he knew who had taken the guidance system. Somehow it had to be recovered, or at least prevented from reaching the Soviet Union.

Superintendent Whitaker had an attic in his Wimbledon home which he used as a studio. He had let a large window into the slope of the roof, and this provided plenty of light, although he didn't claim it came from the north. He knew that his wife, Edie, liked it when he was up there, messing around with his paints and canvases. She knew where he was, and that he was enjoying himself, and that was a comforting feeling. This Saturday he was making a start on a new portrait. He had been very struck by a group of photographic self-portraits that Sergeant Cawston had taken, and the superintendent asked if he could borrow them. 'I think, Snap,' he had said, 'I'd like to have a stab at a portrait of you.'

So it was that Art Whitaker had just got himself nicely organized, his easel set up, palette laid out, and the photographs conveniently arranged, when Edie summoned him down to the telephone to speak to David Rackham. He swore beneath his breath. Not half an hour previously Cawston had been on the blower briefing him about the Andover break-in. It had seemed to him that the local police had got everything well in hand. At any rate, he was reluctant to interfere at this stage.

'Arthur—that Digitalia break-in—'

Why did Rackham's voice always sound so confoundedly cheerful? Whitaker grunted.

'Has Gillian Ward's flat been searched?'

'She's been questioned—obviously. I don't imagine the local boys saw any reason to search her flat.'

'No, I don't suppose they would. Arthur, get them to search it right away. It's important.'

'You're not suggesting she's got the guidance system?'

'Yes. I know she's the last person the police have any reason to suspect—but search her flat just the same. And quickly.'

'Is there anything else you can tell me?' Whitaker asked.

'No.'

The superintendent made a sound of unmistakable displeasure and put down the receiver, only immediately to pick it up again and dial 0264 4311 for the Andover police.

Five minutes later Arthur Whitaker returned to his attic, got his pipe going, and made the first strokes on the canvas. That was a very satisfying feeling. Not a feeling of power, or even of authority, but a feeling of adventure. Where there had been nothing, something would be created, and exactly how it would come out he could not know, and yet it depended upon his skill. He always found this fascinating and stimulating. So the brush went to the canvas again, and more initial strokes were made.

'Arthur!' Edie's voice called up the attic stairs. 'It's Sergeant Cawston again.'

'Blast! Damn and blast! All right, I'm coming.'

The superintendent lumbered down the two flights of stairs to the telephone extension in his study. 'I wonder,' he said mockingly into the mouthpiece, 'if Rembrandt got interrupted like this?'

'Couldn't say, sir,' Cawston answered seriously.

'Imagine painting the *Nightwatch* and—Oh well, Snap, what is it?'

'Andrew Lane hired a two-litre Ford Sierra from Godfrey Davis, and returned it last Saturday. The girl remembers that he was good-looking and wore a full beard. She's seen the German photo-fit of Argus. Thinks it could be the same man.'

'Humph! Address?'

'That's been checked, sir. It doesn't exist.'

'So he's back in London? Or else the bastard's out of the country. Where's the Sierra now?'

'It's been washed, polished, cleaned and hired out again.'

Whitaker rumbled out an angry expletive.

'And while we're thinking of fingerprints, sir,' Cawston continued dourly, 'the Astra at Andover was completely clean.'

'It would be.'

'A bit strange, sir. I mean he takes such care over fingerprints, and doesn't give a damn about the boiler suit.'

'And have they traced where it was purchased?'

'No, sir. It's just about the most common you can get. Available everywhere.'

'Hardly matters, does it?' Whitaker grumbled. 'We know we're dealing with an international terrorist, and the Germans think they know what he looks like.'

'This Argus business, guv. I've been looking it up. He had a hundred eyes—'

'Oh, I see, he'll stop after a hundred killings, will he?'

Cawston politely ignored the sarcastic interruption. 'On the instructions of Zeus, sir, Hermes lulled him to sleep by the notes of his flute. Then he cut his head off. Hera transplanted his eyes to the tail of a peacock.'

'Did she, now? Very interesting, Snap. Can you play the flute, then?'

'No, sir.'

'Pity. We might have caught him. I can see the headlines: COP FLAUTIST LULLS KILLER TO HIS DEATH.'

77

Cawston made a sound that might have been a chuckle. 'But in the end he didn't do too well, sir—having his head cut off, I mean.'

'Sorry, sergeant, beheading went out some time ago, and we don't keep axes in the Special Branch. Well, not that kind,' he added as an afterthought.

'I just thought we might find him a bit of a peacock, sir—rather vain, like you said.'

'Good deduction, sergeant.' Whitaker knew that he was being unusually sarcastic this morning, but he did so want to get back to the attic.

There was a slight pause at the end of the line, which Whitaker soon discovered was Cawston wondering whether he was entitled to a touch of humour as well.

'This Digitalis concoction,' the sergeant said, 'd'you reckon that's part of the Argus business as well?'

'You're witty this morning, Snap. That's what the Friends think.'

'They think this chap Lane pinched it?'

'I don't know. Acton's assistant probably. I'm damn sure they know something we don't.'

Cawston made a sympathetic sound. He didn't like getting tangled with the spy mob, as he called them, either. 'You'll be wanting to go to Hampshire—tomorrow, sir, or Monday.'

'I don't want to poke my nose into the work of the local boys too soon. There's nothing we can do down there about the von Erbacher murder. Andover and C13 between them have done the job. I'm happy to let Andover do the ground work on the break-in before we take a look.'

'Very well, sir—you can get back to that portrait. I'll phone if there are any developments.'

'Oh, by the way, Rackham wants to be kept fully informed. He said closest co-operation. That means us, not him,' Whitaker added, disgruntled.

He put down the receiver and climbed the two flights of stairs. He was quite breathless at the top. Perhaps he wasn't as fit as he used to be, but he was damned if he was going to try that jogging round Wimbledon Common again. Too boring, and it made him look ridiculous. He stared at the first painted outlines on his canvas. Suddenly he thought: Cawston might have something. Perhaps Argus *was* a bit of a peacock.

David Rackham had found it painful to phone Superintendent Whitaker and ask for Gillian's flat to be searched. He'd allowed himself to become too personally involved with the woman, he thought. He'd behaved like an amateur. It was inexcusable, but—there it was. It wasn't only that she was attractive and bedworthy; he was intrigued by her, even felt sorry for her. Immediately his call to Whitaker finished, he rang her. There was no reply.

It was almost two hours before he heard her voice. To his single word, 'Goethe', she said she'd ring back, and immediately cut him off.

It was several minutes before she did, and then she said she was speaking from a telephone box. She gave him the number, and he rang back.

'The police have searched my flat,' she said.

He waited for her to continue, but she didn't. 'I've been trying to get you,' he said. 'I was going to warn you that they might. Once I'd heard that the factory had been—' he paused, and then added significantly, 'broken into, they were bound to pay you a visit.'

'I don't understand why the drawings weren't enough for Stoebel. Surely that's all you needed.'

'I'd hoped it would be. But having the thing itself means we can make it so much quicker. I'm afraid not even I could persuade them that the drawings would do.'

'I see,' she said, full of trust, so that Rackham felt worse than ever.

'Where is it now? I was going to suggest that I came down for it.'

There was a perplexed silence. Then she said, 'But you sent Stoebel for it.'

Rackham thought fast, and responded instantly. 'I told him to collect it tomorrow but I've had second thoughts. Couldn't I come down today? It would be a chance to see you. I decided to check with you before changing Stoebel's instructions.'

'He came today,' she said.

'Blast! Crossed wires.'

If she wasn't convinced, she gave no hint of it.

'Too late,' she said.

'You mean the police have found it? Then why didn't they arrest you, eh?'

She managed a diminutive chuckle. 'I got it to Stoebel before they searched the flat.'

Rackham cursed inwardly and silently. He wanted to ask how she'd done it, but the question was impossible. Instead, trying to sound sincere and enthusiastic, he said, 'That's marvellous. You're wonderful. It's sad I don't see you, but—you have done very well.'

'I've decided,' she said. 'It really must be the last time.'

'H'm,' Rackham mused.

'Will you let that happen? Or am I going to be black-mailed?'

'I shall—we shall let it happen.'

'Thank you.'

He sensed she didn't want to let him go. She trusted him, and he cursed himself for it. What a lousy job he did. 'You—you ought to get away,' he said. 'There is still time. The police haven't found anything.'

'Yes. But I can't yet. I still hope it won't be necessary—' She paused, and what she said next made him feel an even bigger swine, in spite of reminding himself that he was dealing with a traitor. 'But I don't see how the police can prove anything. They might think I did it—I'm not sure they do think that yet; I'm sure Hammond Acton doesn't—but there's a hell of a difference between thinking it and proving it.'

'You're still at Wellesley Court?' he asked impulsively.

'Yes.'

'I'll come and see you.'

'Isn't that dangerous?'

Rackham smiled to himself. 'I wouldn't come if it was.'

'Oh please, Goethe—please come then.'

The whole evening Gillian had seemed preoccupied. Hammond had taken her for a meal at The Keys in

Newbury Street; now he was back at her flat at Wellesley Court. He always felt that the place reflected something of her self-possession, her ordered mind. It was tidy and organized; even the odd magazine on an occasional table looked fittingly in place. The carpeting, curtaining and upholstery were in toning colours of discreet pastel shades. The sitting room was tidy and restful. Only Gillian seemed uncharacteristically disturbed.

She was in the kitchen, making them some coffee. Hammond went to a side table to pour himself a brandy, and then thought better of it. He still had to drive home. Instinctively he realized that he wouldn't be staying the night with her this time.

She returned with a tray set with a bone-china coffee service.

'Shall I get you a drink?' he asked.

She shook her head. He took the tray from her and put it on a low table by the settee and, taking her hand, gently guided her down beside him. He was aware of the fragrance of the perfume he had given her on her birthday. She had high cheekbones, a creamy complexion. He turned her face towards him. The brightness of her blue eyes seemed less intense.

'What is it?' he asked.

She shrugged, then leant forward and poured out the coffee.

'Something worrying you?' he persisted.

'Isn't having the factory broken into, and that equipment stolen, something to worry about?'

'That's my worry.'

'Not mine too?'

He kissed her. 'There's no more we can do about it.'

'I'm going to have some Turkish delight,' she said decisively, and immediately got up and fetched a box from the sideboard in the adjoining dining room.

At least, Hammond reflected, that gesture was in character but he remained puzzled by her distracted air. He hadn't told her about von Erbacher because Rackham had given him the impression that the information was secret. However, he saw no reason why she shouldn't know.

'Hans von Erbacher,' he said, 'he came from West Germany, but he was working for the East.'

Gillian's jaws stopped in mid chew. She looked startled. 'But—how do you know?'

Hammond didn't answer her question but instead said, 'I reckon he was there to suss out the place, find exactly where the system was, so that his mates could break in and take it.'

'And he never got the chance to tell anyone.'

'No. But they still broke in.'

'How do you know it was his lot?'

'Who else?'

Gillian sipped her coffee. She looked thoughtful but said nothing. They finished their first cups in silence, and she poured out more. She stretched across and took his hand.

'Who killed von Erbacher?' she asked.

'I—I don't know.'

'Oh god,' she muttered, 'if we hadn't made that damned guidance system none of this would have happened. I wouldn't have—' she broke off.

Hammond looked surprised. He hadn't expected that reaction from her. 'Something's wrong,' he said.

'Don't you have any feelings about what we make? Doesn't it matter?'

'I don't think I understand you tonight,' he said.

'But that's what it's about. They—everyone's interested in the guidance system to put it in a missile—a nuclear missile.'

'It's got umpteen peaceful applications.'

'Who cares about those?'

He took her hands, looked into her eyes. They were misted with unshed tears. 'You're beginning to sound just like my sister—not like yourself at all.'

She looked away. 'Perhaps you don't know me.'

He sighed, perplexed. 'Well,' he attempted, 'you're a very self-possessed person who knows her own mind. But I'm damned if you are tonight. You'll be off to Greenham Common with Sandra next.'

Gillian smiled unconvincingly. 'Perhaps we should think more,' she said, 'about the use made of the things we make. I mean if that damned guidance system couldn't be used in a

82

missile—well, none of us would have got involved, would we?'

'Involved?'

'Well, what else can you call it?'

They finished the coffee. He looked at her, puzzled, and then took her in his arms. 'Stop worrying,' he said.

She smiled faintly. 'I'll try.'

He kissed her again. 'Do you want me to go?' he asked.

'H'm, I think so.'

He paused by the outer door of the flat, took her by the shoulders and looked into her eyes, as though seeking an answer to a question. 'Take a few days off if you like,' he said, 'although heaven knows how I shall manage without you.'

'I'll see you on Monday,' she answered.

The door clicked shut. She dropped the latch, turned the key of the second lock, and put on the chain. Self-possessed, he had said. She didn't feel very self-possessed, or assured, at the moment. She wished none of it had ever happened.

Back in the sitting room, she poured herself a brandy and slumped on to the settee, staring abstractedly at the dirty coffee cups. Something moved on the periphery of her vision. She turned her head. The door, which she had left ajar, was opening slowly. Breath caught in her throat. Her eyes widened. She felt a sudden thumping at her heart. The door moved again—wider. She jumped up, barking her shins on the coffee table. Standing in the doorway was a man—tall, slim but strong, probably in his forties, but his face was masked. Only the eyes were visible—grey and cold. He wore a well-cut blue lounge suit. Whatever she was going to say got swallowed in a gasp of fear. He took an automatic from his pocket, and pointed it directly at her.

'It was fortunate no one came into your bedroom,' he said. 'I might have had to use this. I hope you're not going to force me to use it now.' He watched her intently.

'Who are you?'

'That doesn't matter.'

Gillian fought to regain self-control.

'I think you'd better sit in the other chair,' he said, indicating with his pistol.

Gillian paused, took a deep breath, and then did as he

83

commanded. She struggled not to appear nervous. The man came and stood a few yards in front of her, looking down at her.

'What do you want?' she asked as firmly as she could.

'Information, Miss Ward, that's all.'

'Do you have to point that thing at me?'

'I don't take chances, even with women. Some of them are karate experts. Very unfeminine.'

'I can't think I have any information that will interest you.'

'Who took the guidance system?'

'Why don't you ask the police?'

'I don't think we need waste time on humour, Miss Ward. But I've got all night if necessary.'

'Then let's try and work it out. I don't know who took it.'

'I think you do. Where did it go?'

She shrugged, beginning to feel that she was getting her fear under control.

'Come on, who received it?' His tone was threatening.

She shook her head.

He took her chin firmly in his left hand, and forced her head back. 'I'm serious, Miss Ward.'

'You should know who had it,' she said desperately.

'I wouldn't be here if I did.' His fingers tightened on her jaw. 'But you're going to tell me.' He threw her back into the chair.

He had no foreign accent that she could detect, and yet he seemed to be speaking very precisely. Did that mean anything? She stared back at him and repeated slowly, 'Who are you? You must tell me.'

'The name, Miss Ward, the name,' he said menacingly. 'Who was it?'

She looked up, saw the pistol facing her. 'Oh god,' she muttered, 'I—' But her words were interrupted by the ringing of the front-door bell.

'Don't move. Not a sound,' he whispered, and held the pistol to her temple.

The bell rang again. Then Hammond's voice shouted, 'Gillian! Gillian!'

The man held up his left forefinger, and twisted the barrel of the gun against her head. The bell rang again, and again

Hammond shouted her name. Then there was silence. He told her to get up. They went into the hall. There was no sign of anyone shadowed behind the frosted glass of the front door. He held the pistol to her ribs.

'Now,' he said, 'you will open the door, slowly and quietly, and don't forget I've still got the gun and I'm quite prepared to use it.'

She did as she was told. The corridor outside was empty.

'I'm sorry,' he whispered, 'we shall have to return to this later.'

He pocketed the gun and ran swiftly down the stairs.

Gillian slammed the door shut and sank back against the wall. After a few moments she felt calmer and forced herself to go back and collect the coffee cups and take them to the kitchen.

Within five minutes the door bell rang again. She ran into the hall, saw Hammond's shape against the glass door. He was shouting her name. She flung open the door, and fell into his arms.

'It's all right, it's all right,' he soothed. 'What is it? Why didn't you answer?' She clung to him. 'The police are coming,' he added.

'Oh no—no,' she muttered. Then suddenly she straightened herself. 'All right, Hammond,' she said, 'all right, so the bloody police are coming.'

By the time the police had arrived, the intruder was at the White Hart Hotel in Bridge Street. The exertion had given his features a rather fresher complexion than they usually had.

He collected his key from the girl at the reception desk and made for the stairs. At the head of the first short flight was an imitation stained-glass window depicting a stag. He conceded that many of his countrymen would find it quaint and enchanting, part of the charm of this old coaching inn. He thought it ridiculous. There was something more genuinely quaint about the situation of the bedrooms. They were in narrow corridors that tilted up and down stairs. His own was reached through a swing door at the top of the second flight of stairs, up another short, green-carpeted flight, and then down three twisting steps to the left—undeniably quaint. The door to No. 3 faced a window that looked down into the old coach-way and the car park.

He was about to slip his key into the highly polished brass Union lock when a minute glint of metal caught his eye. He stopped, bent down to look more closely. There were tiny scratches all round the keyhole. It was one scratch a little deeper than the rest that had attracted his attention. Perhaps it was natural wear, the result of numerous guests not too accurately inserting their latch keys, and scraping the surrounding metal. Yes, perhaps that's what it was. Then again, perhaps it wasn't.

He moved along the narrow corridor to the next room and peered at the keyhole, further on to the room in the corner, and then back, up another flight of stairs to other rooms. There were little pit marks on all the keyholes and marks of wear. All had been highly polished. They weren't, he decided, quite the same. He returned to his own door and peered again. Unlike the patina of wear on the other brass locks, the minute marks here had clearly been made since that day's polishing.

This was a development he hadn't expected. Revenge for von Erbacher? That meant Stoebel was probably still in the hotel. He juggled the key in his hand, looked at the scratches again. No, it wasn't worth the risk. He returned to reception.

'Is Herr Stoebel in?' he asked.

The girl smiled. 'He left, Mr Kerringer, just before you came in. He seemed in a bit of a hurry.'

'Could you arrange for some smoked salmon sandwiches and a half-bottle of champagne to be sent to my room? And I'd like to pay my bill now, too, please. I shall be leaving very early in the morning—before breakfast. I'll be here in the lounge shortly.'

'Certainly, sir.'

But first he went out of the hotel, turned right and made for the pair of telephone boxes on the river bank, by the bridge. There were ducks paddling in the shallow water, and a solitary swan. Kerringer dialled a London number. Stoebel had to be stopped. The voice at the other end of the line was angry and derisive.

As he walked back to the hotel, Kerringer reluctantly admitted to himself that he had been underestimating the enemy. And at what a cost—the best weapons guidance system in the world. But it wasn't only that. He knew well enough that the essence of survival was never to underestimate your enemy.

The hotel doors swung behind him. The receptionist handed him his bill. 'I've ordered the sandwiches and champagne to be taken to your room,' she said.

Kerringer seated himself in a corner near the staircase to check the account. He was still sitting there five minutes later when he heard the sound of the explosion.

Herr Erich Stoebel drove the dark blue Mercedes bearing CD plates at a steady ninety miles an hour along the M3 towards London. Just beyond Basingstoke he pulled into a parking bay, braked to a stop and turned off the engine. Five minutes later a bronze Vauxhall Cavalier drew up behind him. The two men got out simultaneously, each opened the boot of their car.

From the Mercedes, Stoebel took out a package, no more than a nine-inch cube. He placed it in the boot of the Cavalier. The two men nodded to each other, and then Stoebel returned to the Mercedes, switched on the ignition and drove off.

9

On Sunday morning, beyond the skyline of London's West End, white cumulus clouds had begun to bank one above the other. So the sunlight came fitfully to make its patterned shade beneath the plane trees in the gardens of Grosvenor Square. Grant F. Kerringer walked briskly along the enclosing pavement. He paused briefly to glance to his left at the bronze figure in the gardens—his fellow countryman—Franklin Delano Roosevelt, up there on the stone pedestal in his familiar cloak. Kerringer, unashamedly, felt a distinct pride. He, too, he felt, was serving his country, defending the values for which that great democracy was renowned, although perhaps not as efficiently as usual. It was only a momentary pause, but it was enough to stiffen his resolve in what he knew was going to be an embarrassing encounter. He walked on swiftly towards the large white building with its bronze-framed windows that occupied the whole side of the square. In the centre, above its five storeys, stretched the golden wings of the eagle, and above that the stars-and-stripes hung down in folds.

Kerringer took the nine steps in three strides, identified himself at the reception desk on his left, and turned to the lift beyond the bronze-coloured metal curtain that stretched from floor to ceiling. Within a couple of minutes he was facing, across a bare modern desk, the head of the CIA's London station.

George V. Bruton had transferred from the United States army after distinguished service in Vietnam, and he no longer used his military rank, on the ground that it drew too much attention to him. This gnarled-looking man, with deep-set eyes and a thin, hard mouth, preferred anonymity. The fact that the man who sat opposite him was one of the most experienced and skilful of the CIA's agents did not weigh with Bruton in assessing the present operation. He was not very tolerant of failure.

'You goofed. You blew it.' He uttered the words as though he had broken them off a longer sentence.

Kerringer didn't like failure either, and he wasn't the kind of man to be intimidated by Bruton. But explanations, he knew, were irrelevant.

Bruton watched with gimlet eyes as he said, 'Some gook, driving like a maniac, forced Stoebel off the road. He wasn't hurt, fortunately. There was nothing in the boot of his car. The police took him back to—' Bruton paused significantly, 'to the East German Embassy.'

'So where is the bloody thing?'

'That's what you should know, Kerringer. And what about the waiter?'

'He's in a bad way, but he'll live. It was my room. The police wanted to know if I had any enemies.'

Bruton was unsmiling. 'You shouldn't have been there,' was all he said.

'I have a cover.'

Bruton was unimpressed by the obvious. 'Bloody Shokolov's ahead of us.'

Kerringer didn't need to be told, and there was nothing he could say.

Bruton slammed his fist on the desk. 'Christ! The bloody Brits are pathetic. They have the best guidance system in the world, and how do they protect it?'

'What's the Firm doing?'

'What can they do? I haven't been very helpful, but how can I be, when you balls it up?'

'I'll talk to Rackham.'

'Splendid. That'll be a great help.' Bruton was sarcastic.

'There was only Stoebel in the hotel,' said Kerringer.

'But did he take it? It wasn't in his car.'

'If he didn't, then it's still in Andover somewhere. But why should he leave without it? He might have been met. A switch.'

Bruton groaned. 'In which case it's on its way out of the country.' His features were fixed in their gnarled creases as he stared back accusingly at his agent. 'Ever thought of teaching for a living, Grant?'

Sandra had got back early from Hampshire. Not only had she borrowed the plans of Sizewell nuclear power station from her father's drawing office, but she had also pinched a reasonable bottle of claret from his cellar. She had been careful not to take it from the racks which she knew were used only for laying down vintages. By the time Heinze arrived, the beef casserole she had prepared was ready.

He looked at the food and the roll of plans, and smilingly told her she was a clever girl. Sandra glowed.

During their meal she chatted excitedly. A terrible thing had happened, she told him, at her brother's factory. There had been a break-in, and someone had stolen something that was top secret.

'Mind you,' she added, 'I don't approve of it myself. I'm sorry really that my brother—' She broke off, looked adoringly at Heinze. 'Oh, I'm sure you'd like Hammond,' she said. 'He and I have always been close, ever since we were children, although he's six years older.'

'What is it then—that's been stolen?'

'Told you, it's top secret,' she laughed. Then suddenly serious, she added, 'It's an electronic guidance system. Oh, Hammond says it can be used for anything. I suppose it can. He wouldn't lie to me. But it can be used to guide missiles too. Supposed to be way ahead of anything else. Oh god, Karl, I wish he hadn't got mixed up with the wretched thing.'

He looked interested. 'So who's pinched it?'

'They don't know. But everyone's very worried—I suppose in case the Russians get it. I wish there weren't such things. There ought not to be. Perhaps it will all end,' she said dreamily. 'Can we make it end?'

She leant over and kissed him.

'Don't worry your lovely head,' he said, as he stroked her hair and looked longingly at her. There was no doubt she would improve. The prospect pleased him.

After they had eaten and consumed more than half the bottle—the rest, he insisted, they would drink in bed, and there he would anoint her—he unrolled the plans on the floor. They were architect's drawings, and so the measurements would be accurate. He studied them for ten minutes in silence. Sandra knelt alongside him. She wanted to stroke his hands, his face, but, seeing his concentration, restrained herself.

He shuffled the sheets of paper on the floor, and then looked up at her. He said with quiet determination, 'It can be done.' He saw the admiration in her eyes and rewarded her with a smile.

'The great advantage of these drawings,' he went on, 'is that they show me exactly where each reactor is in the main structure.'

'What's that?' she asked, pointing to a large circle with pipes leading from it at the top and the bottom.

'Ah—that contains the core of the reactor. That's where it all happens.'

'What is it, then?'

'It's an enormous hollow ball, made of steel just over four inches thick. It's called the pressure vessel, and—look, you can see, it's sixty-three and a half feet across.'

'What's this grid-like thing in the middle?'

'That's the graphite moderator.'

'I'm no wiser.'

'Actually, it's got twenty-four sides, and it's built of blocks of graphite. See, it's forty-nine feet across and thirty feet high. They put the fuel rods into that stuff, and—'

'How?'

'Well, there are four thousand holes in it, each four inches across. They're fuel channels. Each one of them takes seven separate fuel elements, one on top of the other. The rod itself is uranium, almost all uranium 238. It's about an inch across, encased in a can made from a material called magnox.'

'But how do they get them in there?' She was fascinated. 'People can't just put 'em in, can they?'

He laughed. 'Oddly enough, when they're new, the fuel elements themselves, in their magnox cladding, are quite safe to handle. But no, they're put in by a huge machine —the fuelling machine.' He sifted through some of the other drawings. 'Look, here it is. Twenty-three feet high. It moves over the top of the reactor, and can be positioned exactly over one of the fuel channels. The whole thing is done remotely. A chap can see exactly what is happening on a television screen.'

'All right, so you put the fuel rods down these channels in the graphite—then what happens?'

'Oh, that's the process—that's nuclear fission. Once the fuel is in there, it pushes out enormous amounts of energy in the form of heat. This goes on continuously—a chain reaction.'

She looked at him admiringly, but puzzled at the same time. 'Then why doesn't the whole thing blow up?'

'Because they control it,' he said precisely. 'If the whole process is going on too quickly, they lower rods made of boron steel into the reactor. They're called control rods, and there are more than a hundred of them. They work like blotting paper really—soaking up the free neutrons. So the whole process is slowed down and controlled.'

She looked at him wide-eyed. 'How do they know?'

'There are instruments built in. They can monitor exactly what's going on inside.'

'So how do we get the electricity?'

'Ah, that's where they make use of all that heat being released in the reactor.' He pointed to the pipes shown on the first drawing going in and out of the pressure vessel. The plan showed that they were six and a half feet in diameter. 'These,' he continued, 'carry carbon dioxide gas. It's forced through the graphite at high pressure. That takes the heat out of it, and the pipes carry it away to the boilers.' She followed the movement of his finger. 'It's blown over these tubes. They've got water in them. That condenses into steam, and that drives the turbo-generators that produce electricity.'

'So that's what it's all about?'

He smiled. 'I've been reading it up,' he explained. 'But the problem is this.' His finger pointed to the area surrounding the pressure vessel. 'That's the shield. It's made of rein-forced concrete and is more than twelve feet thick. So any missile has got to get through that, and the steel shell of the pressure vessel.'

'But we're not going to,' she said. 'We're only threatening.'

'H'm,' he replied, and stroked her hair. 'But we've got to have a missile that's capable of it. It's no good threatening with something which they know can't do the job.'

'And is there?'

'Yes, there is.'

'But we can't really get it?' She looked incredulous.

'It's on order,' he said.

She laughed. She felt almost hysterical. She threw her arms round him and kissed him.

He saw she didn't believe him. 'No, I'm serious,' he said. 'I told you I had contacts. The missile would be fired from a ship outside territorial waters.'

He spoke with such authority that she was already believing him again, and yet it seemed impossible. 'I thought,' she said diffidently, 'that we weren't actually going to fire it. So we don't have to have a ship, do we?'

'I know we're not going to fire it. But of course we have to have a ship, and a missile. Is the British Government ever going to believe us otherwise? You can't threaten anyone with nothing.'

He pulled her back on to the floor beside the plans. 'Now, easiest of all would be a heat-seeking missile, because that wouldn't have to go through the concrete shield. That could merely strike one of these pipes carrying the gas coolant, and that would lead it down to the heat source—the core of the reactor. But it's too risky.'

She stared at him, questioning.

'You'd only have to have something like a bonfire on the beach for the missile to be diverted. So we'll have a missile that can break through to the reactor core. It'll be guided along a laser beam.'

She hugged his arm. 'I just don't believe you.'

'Please yourself.'

'But you can't be serious?'

'Look—do you want to do this, or don't you?'

He *was* serious. Suddenly she had no doubt of it. He was determined. It seemed incredible, but he was really going to do it. They were going to threaten the British Government with a missile attack on Sizewell nuclear power station, and that would force the government to do something about nuclear weapons. They wouldn't dare risk people being killed. At last she was going to do something constructive and important. All that crouching beneath canvas and polythene shelters at Greenham, the songs by the camp fires, the watching policemen, the soldiers behind the barbed wire—the camaraderie had been wonderful, but it had all achieved nothing. Now at last—She looked at him, her eyes shining.

'I want to do it,' she said.

'That's settled then.' Whether in fact she would go with him, he hadn't decided. She had already played the only role she could possibly have in the operation—the production of the Sizewell plans. Her only other use would be sexual. He wasn't really concerned with what happened to her afterwards. 'I shall have to go away for a few days soon,' he said.

'Where?'

'East Berlin—Rostock. To make arrangements.'

'It'll be an East German ship?'

'Well, it couldn't be a British one, could it?'

'They're Communists.'

He shrugged. 'We have to get what we need from wherever we can.' He forestalled her. 'Well, it's important, isn't it?'

She nodded. He was right, it was important if the peace movement was ever to get anywhere. Where Greenham had failed, Sizewell would succeed. Suddenly she was determined, as well as excited.

'Next weekend,' she said, 'come down to Hampshire with me, and meet my family. You'll like my brother.'

'No,' he said grimly and decisively. 'It's better that nobody knows me.'

She knew that was true, but she wanted to show him to everybody, and especially to Hammond. 'Then—afterwards,' she murmured. 'I suppose there'll be an afterwards? I mean, we shall succeed? They won't know who did it? After all, we're only threatening.'

He smiled indulgently. He almost replied that he was never found out, but checked himself. 'Of course they won't

94

know,' he said confidently, 'and of course there'll be an afterwards.'

She squeezed his hand. 'It will always be our secret.'

He thought that was pathetic, but said nothing. He wanted to take her to bed.

'Can I borrow your car tomorrow?' he said. 'It would be better than hiring one.'

'Of course. What for?'

'I want to go to Sizewell. I want to see the place, check its position carefully against these plans and a large-scale ordnance survey.'

'But if we're not going to fire the thing—?'

'Detail. It's important—for conviction.'

The explanation satisfied her. She was ready to believe anything he said, and when she walked to school the next morning, she felt almost light-headed with elation.

It was a fresh but sunny morning, and Heinze drove with a certain éclat as he threaded through the London traffic towards the M11. Before he had arrived at Sandra's flat the previous night he had arranged to pick up Philip Strang, complete with tripod and theodolite, near the Waterworks roundabout, and as Heinze drove along the last stretch of straight road by the trees that marked the very fringe of Epping Forest, he saw the gangling, ill-kempt figure of Strang waiting by the roadside.

It was their first meeting. Heinze looked with distaste at the long legs in faded jeans and the slightly grubby open-necked shirt, as Strang edged himself into the car. The man had a sharp, nervous face and long fair hair that looked as though it had never experienced a hairbrush. He was like so many young militants in protest movements whose very appearance advertised their convictions, and Heinze un-hesitatingly despised him.

Before the car moved off, Strang extended a thin hand and said, 'Good to meet you, comrade.'

Heinze ignored the hand, and said only, 'Good morning. Can you measure the position of anything down to the last second?'

'From a triangulation point—yes.'

Heinze let in the clutch, slipped the car through the gears, negotiated the roundabout and drove out along the elevated dual carriageway to the M11. Well, he supposed the Strangs of this world had their uses, mostly as moles in various organizations. But they were small fry. He gave the man a glance and thought how odd it was that the whole idea had originated with him.

Strang fidgeted. 'This should wake the bastards up. Show them we've had enough of their filthy weapons. It'll make people realize just how horrible it would be. Anything to get those fucking missiles out.'

Heinze couldn't be bothered to reply. The speedometer needle rested securely on the 70 mark. He had no intention of running the risk of being stopped for exceeding the speed limit.

'What do I call you, comrade?'

'Argus.'

'I'm Philip. But you know that.'

Again Heinze saw no reason to reply. He drove on in silence, reached the M25, turned right and headed for the A12 to Chelmsford, Colchester and Ipswich. He was aware of Strang shooting nervous glances at him from time to time, and even sensed a certain resentment. It was evident in the man's next remark.

'So you're the professional,' he said. 'The professional terrorist.'

'One man's terrorist is another man's freedom fighter, or, in this case, peace worker.'

That was better. Strang could understand that. 'How are you doing it?'

'A missile.'

'That's great. Shokolov's providing it, is he?'

'It doesn't matter who's providing it. It'll be there. I shall fire it.'

'What happens afterwards?'

'That's my affair. It's being taken care of.'

'Have you done anything like this before, comrade?'

Heinze grimaced at the sound of 'comrade' yet again, and replied only, 'I don't answer questions like that.'

'No, I'm sorry. Of course you don't. You know what I do?'

'I can imagine.'

'The Party's the thing for me. That's why I'm where I am, why I'm a local councillor, too. You can't have revolutions in Britain, though god knows that's what's wanted. The only way to change things is from the inside. So I keep Shokolov informed. We've got Party members and sympathizers on the executive of CND.'

'I know,' Heinze muttered wearily.

'How can we help on this one?'

Heinze practised patience. 'You're helping me today. I've got to get a perfect fix on the pressure vessel. After that, there isn't any more you can do.'

'Do you know where in the building the pressure vessel is?'

'Yes, I've got plans. So, from the outside we can determine, with the help of the plans, exactly where it is. Then we need to have a precise measurement of that position. We need that for guiding the missile.'

For the rest of the journey Heinze talked as little as possible. He saw Strang as no more than a fanatical informer. Had he not had surveying experience, Heinze would have ignored Shokolov's advice to use the fellow on this occasion.

In the centre of the busy little market town of Saxmundham, Heinze turned right on to the B1119 to Leiston, with Sizewell another couple of miles beyond. Almost opposite a pub, the Vulcan Arms, a private road curved to the left between well-planted shrubberies, trees and close-mown grass. Heinze drove straight on for a few yards to where the road ended in a left turn, fronting the sea. He parked the car just beyond the white-pillared porch of Gap House and before what looked like a Georgian red-brick cottage bearing the name Ocean Cottage. Beyond, standing back from the sea, were the squat, concrete blocks of the power station.

Heinze got out and crossed the narrow road to the greensward and the low dunes. Beyond was a ridge of pebbles and, beneath that, long stretches of silver sand. It glistened in the summer sunlight, and even the scarcely wrinkled grey North Sea appeared to be smudged blue as it seethed on to the sand. Like two miniature oil rigs, stuck in the sea just offshore, were the structures that take in cooling water to the power station and later discharge it, some ten degrees centigrade warmer, back into the sea. Strang stood on the grassy sand beside him. To their right, at the edge of the shingle ridge, was a black boxlike building with a window facing the sea. Heinze assumed it was a coastguard look-out, but he couldn't see anyone inside.

'I guess you've been here before,' said Heinze.

'Several times—demonstrations. And during the inquiry into the second power station, I'd get away sometimes, come down here to the Vulcan Arms. The beer's good.'

They walked along the ridge of the beach towards the power station, and Heinze indicated the building containing the two reactors. Then they went back to the car and Heinze spread out the architectural drawings over the steering wheel, pointing out the exact position of the reactor which was their target. Then he and Strang studied the large-scale ordnance survey, and Strang confirmed that, from the triangulation point at Goose Hill, a little over a mile away, he would be able to plot the position of the target to the nearest second.

'Come on, then.' Heinze threw the maps and drawings on to the back seat, turned the car round, and headed towards Leiston. 'If anyone wants to know who we are, we're from the Nature Conservancy, surveying this stretch of coast—OK?'

Strang grinned his acknowledgment.

From Leiston, Heinze drove north for a mile, and then turned right up a minor road, signposted East Bridge. Very soon, however, he turned right again into a gravel roadway, between hedgerows high with cow parsley, that led to an old farmhouse with a windpump called Upper Abbey. He stopped, consulted his large-scale map and then slowly threaded a way through brick-and-tiled barns, past a huge wooden barn with a fine roof of thatched reed, and then turned left along a deeply rutted track between trees and hedgerows.

After about two hundred yards, he stopped by a wide gap in the hedge on the right. It was marked 'Private Road', and ran for about half a mile alongside a field of sugar beet. 'This is it,' he said. 'That's Ash Wood, over on the left there.' At the far end he turned right. The track was even more deeply ridged, and was clearly used only by tractors. 'Come on, we'll walk the rest,' he said.

Strang took the theodolite and tripod from the back of the car, humped it over his shoulder, and they followed the track for about a quarter of a mile to the triangulation point just twenty-nine feet above the sea no more than another quarter of a mile away.

From this moment even Heinze had to admit that the behaviour of the egregious Strang became contrastingly professional and efficient.

'This is a fairly sophisticated device,' he said as he set up directly over the triangulation point. 'It's a gyrotheodolite with E D M.'

'E D M?'

'Electro-magnetic distance measurement. I can read off the measurements on this digital display at the top of the instrument. If we'd been able to get a reflector fixed on to the power station it would have been easier. Without it, we shall have to set up another point here. That'll give us the base line of the triangle.'

He led Heinze to another point about 250 yards away, marked a position very precisely with a pole, and instructed Heinze to hold a prism on the top of it. Strang went back to the triangulation point, sighted the prism, and read off the horizontal and vertical angles and the distance. Then he sighted a predetermined point on the power station and noted the vertical and horizontal angles. Next he went to the position where Heinze was standing, sighted the power station from there, and read off the two angles again.

'We've now got all the information we need,' he said, as he pulled out a pocket calculator, keyed in the measurements, and then scribbled the results on to a slip of paper. 'That,' he added, 'is a precise latitudinal and longitudinal fix on the reactor, measured to the nearest second.'

Heinze, for him, was unstinting. 'That's very good.'

'I'll check it,' said Strang, and immediately repeated the whole operation. At the end he gave Heinze a smile of satisfaction. 'That,' he said, 'will ensure a direct hit.'

10

Superintendent Whitaker's pipe had gone out. It hung in the corner of his mouth. He sucked involuntarily, and it made a gurgling sound. He was thinking, and not, he had to admit, to any great effect. He was puzzled by one or two apparently disconnected happenings. He took the pipe from his mouth and tapped the remaining dead tobacco into the glass ashtray. He got up from his desk and wandered across to the window. There were white cumulus clouds in the blue sky. The sunlight was forced out of them in intermittent shafts, so that the rooftops passed in and out of shadow, almost like waves. From where he stood, the superintendent could see the Victoria tower, Big Ben and the Houses of Parliament, even the green of the young trees in New Palace Yard that covered the M Ps' underground car park. He wondered how long it would be before there were questions in the House about the events in Andover.

During the weekend there had been three more developments—a mysterious intruder in Gillian Ward's flat; an explosion in a bedroom at the White Hart Hotel, injuring a waiter; and a German diplomat's car forced off the road. According to C13, the lock of the bedroom door had been wired to a bomb. The room had been occupied—although not at the time—by an American diplomat, Grant Kerringer. Also staying in the hotel had been an East German diplomat, Herr Erich Stoebel. He had been driving back to London when his car was forced off the road by some lunatic driver who had disappeared, and Stoebel hadn't noted the number.

Were the incidents related, and had they got anything to do with the murder of von Erbacher or the break-in at the Digitalia factory? Whitaker had no answer. That in itself would not normally have troubled him too much, because experience told him that painstaking routine frequently provided the answers. What, however, did trouble him was the growing feeling that all these things had a common source, and that it was an international affair—a messy business of terrorism and espionage. Why else was David Rackham so interested? It was evidently more an MI6 affair than MI5.

Meanwhile routine was grinding on—checking the hotel door for fingerprints, and Stoebel's car; collecting the remains of the explosive device into carefully tagged plastic bags; questioning the hotel staff, and getting a statement from Kerringer. And none of it yet provided an answer to the memo that was hidden in a folder on his desk. It came from the Metropolitan Commissioner, and it was brief and to the point. The Prime Minister would need, very soon, to have something concrete to say both to the Federal German ambassador, and to the House of Commons.

He was beginning to think that perhaps in his own interests, if for no other reason, he would have to make a trip to Andover, when a firm precise tap at the door announced the entrance of Sergeant Cawston.

He was holding a collection of photographs, all the standard eight by six inches. 'D'you think these might be of any use to the department, sir?'

'What are they?'

'They're photographs of foreign embassies in London. Well, you remember my London monuments, and my architectural gems, as I called them? I thought I'd also have a bash at the embassies. Some of them are very interesting —the American one for instance. The photos are all very recent. I've done them in the last few weeks. No trouble printing an extra copy of each.'

Already he had put them on Whitaker's desk, and the superintendent walked over and began to riffle through them.

'These are very good, Snap. Quite nice buildings—some of them. Yes, why not? They might come in useful. Who knows? Let's have them. Thanks, Snap.'

The superintendent was still shuffling them on the top of his desk, pausing every so often to look at the more interesting. 'Oh,' he exclaimed suddenly, 'that's the Russian Embassy, isn't it? Odd building, that.'

'Yes, isn't it, sir? Doesn't look quite real—those buttresses and things. I took another one of the roof just for us, so we had a picture of their latest aerials.'

Whitaker grinned, but he was now looking closely at the original print of the embassy itself. 'H'm,' he mused, 'I wonder?' He looked up at the sergeant. 'When did you take this?'

'Oh—let me think. That's the most recent. A week ago. Last Monday—that's right.'

'And who's that coming down the embassy steps?'

Cawston picked up the print and stared at it. The figure was far too small to identify, even if Cawston knew him.

'Just a hunch,' Whitaker added. 'Get the figure blown up, sergeant, as quick as you can. Let's have a look at him.'

While Cawston was absent, the superintendent returned to Kerringer's statement. It was immaculate, and it intrigued him. The man had been staying at the hotel the whole of the time. He was not dissimilar from the description given by Gillian Ward, except that she was sure her intruder was not an American, and Kerringer had a distinct accent. He telephoned Rackham to discuss the similarity, but the latter dismissed the superintendent's suspicions in a characteristic way.

'Oh, impossible. I know Grant well—not his line.'

Whitaker made a growling sound. 'Then what the hell was he doing in Andover?'

'Better ask him, Arthur. The Americans have a real interest in that thing Acton's making, you know.'

'Yes, and someone has sufficient interest in Kerringer to want to blow him up.'

'Very distasteful.'

By the time Whitaker put down the telephone he was under the distinct impression that any inquiries made in the direction of Grant Kerringer would meet a diplomatic brick wall. It made him angry. Bloody Rackham expected to be given the fullest information but, from his side, only dished out what he thought the police should know.

Whitaker was considering the possibility of seeing Kerringer himself, and paying a visit to Miss Ward, when Sergeant Cawston returned with an enlargement of the figure coming down the steps of the Soviet Embassy. There was a slight smile on his face.

'It is,' he said, 'isn't it?'

Whitaker peered at the photograph, pulled across a folder and took out the German photo-fit. He looked at them side by side, then nodded with quiet satisfaction.

'It's Argus, alias Andrew Lane,' he said, 'without a beard. Well done, Snap.' Whitaker thought for a moment. 'So what's he doing at the Soviet Embassy? The man who killed von Erbacher, a West German industrialist, has links with the Russians. I don't like it. O K, Snap, get copies made —lots of 'em—out to all the local forces—a check made on all London hotels. We've got something to show 'em now.' He retrieved his pipe, began filling it, and fiddled for his Swan Vestas. 'And we'll take copies with us tomorrow morning—down to Andover.'

When he was alone again in his office, Whitaker drew pleasurably on his pipe and sent a cloud of smoke towards the ceiling. He gave himself a few minutes. Then with a small feeling of triumph, he picked up the telephone and punched out David Rackham's number at Century House.

'We've got a photograph of Argus,' he said. 'He's coming out of the Soviet Embassy. There's a date on it, too.'

There was a momentary silence. Then, with what Whitaker detected as false enthusiasm, Rackham said, 'Splendid. Lob it over.'

'It was taken after the murder of von Erbacher,' Whitaker added.

'Oh, really.'

'What's he doing—collecting his reward?'

'I shouldn't think so,' was all Rackham guardedly said.

'Have the Russkies any reason for wanting to get rid of von Erbacher?'

There was another pause. Whitaker was irritated. He felt that Rackham was again wondering how much he could pass on. Then the reply came.

'No. No, not von Erbacher.'

'Then what's the bastard doing at the Soviet Embassy? And why's he carrying a plumber's bag?'

This time the pause was shorter, and the reply, Whitaker felt, was genuine.

'I wish I knew,' Rackham said. 'I wish I knew.'

Superintendent Whitaker first established friendly relations with the local police and complimented them on their achievement so far. The tribute was sincere. They had worked fast and efficiently. Having established his credit-worthiness, Whitaker and Cawston left for the Digitalia factory with goodwill.

The superintendent liked Hammond Acton on an instant hunch—and, after all, Edie always told him that his hunches were right. He assessed Acton as a go-getting, but sincere and intelligent businessman. So when the superintendent praised the security system, it was his second genuine compliment that morning. In addition to quite sophisticated electronic screening of the whole office block and factory, there were automatically controlled video cameras covering the entire outside of the premises. Moreover, they were fitted with night-sights, so that any after-dark intruders would also be recorded on video-tape. Yet none of this had worked, and for the simple reason that it had been switched off. Apart from Acton, there were only two other people who had access to the control—the factory manager and Gillian Ward.

Whitaker checked through Acton's statement, and the factory manager's. It was obvious that the latter shared his boss's pride in the firm's products, and his pride in the guidance system was so enthusiastic that he might have invented it himself. So Whitaker was left with Gillian Ward.

He presumed her office showed her own taste. The carpet was a soft cherry colour, the patterned curtains matched; the furniture was modern office furniture, but clearly chosen for its comfort. There was one easy chair, and Gillian Ward unhesitatingly occupied this herself, waving the superintendent and the sergeant to more functional ones. Whitaker studied her. She was strikingly attractive rather than pretty, with dark hair and disconcertingly bright blue eyes. She was slim and lithe and as she sat down she crossed her legs elegantly. She had a kind of inner authority.

She was not the least put out by the fact that she couldn't

explain how the security system came to be switched off. She looked straight at Whitaker and told him that she had checked it before leaving, and it was working. Yes, it was true, no one could have broken in without being observed electronically. Then how had it happened? She gave a little shrug, and said it was a mystery. She was convincing. Whitaker could understand why Acton valued her so highly.

The superintendent nodded to Cawston, and the sergeant produced two photographs and handed them to Miss Ward.

She looked at the bearded photo-fit first. 'I've already been shown this,' she said. 'I don't recognize him.'

'Well, that's a reconstruction,' said Whitaker. 'Try the other one. It's a real photograph. Try putting a beard on it.'

Gillian knitted her brows. 'No,' she said thoughtfully, 'I don't think I've ever seen him.'

'He was staying at the White Hart, wearing a beard, though.'

'No,' she repeated.

'Not even when you went to the White Hart?'

If the question surprised her, she didn't show it. She only said confidently, 'No.'

'But you did go to the White Hart at this time. The receptionist remembers you.'

'Then, unless she's made a mistake, I did.'

'So what were you doing there?'

'I expect I was having a drink.'

'By yourself?'

'Really, Superintendent, how old-fashioned you are. Why not?'

'I thought perhaps you were meeting Herr Erich Stoebel.'

Gillian raised a well-shaped eyebrow, but said nothing.

Whitaker added, 'He was staying at the White Hart.'

'I didn't meet him,' Gillian said emphatically.

'Have you any idea who the man was who broke into your flat?'

'No. I've told the police. I've given them a description.'

'Yes, I have that, Miss Ward. You said he asked you who had stolen the guidance system.'

'That's right, he did.'

'Why should he think you would know?'

'That puzzled me at the time. It still does.' Gillian uncrossed her legs, and recrossed them.

Whitaker admired her self-possession. He took from his pocket a photograph of the American diplomat, Grant Kerringer. 'Is this the man?' he asked.

'It does look a bit like him.'

'But you're not sure?'

'No.'

The superintendent nodded slowly. He changed tack, asked her how long she had known Mr Acton, and how long she had worked for Digitalia, and she reminded him politely that he already had the answers to those questions. He smiled gently, and asked her if she was Mr Acton's fiancée.

'No.' She paused before adding, 'Not exactly.'

'A little inexactly, then?' Whitaker mused, and she smiled in response. 'So,' he continued slowly, 'you must share something of his pride in having developed this new guidance system? I gather it's way ahead of anything else.'

'By all accounts it's very remarkable,' she said.

'But you don't approve?' He added, by way of encouragement, 'I don't think Mr Acton's own sister does.'

Gillian shrugged. 'I have sometimes thought,' she confessed, 'that had we not made the guidance system none of this would have happened. I said as much to Mr Acton.'

Whitaker said reflectively, 'Von Erbacher wouldn't have been murdered, the guidance system wouldn't have existed to steal, your flat wouldn't have been broken into, an attempt wouldn't have been made on Kerringer's life at the White Hart, and you would not have—'

'Been sitting here answering your questions,' she interrupted sharply.

Whitaker stood up. 'True,' he muttered. 'But that's not what I was going to say.' He paused, looked hard at her. 'Miss Ward,' he said, 'how long have you been working for the Soviet bloc?'

Gillian Ward's facial muscles tightened. She returned the superintendent's stare unwaveringly. She said nothing.

11

On Tuesday evening—the day after his trip to Sizewell—
Heinze and Sandra had a meal in a Kensington bistro, and
then returned to his Knightsbridge hotel. Sandra thought his
rooms were comfortable, even luxurious, without being
ostentatious. They were, she decided, in character, the kind
of place she would have expected him to choose. Karl liked
things to be orderly, comfortable and elegant. He was careful
about his own appearance. She liked that, and was rather
proud of him. He brought the same kind of elegance to his
love-making. Moreover, he was teaching her things she had
never guessed. She was sure she was improving.

After they had made love this evening, he told her he
would be away for about a week. She looked alarmed.

'It's all right,' he said. 'I'm going to East Germany—to
Rostock. Arrangements have to be made.'

She still found it hard to believe. Perhaps he was just going
away and would never return, and the whole plan was a
fantasy they had shared. No, she couldn't believe that of
him; it was impossible. He was too—she searched for the
word in her mind—confident, assured, authoritative.

'What are you going to do?'

'There's the master of the ship to meet. I want to know
who the crew will be, when the ship is arriving, when it will
be ready to leave. There are details,' he said with the slightest
touch of impatience.

Yes, it was happening. It was really happening. 'When,'
she said, scarcely believing that she was uttering the words,
'when do we issue an ultimatum?'

He looked at her strangely, with a half smile. 'When we're
at sea.'

'That'll put them in a tizz.' What would happen? There'd
be an emergency meeting of the Cabinet. The government

would consult its allies. Then—'Won't they send out a warship or something to stop us?'

'What—an East German ship outside British territorial waters? And risk a Soviet response? Like hell they would.'

'You won't be back before the weekend?'

'No.'

'Then I'll take those plans back before they're missed.'

He fetched them for her from his briefcase and put them in a large envelope. She held on to his hands, not wanting to let him go. She had intended getting a taxi back to her flat, but now she told him she would rather stay, and go straight to school in the morning.

'No,' he said quietly but firmly, 'you go home. I've work to do anyway.'

She was disappointed, but she must do what he wanted.

In fact Heinze had a very good reason for not wanting her in the hotel the next morning. He had an early appointment beside the Serpentine with Dmitri Shokolov. They walked together by the water's edge.

'It's indecent,' grumbled the stocky Russian. 'They've started to tail me.' Heinze looked round. 'No—not this morning. Perhaps I was too early, eh?'

'The fee?' said Heinze.

'It's agreed. A hundred thousand in cash before you leave. The rest paid direct into your Swiss bank account.'

'No. Half and half. A hundred and twenty-five thousand cash.'

The Russian nodded his square, close-cut head.

'I may want an additional passport, visa.'

Again Shokolov nodded.

'What about the master and crew?' Heinze asked.

'The master and two chief officers are hand-picked, as you instructed. They will be briefed on the operation. You have to arrange for them to be armed, if that's necessary. You have to recruit as many substitute crew as you need. The master will then lay off the same number of regular crew at Rostock. You must collect your own arms. You may need them for emergencies.'

'There should be none.'

'I know.'

'And the missile?'

'The SS-N-2C Styx is a reliable weapon, but the production model wouldn't do the job. However—' The Russian paused for the thinnest of sardonic smiles, 'if it's fitted with a hollow charge, it will more than do it. A weapon of half the diameter would go through your twelve feet of concrete and another four inches of steel. But with a hollow charge of nearly seventy-five centimetres diameter—' Shokolov threw up his hands in a gesture that implied incalculable damage. He added, as though quoting from a brief, 'With a hollow charge of that diameter, the stand-off distance would be about 150 centimetres.'

Heinze didn't have to be told the effect of this. The cone of the hollow charge would cause the explosive force of the weapon to implode instead of explode. Thus it would go tearing into the reactor at about 8,000 metres a second with a huge implosion of white-hot metal and white-hot gas.

'The missile,' Shokolov continued matter-of-factly, 'will be housed in a forty-foot container mounted on a turntable.'

Heinze smiled. 'Very satisfactory. What about targeting?'

'As you wanted—laser target-designation, gyroscopically mounted on the bridge. Missile is fitted with a laser seeker in the nose cone.'

They turned about and retraced their steps. A mallard scutted itself into the air from the water alongside. A few other people were beginning to appear from various parts of the park. The morning was overcast, not with the haze of impending heat, but with the threat of rain.

'And the route?'

'The ship is the *Argus Viktor*. Like it?' asked the Russian, with the hint of a smile. 'It's flying the flag of the German Democratic Republic, carrying arms to Angola.'

'The helicopter?'

'Exactly in accordance with the plan which you drew up. You are a desperate Western terrorist, who has taken over the *Argus Viktor* and is holding the master to ransom. A vessel of the GDR navy will monitor the operation. From its deck a helicopter will make a raid on the ship and capture you. Piracy at sea cannot be tolerated, and you will be taken away to your fate in the Democratic Republic.' This time the Russian did smile.

'Very good.'

Shokolov nodded. 'Your paper planning was meticulous. Centre were very impressed. Worthy of a star pupil, eh? You see, my friend, when the KGB makes a decision, nothing stands in the way.'

'I'm going to Berlin tomorrow. I shall stay as long as necessary to recruit substitute crew. I shall use as few as possible. I will also arrange for arms to be collected at Rostock.'

'So, nothing can go wrong, eh?'

'I don't make mistakes.'

'We know.'

They parted, walking in opposite directions. Heinze was satisfied. At the very least he would have £125,000 in his pocket. Not bad, when the Soviets were providing the vessel, the missile and the necessary reconstruction of the ship's main deck. On the other hand, they had only followed his instructions. As Shokolov had said, his paper work had been meticulous. He wondered if Strang was getting anything. After all, the original idea had been his, but then he wouldn't have had a clue about how to implement it. Heinze assumed the poor chap would be getting nothing; he was one of the idealists the KGB were ready to use for their own purposes. If the fool didn't ask for more, that was his fault.

There remained Sandra. As he walked slowly across the grass in the direction of Park Lane, he considered her role. In the operation itself, it was already finished. It had ended with the provision of the Sizewell plans. Her only possible justification now was sexual. Well, that had often been the case. There had been no problems up to now. He would like to have her with him in Rostock and on the ship. She was really getting rather good. He had found before that it wasn't unusual for some girl, totally inexperienced, suddenly to discover what it was all about, and then go completely overboard. For him it was very gratifying. Then should she be lifted off with him, or left on the ship? Well, that was up to her. He didn't really care one way or the other. Back in East Berlin, he would rest a while before deciding where to go. He might even retire from 'active service'. He would certainly be rich enough. Would he be interested enough? For that matter, would his clients be prepared to let him go? He was, he thought to himself, about the best operator available. But sod them, if he wanted to get out, he would. Meanwhile there was Sizewell—quite the most interesting project he had tackled, a change from straightforward assassination.

He reached Park Lane. The traffic streamed away from him towards Hyde Park Corner. Eventually he managed to cross and pick up a taxi near Grosvenor House.

For the rest of that week, Sandra was surprised at how suddenly lonely she felt. She thought of Karl Heinze incessantly—good-looking, with strong, regular features, and the deep brown eyes, sometimes meltingly soft, sometimes hard and determined. After the first night she missed him. Lying alone in her bed, she fantasized until her desire was almost unbearable. She was glad when the weekend came, and there was the excuse to do something different from the daily routine in the classroom. So early on Friday evening she again headed out on the M3 to Hampshire.

Her mother, with a vague air of gratitude, said how bright and happy Sandra was looking, and then added—as though she had found the explanation—that teaching very young children must be most rewarding. Sandra longed to tell her about Karl. The words were threatening to spill excitedly from her lips, but he had insisted that, at least until their operation had been completed, it was better that they did not know about him. After all, she had admitted that they would not approve. If that was what Karl wanted, then that was that. But she longed to talk about him just the same. Perhaps to Hammond. They had always shared their secrets.

She found him in his own flat. He was sitting by the window that overlooked the parkland, a file of papers open on his knee.

'Hi!' she greeted. 'Any news?'

'You're interrupting one of Britain's successful young captains of industry just when he's about to make a decision.' He smiled at her as he tidied the papers back into the file and closed it.

'Oh, don't give me that guff.'

'No, not really,' he said, 'only a little homework. As for news, none, I'm afraid.'

'Who broke into your factory? Don't the police know?'

'No.'

'You mean they haven't a clue?'

'Oh, I don't know. They keep their clues to themselves. But as far as I know they haven't the least idea, any more than they have about who killed von Erbacher. But I get the impression that they're not bothering about him any more. Almost as though it is irrelevant.'

Sandra looked horrified. 'Are the two things connected?'

Hammond shrugged. 'I guess so. But the police don't understand how anyone could have got into the place to deal with the alarm systems. Nor do I. The entire staff have been questioned, and questioned again.'

'How much does the theft matter?'

'Depends who's got it.'

She raised her eyebrows interrogatively.

'It might be the Russians,' he said, 'or more likely the East Germans. Same thing in the end.'

'And you said it wasn't a military project?'

'Well, it isn't. But it could have military uses, of course it could.'

She sighed despairingly.

He patted her hair. 'You don't have to worry yourself,' he said and then, looking straight into her eyes, he added, 'You're looking very perky, anyway.'

She laughed. 'I feel perky—if that's what you call it.'

'Call what?' he asked with a smile.

They laughed together. Sandra was grateful. It was just as it used to be when they were younger.

'Something's happened, hasn't it?' he said.

She was bubbling to tell him. She nodded excitedly.

'Come on then, out with it.' He saw the glowing look in her eyes. 'My little sister has met a knight in shining armour on a white charger, hasn't she?'

Again Sandra nodded. 'It's our secret, Hammond, isn't it?' she said, almost childlike.

'All right then.' He took her hand. 'Promise.'

'He's wonderful,' she said.

'Of course, they always are,' he teased. 'Who is he?'

'His name's Karl Heinze. I met him at a concert at the Festival Hall. He was born in Germany, educated there and in London. He's—'

'What does he do?'

Sandra paused. 'He's—he's a sort of consultant, on economic and political affairs, to large firms, sometimes to governments. He travels a great deal. He's—' She stopped lest, in her enthusiasm, she betrayed herself.

'He's what? Abroad at the moment? Otherwise, you would have brought him home.'

'Yes,' she said. 'I think it will be several weeks before he can get away to come down here. But yes, yes—of course I'll bring him home. You'll like him, Hammond, you will, really.'

He smiled indulgently. 'I'm sure I shall.'

Most of all she would have liked to tell her brother about what they were doing; how they were going to force the British government to abandon its nuclear weapons; how they were going to do more for peace in one day than the politicians had done in years. She was sure of it. They couldn't fail. Faced with such a horrifying threat, the government would have no alternative. She and Karl—together they were going to do this thing. Yet she couldn't tell Hammond. He disagreed with her about the bomb. Damn it, he'd even made this wretched guidance system. Neither of them allowed this difference to interfere with their relationship, but it did prevent her telling him everything, and that was what she wanted to do more than anything else. She wished he could understand. She looked up brightly.

'And how's Gillian?'

His eyes clouded. 'I don't know, I really don't. She's not the same. Oh, she does her work as efficiently as ever. I don't know how I could manage without her. But it's as though we'd had a bloody great row or something. There seems a curtain between us.'

'Oh, I'm sorry. I thought the pair of you were made for each other. Perhaps it's just that recent events have upset her.'

'They've done that all right, but surely that should have brought us even closer. Yet there's this—oh, I don't know.'

'What about the man who got into her flat? You told me about him last Sunday.'

'Again nothing. He was wearing a suit similar to one worn by a chap called Kerringer, who was staying at the White Hart. But it obviously wasn't him.'

'Why? Who's Kerringer?'

'Some fellow at the American Embassy. Got an accent too. Gillian's sure the chap who broke in hadn't an American accent. Anyway, it doesn't make sense.'

Sandra was about to agree, but was stopped by his worried frown. 'What is it?' she asked.

'It seems there may have been some attempt on Kerringer's life too. A waiter going into his room was blown up when he put the key in the lock. He's badly injured.'

'I didn't see it in the papers.'

'No, that's the odd thing. It's been kept quiet. I didn't hear about it until some days afterwards, and I wouldn't have known but for an old friend who is—well, involved in all this.'

'When did it happen?'

'On the Saturday night after the guidance system had been stolen. And even the local press haven't heard about it—I don't believe it.'

'Well, I haven't seen it anywhere. And you suppose they—whoever they are—were after this man Kerringer?'

'That's the idea. Although don't ask me what the hell it's got to do with anything. I just don't understand it. But anyway it obviously couldn't have been Kerringer who broke into Gillian's flat.'

'I suppose not. By the way, why doesn't she come here? There's plenty of room.'

'I suggested that. She won't. We've had new locks and bolts fitted to her flat. She insists on staying there. Yet she's obviously apprehensive.'

'Will she be coming here this weekend?'

'I don't think so. I did ask her. She said she'd try, but she didn't think she'd be able to make it.'

'What's stopping her?'

114

'That's just it—nothing that I know of.'

Sandra was disconcerted. She was so bubbling with happiness herself, as well as feeling the enthusiasm of a sense of mission, that she didn't like to see Hammond unhappy and worried. She would much rather that he could share her own feelings.

Something of this emotional disparity permeated their family meal that evening. She was in a chatting mood, and Hammond did his best to keep up with her but was plainly preoccupied. Her mother was, on the one hand, upset because of Hammond and made matters worse by wondering why on earth Gillian couldn't be with them, and on the other hand was plainly delighted by Sandra's cheerful manner. Her father, understanding about Hammond, was clearly puzzled by her but pretended not to notice. He disturbed her; he always had. Yet Hammond, in many ways, was like him—the same kind of charm, the same inevitability of success. But with her brother there was an abiding closeness; with her father, a tension, a separation. Hammond was always willing to understand even when he disagreed; her father was not. At least that was how it seemed to her. He just wouldn't understand.

The last thing Mrs Acton could have known—or her son Hammond could have suspected—was that the reason Gillian was unable to have a meal with them that Friday evening was because she was with David Rackham or, more precisely, he was with her.

When she opened the glass door of her flat in Wellesley Court, she stood for a moment, slim and erect, apparently full of self-assurance. Immediately the door was closed, however, she fell into Rackham's arms, murmuring, 'Goethe, oh Goethe, I'm so glad to see you—relieved, and—' She looked at his smiling, freckled face and added, 'and happy. Even if it's not for long, I'm happy.'

For Rackham it was becoming an effort to maintain the occasional thickened vowel or consonant to suggest, behind his mastery of English, a German origin.

She prepared a light meal of cold meats and salad, with strawberries and cream to follow.

Rackham watched her, and wondered what kind of an idiot he was in being there at all. He could imagine what his boss, Sir Dick Randle—a tall, lean, ascetic-looking figure —would have to say about it. He consoled himself with the thought that it had never happened before, but that wasn't much justification.

Her cheekbones were high, her skin creamy. He reached out and touched it. She smiled. He could feel her gratitude. Again, for her, this was a great escape—a necessary escape.

He undressed her very slowly, and then stood looking at her, painfully aware that this was the last time he would ever see her like that. He made love to her just as slowly, trying to impress every moment of it into his memory. She gave herself to him with a fulsome desperation. It was a wonderful night, in which even Rackham's guilt was eclipsed by the ecstasy with which they explored each other.

The early dawn came with a shattering of bird song from the golf course, and it was only then that each spoke of the one thing that was uppermost in their minds.

She whispered, 'I'm going on Monday morning.'

'Good.'

'I don't think the police can prove anything,' she said, 'although a Superintendent Whitaker asked me about working for the Soviet bloc. But they've found nothing to link me with the theft. And the very idea of it would be unthinkable to Hammond. It's just that it's impossible to break into the factory. I'm sure the police are reluctant to think that it's an inside job. They've spent so much time trying to discover ways in which someone could have got in. But I just can't stick it any longer.'

He said, 'The police will prove it in the end,' but he acknowledged to himself that it was the evidence in his possession that would prove her guilt. And he would use it, he would have to.

'Well, they might, but—oh, I've just got to end it all. Make a new beginning. You—you won't let them stop me?'

'No, of course I won't.' And Rackham had already decided that he wouldn't stop her. He wouldn't summon the police to her flat after he'd left, or see that she was apprehended at London airport. There was nothing to prevent her leaving

the country. She hadn't been charged. Of course, her depar-
ture would signal her guilt, but it would be too late then,
providing she went to the right place.

'Where are you going?' he asked.

'South America. I've got some money. I can get by for
quite a while, and I can read Spanish. Maybe I ought to learn
Portuguese.'

They each tried to smile, not very successfully.

She added, with obvious guilt, 'And you know how gener-
ously Stoebel paid me. I—I wouldn't have taken the money
but for having to get away.'

Rackham nodded. 'You should be quite safe there.' He
added reluctantly, 'Don't try to get in touch.'

There were tears in her eyes as she murmured that she
wouldn't.

When he left her flat an hour later he had never felt so
wretched in his life. He was also disconcerted by his own lack
of professionalism. He had succumbed to feelings that he had
repeatedly instructed agents to ignore. It was pathetic. It was
even worse momentarily to think that if only he could give it
all up he would. Crazily he imagined escaping to South
America with Gillian, perhaps on some silver beach con-
fessing everything to her. It would no longer matter. They
would love each other.

He shook the thought away, like a dog shivering water
from its back. Ridiculous. He kissed her. She held on to him.
He prised himself away, and ran down to his car.

David Rackham, oppressed with feelings of guilt and his
own uncharacteristic ineptitude, drove back to London
much faster than the speed limit allowed.

Rackham was already back at his flat, staring disconsolately
down at the Thames, when Sandra Acton was made acutely
aware of what she regarded as her father's unwillingness to
understand. She had gone to his drawing office, at the far end
of the house, to return the power-station plans. She had
chosen a moment when he was nowhere to be found. The
small room looked towards a coppice at the end of their
property, and beyond it the landscape sloped away into low
hills. Everything looked exactly as it had on her previous

visit. The same little pile of architectural magazines, a few sheets of paper covered with the broad black scrawlings of doodled ideas, and on top of the drawing table a neatly finished plan of some large building.

She pulled out the second drawer down. Inside were the same sheets of power-station plans she had seen before. She was taking the Sizewell plans out of the large envelope she had brought with her when she was aware of another presence. She stopped, the papers in mid-air, holding her breath.

'I wondered what had happened to them.'

She turned. Her father stood there, smiling faintly, looking, as always, distinguished and infuriatingly unruffled. She felt guilty. She told herself that there was no reason why she should, but that only aggravated the sense of guilt, and made her angry.

'I—borrowed them,' she said, as indifferently as she could. 'I hope it hasn't inconvenienced you.'

'Not at all. They're only of historic interest, not practical use. I haven't needed them.'

'That's all right then.' She was irritated.

'Except, does one—even one's daughter—usually take things without permission?'

She felt he was reprimanding her and teasing her at the same time. It added to her irritation.

'I didn't think it was necessary,' she said.

He relaxed, smiled. 'Oh, come on, darling, let's not be silly. What's it all about?'

'I wanted to see them, that's all.'

'Couldn't you have asked me? Was I likely to refuse?'

'You made such a fuss about it when you told me you were designing one of those bloody things.'

He looked surprised. 'I thought *you* made the fuss, darling. Said I was designing a bomb factory.'

She sighed impatiently. 'You don't have to design it.'

'It's my job to design things.'

'Oh, go on, tell me that's what paid for my education, and Hammond's, and—'

'Well, of course it did, but I wouldn't want to labour the point. You're being very sensitive, Cassandra.'

She looked straight at him. He was still smiling, gently, indulgently. He knew that name irritated her. All the time she had been holding the plans in her hand. Now she put them into the drawer and closed it.

'You still haven't told me why you wanted them,' he said.

'I said I just wanted to see them.'

'I know that's what you said. You didn't want them for one of your damn silly CND things, did you?'

God, if only she could tell him. 'That's my business,' she snapped.

'But my property.'

She hated his calmness, his rightness. 'It doesn't matter,' she said.

'No, I suppose it doesn't,' he said tolerantly, 'except I don't understand why you can't be honest with me. If it was just personal curiosity, you could look at them at any time. You didn't have to take them away. Now, why did you?'

'I—I don't approve of nuclear power stations, you know that. I—I just wanted to see if they're as safe as they're supposed to be.'

He pursed his lips, looked at her sceptically. 'And are they?'

'No.'

'Indeed. Sandra, I don't think I believe you, darling.'

She shrugged. 'Please yourself.'

'I admit I can't imagine what on earth you would want them for. But I think it is something to do with your CND loonies. I can't see what else it can be.'

'It's not loony to have a different opinion from yours.' She was suddenly angry. 'It's not loony to want peace—'

'The implication is that I want war,' he interrupted. 'I want peace too, Sandra. I think I am a little more realistic about it than you are.'

'You can't have a nuclear war if you don't have nuclear weapons.'

'True. But you can if *you* don't have them and someone else does. Someone, for example, who is happy to march into Czechoslovakia, into Hungary, Afghanistan; someone who clamps its dissidents into jail or a psychiatric hospital. I'm just not as ready to trust that someone as you are, my dear.'

She thought he sounded superior, and for her that was insufferable. She didn't answer him. She said angrily, 'This country needs a shock—something to shake it into reality.'

He smiled tolerantly. 'We're getting away from the point. Why did you want to take the Sizewell plans away with you?'

'It wouldn't occur to you that I might want them at school—to explain nuclear power to the children?'

'No, it wouldn't, not to—what, five- to eight-year-olds?'

'All right then, think what you bloody well like.'

She pushed past him, ran along the short corridor into the square hall, and then out into the garden. She walked up and down the lawn angrily, not noticing her mother, snipping some early roses with her secateurs, until she stopped. Then she saw her mother just a couple of yards away, staring at her, bewildered.

The elder woman shook her head sadly. 'I don't know,' she said, 'you were looking so jolly. Now you look as though you could murder someone.'

12

Geoffrey Acton spent the afternoon watching Hampshire play Essex at Southampton. His son and daughter went for a walk together across the parkland and along the Hampshire lanes, and his wife could always find work to do in the garden. While they were all so occupied, Gillian Ward was confronting herself in her own flat, wondering what she was going to do. She was annoyed with herself for losing control. She had thought she could always manage things efficiently. Well, so she had mostly, but at some cost to her conscience. Or perhaps it was her pride that was hurt.

When the doorbell rang she almost didn't answer it. She was sure it would be Hammond, and she didn't think she could face him again so soon. But it rang again, repeatedly, insistently. She checked herself in the mirror that hung above her sideboard, patted the waves of dark hair. She slid back the latches, preparing herself for Hammond's smile.

But the man standing there had stern, slightly angular features and cold grey eyes. He was slim but obviously strong. Before she could slam the door shut, his foot had moved swiftly across the threshold. He put out his left arm and pushed her aside. In one quick movement he was in the hall and closing the door behind them.

'I think we need a talk,' he said, not trying to hide his American accent, and led the way back into her lounge.

Gillian fought to recover her self-possession. She mustn't let him see that she was afraid, if indeed she was. She was not certain.

'Who are you? Are you the bastard who came here before?'

He shrugged. 'My name,' he said, 'is Grant Kerringer.'

'Where's your gun? I thought you didn't take chances, even with women,' she mocked.

She didn't notice where the weapon came from, but suddenly the pistol was in his right hand. He was watching her intently. He said, without turning his eyes from her, 'I don't really think this will be necessary.'

'At least now that I know your name I can tell the police.'

'I somehow don't think you will, Miss Ward. That would be very silly, wouldn't it?'

She didn't reply.

'Sit down,' he commanded.

She lowered herself into the corner of the settee, and crossed her legs. Kerringer took an upright chair and sat opposite.

'Where is the guidance system, Miss Ward?'

'How should I know?'

'Stoebel didn't have it when he got back to London.'

She half raised an eyebrow, checked herself. 'And who is Stoebel?' she asked.

He ignored the question. 'No one with him, so presumably he handled the whole affair himself. What happened? Why wasn't the guidance system in his car?'

Gillian looked at him quizzically. She felt in control again, no longer had doubts about herself. 'Perhaps you might like to answer one of my questions first, Mr Kerringer. Who killed von Erbacher?'

'It doesn't matter. It wouldn't have made any difference to you. Unfortunately, I didn't know that at the time, didn't know that the removal of von Erbacher wasn't the removal of the threat. You still haven't answered my question.'

'You haven't answered mine.'

'I'm in the stronger position. The police would be very interested in your activities, Miss Ward.'

'As they would in the killer of von Erbacher.'

Kerringer's thin mouthline twisted grimly. 'Not me. That's not my scene. But I'm assuming it was Stoebel who tried to kill me off at the White Hart.'

'Certainly not me,' she mocked.

Kerringer's eyes narrowed. He'd had enough. 'We can come to an arrangement, Miss Ward. You can tell me what happened to the guidance system, and where it is now, and I can decide not to go to the police about your activities.'

Gillian straightened herself, looked directly into his eyes. 'You can tell the police what you like. That's rather different from proving it.'

Kerringer got up from his chair, stood above her threateningly. 'You tell me, Miss Ward, or when I leave here I go straight to the police station.'

'I don't know,' she said emphatically. 'I don't know what's happened to it.'

He considered for a moment. 'Is it in Andover? Or did Stoebel get it away?'

'I don't know.'

'Stay where you are.'

Kerringer immediately began a quick and professional search of the flat, moving the furniture, opening cupboards. He spent most time in her bedroom and the kitchen. Eventually he returned. Gillian was still sitting very upright in the corner of the settee.

'It's not here,' he said.

'I know. I told you I don't know where it is.'

For a few moments he stood looking at her, thinking, wondering if he could afford forcing the information out of her. He saw her eyes watching him, steady and unafraid. She was also very attractive, but he was unmoved. He had no compassion. He couldn't afford it. He thought of Bruton, leaning across his desk in Grosvenor Square, reminding him that he'd goofed. His pride was hurt. Grant F. Kerringer didn't goof. Yet this bloody woman—an idealistic amateur —had outsmarted him. At least, he assumed she was an amateur. She hadn't the look of a professional. She had a certain calm confidence, an authority, but she didn't have that indefinable bearing of the professional. He wondered if Rackham knew her. He thought about Rackham. Bruton had been dismissive. That was a mistake. Rackham *was* a professional. He thought he saw the hint of a smile in the woman's eyes, mocking. That was too much. For a moment, he could have swiped her, but he held back. There was no point. The damn thing wasn't in her flat. It must be in London, or out of the country already. As Bruton said, he'd goofed, he'd bloody goofed. There was only left the humiliation of a deal with Shokolov. But what the hell had

Kerringer to offer? He racked his brains. It would need a political decision in Washington—something substantial, something from the President. Well, the least he could do was sound out the bloody Russian.

Kerringer straightened his tie—a diminutive gesture of defiance. 'I'm going straight to the police station, Miss Ward. Goodbye.'

She said nothing, watched his straight back disappear into the hall. She heard the outer door shut with a hard slam of finality.

The short, thickset man with the grey hair, crisp and waved, sat in one corner of a slatted seat in front of the orangery at Kenwood, the great expanse of Hampstead Heath falling away before him. The sunshine of the past few days had been replaced by an overcast sky, but it didn't look like rain, and neither was it cold, but there were fewer people than usual strolling with their children and dogs on the grass slopes beneath.

Within three minutes another figure came and sat beside him—lean, angular face, in its way as impassive as that of Dmitri Shokolov. Grant Kerringer spoke first. 'It's some time since we met,' he said.

The Russian's broad head nodded. 'I hope you are well, Mr Kerringer.' He turned his head so that the American could see the thin smile.

'Thank you. And you?'

Again the Russian nodded. 'I'm liking London,' he said. 'Things go well.'

'Too well for you, Dmitri. Not good enough for me.'

The square shoulders hunched. 'It's the luck—one day my way, one day yours.'

'There's luck and luck,' muttered the American.

A labrador ran in front of them and down the slope, pursued by a shouting boy, and nearly collided with a child flying a kite.

Shokolov twisted his head. 'So you have a kite to fly, too, eh?'

'Not yet. I just want to know what kind of kite might interest you.'

The Russian made a little chortling sound of satisfaction. 'We have the string, or will have.'

'I assumed it was already yours.'

'As good as.'

'Stoebel's got the string, so it goes to East Germany,' said Kerringer.

Shokolov nodded. 'A pity there are clouds,' he said. 'We have had such sunny weather.'

'H'm. If I'm to fly my kite over Hampstead Heath, Dmitri, what's it got to be?'

'I asked you—what have you got to offer? You do not know. My friend, you will have to ask your President what it's worth. I haven't the authority in London, you know that.'

'No more than I have. We each have the channel.'

Shokolov nodded. 'It'll have to be something good,' he said. 'Real concessions, I mean—cruise and Pershing, a halt to the next generation—something like that. I guess, my friend, no more than guess. But why should we settle for less than most, when we hold the string?'

A young mother, holding her husband's hand, wheeled a push-chair and child along the pathway immediately in front of them.

'We talk on a bench at Kenwood, Dmitri, and—' he inclined his head in the direction of the family, 'and it is from such apparently casual beginnings that we might even be deciding their future.'

'All Americans are sentimental at heart,' the Russian mumbled. 'But it's not us, my friend. It's the kite makers. You go find me a nice kite, eh?'

Kerringer got up. 'I hope the weather improves,' he said, and strolled away.

The boy flying the kite began to walk up the slope towards the house, jerking the string and slowly pulling the kite in.

So it looked as though the Cousins were going to be a little more helpful. David Rackham peered out of his window at Century House that Monday morning towards the buildings of Parliament, and prepared himself for a visit from Grant Kerringer. It was at the American's request, which was why

Rackham assumed that a higher degree of co-operation might be imminent.

A summer shower had wet the pavements, and he was amused, looking down to street level, to see Kerringer get out of a taxi complete with umbrella. It somehow didn't look characteristic of the lean, slightly gaunt-looking American.

Rackham was smaller in stature, but with the same kind of wiry strength. As the American came in he held out his hand in friendly greeting. He waved his visitor to an easy chair and, with a grin of undisguised pleasure threw him a photograph taken from a folder on his desk.

'Yesterday, I think, Grant.'

Kerringer stared at a colour print of himself and Shokolov sitting on the bench outside the orangery at Kenwood.

'Now I suppose you're going to play me a recording of what we said,' he muttered.

Rackham's expression was one of boyish mischievousness. 'Oh no, not of an ally,' he teased. 'We wouldn't dream of it. Just keeping an eye on old Shockers, that's all. Got quite an album of him now. His main task here is organizing some new agents. Think we know most of them.'

Kerringer shifted. 'I know.'

'Too early for the hard stuff, Grant. Do you think you can bear some of Century's coffee?'

Kerringer nodded, and Rackham picked up the telephone receiver and ordered it. Within a couple of minutes it was there.

Kerringer was liberal with the sugar, and stirred the brown liquid vigorously. Then he looked up, gritting the words between his teeth. 'Fuck it, David, we're in the shit, aren't we? Both of us.'

'Oh, I don't know. It's not as bad as all that.'

Kerringer was a controlled man. He had to be. But he found the Englishman's light-hearted manner infuriating. No wonder they let the bloody Jerries pinch their hardware.

Rackham was sitting on the corner of his desk, swinging his legs and using his spoon to pursue a bubble on the top of his coffee. Suddenly serious, he said, 'You should have told us you were getting in on the act. Von Erbacher, I mean. We didn't know you'd arranged to take him out.'

'You didn't know they were going to nick the system,' Kerringer retorted, reprovingly.

'True. Very true. One up to you. But,' Rackham grinned, 'having eliminated von Erbacher you thought the thing was saved. No further threat. Was that naïve? I only ask the question.'

'As I said, David, we're both in the shit.'

'I confess I didn't think there was any further threat either. Not until it was too late. Some things are so bloody obvious you don't see them.'

Kerringer nodded sympathetically. Rackham's phone buzzed. It would not have been put through while Kerringer was there unless it was urgent. He picked up the receiver. All he said was, 'Rackham,' and then listened for the best part of two minutes. 'Thank you, Arthur,' he said, and put down the receiver. He looked up at the American. 'The police have arrested Gillian Ward,' he said.

Kerringer smiled sourly. 'I'm not surprised. I went to see them yesterday. I'd called on her on Saturday—just to convince myself that she hadn't still got the bloody thing.'

'Why didn't you go to the police on Saturday?' Rackham asked.

'I didn't see it was that urgent, and obviously I couldn't give them evidence to justify an arrest. But there was nothing more she could do either. I saw them first thing Sunday morning, before I came back to town for that meeting with Shokolov.'

Rackham nodded, and turned on another boyish grin. 'They arrested her at London airport,' he said.

'Jesus!'

The exclamation reminded Rackham. 'Did I ever tell you that story about—?'

'Oh, for god's sake, David, not now.'

Rackham shrugged, and looked disappointed. 'Oh, well . . . Of course, she's not going to be any use. I mean the only important thing now is getting back the guidance system. She won't be able to help with that.'

'Right,' Kerringer grumbled. 'The only thing that can help that is a decision from the other side of the Atlantic—a Presidential decision. We'll have to offer the bastards something big. I think yours truly will be looking for another job, David.'

Rackham gulped down the last inch of coffee. 'It might not be as bad as that—yet,' he said.

'You have influence with the President?' Kerringer muttered sarcastically.

'No. But with a mutual—I hesitate to use the word *friend*—shall we just say someone who might be able to help? No.' Rackham held up his hand to silence an interruption. 'No, this time I think you're better on the sidelines—just waiting.' He grinned.

'But by now the Russkies have got the bloody thing.'

'I don't think so. I'm not sure that it has yet left the country. But if it has, it's only just gone—and not to the Soviet Union, Grant. To East Berlin. The Eastern bloc's best expert on missile guidance is there.'

Kerringer looked up with an expression of gratitude, even anticipation. 'Leave him to us,' he said.

'No. Stay out of it, Grant.' Rackham's manner had changed. It was a command. He saw Kerringer's surprise. 'Mind,' he continued, 'it's going to cost a packet.'

'That's the stuff we've got, David. A lot more than you.'

'If we want a sub I'll come to Uncle Sam. But meanwhile, I said stay out of it, Grant. I meant it.'

Kerringer was silent, thinking.

'You can tell that Brute of yours,' Rackham continued, 'that things are in hand. He needn't know. As far as we are concerned, not even the Prime Minister is going to know. Not until afterwards. Go to ground, Grant. I'll keep in touch.'

Rackham strolled across to the window, looked down at the streaming traffic. 'Look, it's stopped raining. The sun's even coming out again. There—that's a good omen, Grant.' He paused. 'Know anything about a Russian container ship, just refitted at Leningrad, renamed *Argus Viktor*?' he asked.

Kerringer got up, shook his head. 'Nope. Should I?'

Rackham shrugged. 'Just wondered, that's all.'

The lift doors could scarcely have closed on the American before Rackham's phone buzzed.

'Mr Hammond Acton's been trying to get you,' Rackham

was told. 'He says it's very urgent—desperately, was the word he used.'

'Get him for me, would you?'

When the phone buzzed again, Rackham only had the chance to announce himself before the anxious voice at the other end burst out, 'What the hell's going on, David? They've arrested Gillian. Did you know? What the hell for?'

'She didn't come in this morning?'

'No, of course she bloody didn't. That had me worried. What was she doing at London airport? Why have the police got her, David?'

'They'll explain everything. They'll be coming to see you—want to question you, obviously. What did you know about Gillian, Hammond? Really know about her, I mean —her background and so on?'

'Damn it, David, she's been with me from the beginning —almost a partner, you might say. I'd trust her with anything. This is mad, David. It's daft.'

'I'm sorry, but I don't think it is. I know it's a hell of a shock, but—'

'You're not telling me she stole the—?'

'Yes, I am.'

'Don't talk rubbish, David. You're letting all this secret stuff go to your head—getting things out of proportion. Gillian couldn't do that—not possible.'

'We'll see, Hammond. After all, nothing's been proved yet,' he added emolliently. He was painfully aware that the proof might depend on his own evidence. Why had the girl left it so late? She should have got out before. If only she had—

'No, of course nothing's been proved. Nor will it be. Isn't there anything you can do?'

'She's being very properly treated. You needn't worry on that score.'

'But—' Hammond broke off, exasperated. His friend didn't seem to understand.

Rackham let the silence persist for a few seconds. He knew exactly what Hammond was feeling—as though he was banging his head against a brick wall. Then he said quietly,

'I'll give you another ring shortly. We'll meet. I'll explain things. As best I can, anyway.'

There was a pause. Then Hammond's voice sounded calmer, more precise. 'What can I do?' he asked.

'Just stay put, Hammond. Help the police all you can.'

'But what can I do to help Gillian?'

'There's nothing you can do.'

There was a sigh at the other end. When eventually Rackham replaced the receiver, he wondered what Gillian would feel when she discovered the truth about him. Betrayed. As she had betrayed. But there was no justice in it. Only guilt.

As he reflected, he wondered if there was any possible connection with the latest report from the man in Leningrad. It seemed remote to say the least. He returned to his desk, pulled open the drawer and laid the folder in front of him. He read the contents again, slowly. The *Argus Viktor* had left Leningrad with a mixed container cargo, but most of it was arms destined for Angola. The flag at the stern had broad black, red and orange stripes with wreathed compass and hammer in the top left-hand corner—the ensign of the East German merchant fleet. She was fully loaded, mostly with twenty-foot containers, except for the main deck amidships, where there was one forty-foot container mounted on a turntable slap in the middle of the deck. Estimated dead-weight—that's to say fully loaded with cargo, crew, fuel, water and everything needed—was 28,500 tonnes. She was about 200 metres long with a draught of 10½ metres. The crew numbered about twenty. Her route was through the Kiel Canal to the North Sea, the English Channel, and then into the Atlantic and down the west coast of Africa. But she would make a first stop at Rostock, where a small amount of cargo would be discharged. The vessel had had a refit at Leningrad.

So what? All very interesting. And puzzling that a Soviet merchant ship should be refitted, have a turntable built amidships, have her own markings painted out, and be transferred to the East German merchant marine. But surely it was no more than intriguing information for the file? Rackham couldn't see that it had any immediate significance for any current inquiry or project. It would be passed to the Soviet and East German sections.

Nevertheless, his curiosity led him to call for the three-volume *Register of Ships*, which gives, among other things, the name, tonnage, owner, country of origin and type of cargo of every registered vessel in the world.

He thumbed through the red A–G volume. *Argus Viktor* was not there. He tried V in the green P–Z volume with no greater luck. Next he searched *Lloyd's Confidential Index*, a work of reference that is not available even to shipping companies. The *Argus Viktor* didn't exist in a book that listed every ship in the East German merchant navy.

There was nothing in the daily *Lloyd's Shipping Index* either. He wouldn't expect that. There were no Lloyd's agents in the Soviet Union. The first time *Argus Viktor* was likely to appear in either *Lloyd's List* or *Lloyd's Shipping Index* was when she was picked up by one of Lloyd's agents in another port. Meanwhile, the ship had no registered identity.

He made some notes on the report, closed the file, and put it in his out tray.

Gillian Ward had been cautioned, interrogated, and had refused to make a statement. Hammond Acton, however, had made a very full statement to the Andover police about his knowledge of Miss Ward and their relationship. On the face of it, she was not only highly competent, but had, in a supporting role, been well nigh essential in the development of the company.

Superintendent Whitaker, looking out over the roofs of Victoria and Westminster, was intrigued. 'You never can tell,' he muttered to the attendant Cawston.

'Bernard Shaw, sir.'

'Hm?'

'Play by Bernard Shaw, sir—*You Never Can Tell*.'

'I know, Snap. I even saw Sir Ralph Richardson in it. I meant human nature—this girl Gillian Ward, what do you make of her?'

'Accomplished spy, sir? She's certainly a cool one.'

'But all the time she's been working for young Acton, do

you suppose she's been peddling stuff to the Russians? Or was there a moment since when, for some reason unknown to us, she suddenly defected? And for what motive?'

Cawston shook his head. 'She's a hard one, sir,' was all he said.

Thus it was that Superintendent Whitaker took the unusual step of having Gillian Ward brought to his own office —just on the off-chance that the more relaxed atmosphere (he assumed his portraits that lined the walls contributed to this) might help. He even left his pipe undisturbed, among the coronet of scorched tobacco in the glass ashtray. He saw that she was seated in an easy chair by the window. She had a view towards the towers of the Palace of Westminster. He relaxed in a similar chair opposite, and Cawston remained on a straight-backed chair behind her, and out of sight. Whitaker had coffee brought in.

Gillian Ward appeared to have no trace of nerves or of apprehension. She looked almost casual as she drank her coffee, glanced round the room, and then remarked on the painted portraits.

Whitaker confessed that he had painted them, and she complimented him. Only when she had put down the coffee cup and looked up expectantly, a small smile quivering on her lips, did Whitaker begin the questioning.

'The last time we met, Miss Ward, I asked you a question which you didn't answer. Let me try again: how long have you been working for the Soviet bloc?'

'You don't know that I have.'

'I'll put it another way. Did you arrange for Stoebel to collect the guidance system from the factory, or did you deliver it to him at the White Hart?'

'I did neither.'

'The punishment for espionage, Miss Ward, is very severe. If convicted, you will face a long prison sentence. Fullest co-operation will help you. Oh, conviction will still result in a term of imprisonment, but it could be less severe. Moreover, if your information were to lead to the conviction of other spies—well, then you could be in a different position altogether.'

'You're presuming my guilt,' she said, equably.

'You've been under surveillance, Miss Ward.' Whitaker forebore to admit that this had been done not by the Special Branch but by colleagues of Kerringer, not to mention Rackham.

She inclined her head. 'Indeed? Then you should know that I'm not implicated in the theft of the guidance system.'

'You were seen with Herr Stoebel at the White Hart Hotel.'

'If I were, what's wrong with that?'

'Come, Miss Ward, we know this gentleman is not what he seems, don't we?'

'You may. I don't. I understood he came from the West German Embassy.'

'It would still be theft, Miss Ward, if you'd handed the guidance system over to an ally.'

'Of course—if I had.'

And that was something which had *not* been observed. The Americans were as much in the dark as Whitaker. For one wild ridiculous moment of wish-fulfilment, Whitaker thought perhaps the damned thing hadn't been stolen at all. It hadn't been, as expected, in Stoebel's car. No one had seen the hand-over. But, he reminded himself, it *was* missing from the factory.

'Your fingerprints, Miss Ward, are all over the controls of the electronic security system at the factory.'

'Of course they are. I mostly switch it on.'

'And switch it off,' he muttered.

She made no response.

The superintendent drummed his fingers on the arm of his chair. He tried another tack.

'You've been with Mr Acton from the very beginning. You've obviously done a remarkable job. Don't you feel a sense of commitment to it?'

'Yes.'

'A loyalty to Mr Acton?'

'Of course, Superintendent. You're the one who is making other assumptions.'

'I believe it was even expected that you and Mr Acton might marry?'

'Probably.'

'That would have given you some difficult moral problems, some issues of conscience, wouldn't it?'

'On your assumptions, yes. You're short on fact, Superintendent.'

Whitaker's manner changed. 'We can prove your implication in the theft of the guidance system. We can prove your association with agents of the East German government. You would be advised to make a full statement, naming your associates. Sergeant Cawston here will give you all the help you need.'

The superintendent got up, returned to his desk. She sat for a moment, and then rose herself. Sergeant Cawston escorted her from the room.

13

It was Wednesday before Karl Heinze got back to London. Sandra had only just returned from school when her telephone rang, and she heard Heinze's voice say laconically, 'I'm back. Can we eat at yours tonight? There's a lot to talk about.'

She rushed out and bought some beef and vegetables for a casserole, hurried back and got the meal cooking as quickly as possible. She wanted time for a bath and to make herself look her best. Now, when she contemplated herself in front of the bedroom mirror, it was with a feeling of pride. She was confident in her appearance. She really was rather attractive, and even if her hair was not distinctive, its pale brown was at least soft. She even thought the slight tilt to her nose was provocative, and her large hazel eyes were shining. Romantic novelists called it love-light, and now she saw why. She laughed at herself with happiness. After her bath she took great care with the minimum make-up that she used and, as it was a warm evening, she put on her thinnest dress, so that the shape of her body was visible.

When he came in, she paused for a moment just to look at him. Then she rushed towards him, and he kissed her passionately.

Heinze, too, was looking forward to the latter part of the evening. He'd missed her body. He held her away and looked at her dispassionately. Yes, she was desirable, very desirable.

'I've got a lot to tell you,' he said, 'after we've eaten.'

But as they ate and drank she was full of questions. 'Where've you been? What have you done?'

'Berlin—East Berlin. Rostock. I've finished making the arrangements. Everything's ready.'

She stared at him, her eyes bright. She couldn't believe it. He had organized it. How? Who with? But the questions

135

weren't important. It was enough that he'd made the arrangements. She had been able to help, if only in a small way. She had helped, and she'd given him her support, she'd given him her love. Now, where the CND demonstrations had failed, *they* were going to succeed. She was sure of it.

Only when she had cleared the things from the table, made some coffee, and they'd taken their last glass of wine to the divan against the wall with its scattering of bright cushions, did she ask him what exactly it was that was ready.

He looked at her, dark eyes unwavering, assessing her. He said quietly, 'The *Argus Viktor*, a container ship loaded with cargo for Angola, will off-load some of it at Rostock. We shall pick it up there. The master, chief officers and some of the crew have been specially picked. The action is code-named Operation Argus. The master is in charge of the ship. I am in charge of the operation. The vessel is armed amidships with an SS-N-2C Styx missile fitted with a hollow charge so that it can penetrate the protective shield and reach the core of one of the reactors at Sizewell nuclear power station. The *Argus Viktor* will anchor outside territorial waters.' He paused, smiling faintly.

She stared at him, wide-eyed. He was serious. How had he done it? 'You said, *we* join the ship at Rostock.'

'Yes, you're coming.'

She didn't know what to say. She wasn't even sure what she felt. She stuttered something about the school.

'You'll have to be ill—an excuse. You'll be back within a fortnight. No one will know where you've been.'

'You said the ship was going to Angola.'

'So it is. But we shall be lifted off by helicopter, taken back to East Berlin, and—'

'But will they give in to a threat as soon as that?'

'A threat to blow open a nuclear power station? Of course they will. You'll see.'

She took his hand, looked into his eyes. She saw his determination, his authority. There was no doubting him. This was big. This was important. The government wouldn't risk having people killed by radiation. They wouldn't dare. There'd be such a public outcry. So they would have to start withdrawing the cruise missiles. They would have no alternative. She was sure of it, because Karl said so. And he needed her with him. He had said she was going too. She could scarcely believe it, but she had no alternative either.

'When do we go?' she said.

'Saturday.'

'I'll write to the headmaster.'

'You won't, of course, tell anyone what we're doing.'

'No.' She shook her head. 'Oh, Karl—'

He smiled, withdrew his hand, and felt in the inner pocket of his light grey suit. 'Here,' he said, 'this is your passport, in the name of Sandra Heinze, and your visa for the German Democratic Republic. Here's a special pass for the Warnemunde shipyard and docks. It explains that you are my wife, accompanying your husband. Check that the number on the visa is the same as your passport. I will get air tickets—don't worry. There are flights via Amsterdam, but we shall fly Czechoslovak Airlines to Prague, and then get an Interflug flight to Shonefeld airport—that's East Berlin. We shall get a train from Berlin to Rostock. It's a very good service.'

She shook her head in astonishment. 'Karl—you're marvellous. But—where did you get all these?'

'I told you I had contacts. The visa has been issued by the GDR embassy—all quite legitimate.'

She laughed. It was all so exciting—wonderful. And what they were going to do would benefit all mankind. It was for peace. She was almost trembling.

He looked at her and smiled faintly to himself. She would be marvellous tonight—that was certain. She was quivering with desire as it was. Casually, he wondered what would happen to her after he had been lifted off the *Argus Viktor*. Well, she might make a good screw for the master if he left her on the ship. Or should he take her with him? If he did, how much longer would he want her? That might depend on what he was going to do, and he hadn't yet decided. His musings were interrupted.

'How long will it take from Rostock to—well, near Sizewell?'

He shrugged. 'Oh, about three days.'

'And when do we issue the ultimatum?' She was going to

137

add, 'And how do we do it?' but decided that Karl would regard that as a silly question. A man who had done all he had done wouldn't have any difficulty about getting an ultimatum to the British government.

He looked at her curiously. 'When we're at sea.'

She nodded, looked serious. 'Have you decided what it will say?'

He chuckled. 'Not the words—yet. It'll be quite frightening, leave no doubt about our intentions.'

'No,' she said, now very serious, 'they must have no doubt that we mean business.'

'You're not afraid?'

'No, of course not. Why should I be?'

'A lot of people might describe it as terrorism.'

She still looked solemn, but there was excitement in her eyes too. 'We've been through that,' she said with a decisiveness that surprised herself. 'It's for the greater good. Anyway, you said no one will know I've been away. Just sick, that's all. And they won't know it's you either, my darling. No one will know. It will be our secret always.' She had no doubts in her mind about the success of the operation.

Neither had he. Half the money was already in his bank account. Moreover, no one ever found *him*. There was a bigger group involved in Operation Argus than he would have liked, but some of them he had picked himself in the past few days. He trusted them, but even if there were circumstances in which they could no longer be trusted, it wouldn't matter. He would have disappeared long before then.

'Yes,' he said softly. He didn't really want this conversation to continue. His loins had better ideas. He stroked her hair. She turned her head towards him, smiling. He kissed her, ran his hands over her shoulders, down over her breasts. She'd got almost nothing on. He wondered whether, for the first time, they should stay on the divan or go straight to her bedroom. He decided on the divan, and began slowly removing her clothes.

Heinze was back in his hotel suite by nine o'clock the next morning. He bathed, put on clean clothes and another suit, satisfied himself upon his appearance, and then settled in a chintz-covered chair by the window and opened a copy of that morning's *Times*. He felt pleased with himself. He'd had no problems in Germany. The plan was complete, the *Argus Viktor* was on its way, and last night Sandra had been her best yet. He wondered how much more there was in her before he needed a change. She'd certainly see the operation through and, if he decided to take her with him, she'd probably still have some weeks in hand. Perhaps that was the advantage of a virgin. The trouble was, there weren't many of them left. Today he would get the air tickets; that would be no problem. He turned to the troubles of the world. He liked to be informed, and *The Times* was as reliable a guide as any. He had reached the leader page when the telephone rang.

The voice said only, 'Argus?', and then in a light, almost cheerful tone, announced a code that Heinze recognized. He acknowledged both himself and his recognition of the caller.

'So why do you call?' he asked.

'I—er, wondered if you were free to accept a commission?'

'On a hotel telephone line?'

The caller chuckled. 'Such business is, of course, confidential. I would give you the details when we meet.'

'Why should I be interested?'

'Because it *is* interesting, and difficult. And the fee would be commensurate. Why not come to see me?'

'In your office? Don't be silly.'

The caller laughed. 'Would it matter?'

Heinze considered. It probably wouldn't, but he couldn't be sure that Shokolov was not having him watched.

'The police might see me,' he said. 'But if the fee is large enough, I'm interested. Let us say twelve noon, Victoria Gardens. I'll be leaning on the river wall.'

Heinze reckoned he would be able to approach the gardens sufficiently circuitously to shake off any tail if there was one. He was, after all, experienced enough.

'That'll do,' said the voice. 'See you then.'

After the meeting, Heinze took himself to the Savoy Grill for lunch. He even had a half-bottle of champagne to celebrate. It didn't occur to him that he was being premature. The assignment would be difficult, that was true enough, and he hadn't got much time to plan, but he had confidence in his ability. He hadn't suspected that the payment would be so large—not from that source. And direct into his Swiss bank account when the operation was completed. And whereas he couldn't be one hundred per cent certain that Shokolov would make the second payment into the Swiss account —that was why Heinze had insisted on half the money in advance—he was sure there would be no defaulting on this one. All very satisfactory.

There were not many of his calling, he reflected, who would, even if they could, take lunch at the Savoy. They were too obsessed by muddle-headed ideologies, too patheti-cally anxious to work for nothing, and although some of them were very able, most of them were ultimately victims of their own ideas. He watched the bubbles of champagne rise up the tulip-shaped glass and felt a comfortable contempt for all of them.

It would be necessary first to go to Rostock, get Sandra settled. He wouldn't be able to take her with him on the new assignment, but she could keep herself amused for twenty-four or forty-eight hours, and then when he returned, they would be ready to sail. He considered how it might be done. With just one day for reconnaissance and planning and another for execution it was pretty tight. But he didn't see an alternative. O K, it was complicated, but that's why they'd come to him. That's why the pay was big.

Heinze summoned a waiter.

He would like, he said, a rosebud for his buttonhole. Red would look rather good on the grey suiting.

14

All day at school on Friday Sandra complained of feeling peculiar. Perhaps she wasn't well. By the time school finished, her headmaster was feeling quite anxious about her. That night she would write him a note, explaining that her doctor had ordered her to take a brief holiday immediately, otherwise he foresaw a breakdown. It was true she wouldn't be able to enclose a medical certificate, but that was something she would somehow deal with when she got back. It was of no consequence compared with the momentous undertaking that faced her.

She was not seeing Karl that evening. They had agreed that each had a lot to do in preparation. Anyway, she felt she needed a little time, not only to pack, but to be by herself and to think about what was happening.

She didn't have any doubts. Karl had swept them away, and she had only to think of him for a moment or so to know that she was doing the right thing. Her thoughts turned to herself. She had not only become a woman, she had grown up, matured. She understood the difference now between sharing cold nights of comradeship round a camp-fire with tousled-looking women at Greenham Common, which was never going to achieve anything, and being imaginative enough to conceive the impossible and then to make it real. Karl had shown her the way.

She was surprised at how methodically she packed. She did that immediately after she had composed the letter to her headmaster, which she would post in the morning on the way to Heathrow. She cooked herself a simple meal, and then, with nothing to do, she thought for the first time of her brother. She wished he had been able to meet Karl. Not that she could have told Hammond about Operation Argus; of course not. Hammond, anyway, wouldn't have understood.

That was sad. But he would have understood about her relationship with Karl, and he would have been happy for her. She was sure of it. Now he was having this awful business over Gillian. God, how terrible he must feel. She felt suddenly close to him. Impulsively, she dialled his number.

Immediately she spoke to him she knew he was aware of her closeness. She hoped it comforted him. No, he said, there was nothing fresh from the police. They were still questioning Gillian, and he hadn't been able to get near her. He couldn't understand it. What the hell did they think they were about? Sandra couldn't say to him that she was sure it was all a mistake, because that was a trite and empty thing to say. She knew he believed it; she also thought it must be true, and so there was no point in mentioning it. Yet she sensed that there was an underlying anxiety, and there was nothing either could do to eliminate that.

'Shall I see you this weekend?'

'I—' She paused, searching for words. 'Well, I'm not sure. I—'

'You haven't got a CND demonstration or something, have you?'

'No—not exactly.'

'What do you mean—not exactly?'

'Nothing. That is, no, I'm not going to a demonstration. It's just that I'm not sure if I can get down.'

'You're doing something with—' He hesitated, trying to remember the name, and then went on, 'With—er, Karl —isn't that his name?'

'H'm. Yes.'

'It's just that I would have liked a chat with you—that's all.'

She felt awful. They had always supported each other and now she was letting him down when he needed her most. She wished she could tell him, but—it was no good, that was impossible.

'Yes—yes, well, we will talk, Hammond—soon.'

'All right—when you can.'

He sounded disappointed—sadly resigned and disappointed.

After she'd replaced the receiver, she sat staring at it for several seconds, feeling miserable, wondering what she could do.

She slumped down at a small Victorian desk she had found about a year ago at a country auction Hammond had taken her to. She pulled some paper towards her, picked up a pen and began to write.

I know you wanted one of our old talks together, she wrote, *and this time it would have been so important. Oh, I do understand, Hammond, really I do. I would like to be with you, like to talk. I've got so much I want to tell you as well. There isn't anyone else—is there?—that either of us can talk to. It's helpful just to talk to each other, and be with each other.*

She paused, read over what she had written, and shook her head sadly. It wasn't good enough, not explicit enough. But he would understand. She put pen to paper again.

And yet I can't tell you—not yet. That hurts. I'm so happy, Hammond, excited and happy. But beneath it is the hurt of not being able to tell you. I'm just bursting to come out with it all—tell you the whole wonderful story. So, why can't I? No, I can't, I just can't at present. But you will know and you will understand. You might not agree. But I know you'll understand. It's so important, Hammond.

How much more could she tell him? She longed to let the pen fly across the page, revealing everything.

I couldn't come down this weekend, she wrote, *because I'm going away for a bit. No, the school don't know. They think I'm ill. But I'm just having to take a fortnight's break. Yes, with Karl—you'd guess that. We're going to Rostock.*

She stopped, stared at the word she had written. It had appeared on the paper automatically, before she realized what she had written. It was important that Operation Argus should be completely secret. But—well, she hadn't said anything about that at all. Surely there was no harm in Hammond knowing where she was going? He would keep it to himself. She could rely on him, she knew she could.

An odd place, you might think, she wrote hurriedly, as though it wasn't of the least significance, *but you'll laugh when I tell you.*

Now that wasn't true. That was the first utterly false thing she had written. He would know that. There was nothing to laugh about. It was deadly serious.

Well, I don't know about laugh, she continued. Now she was confused. She didn't know how to go on. *Perhaps amused understanding would be a better description. Oh dear, Hammond, I'm getting myself tied in knots—how silly. Anyway, you don't have to worry.*

She was almost out of control now, simply putting words down on paper, trying to recover herself. She wondered whether to tear the whole thing up. No, she couldn't do that—not after their telephone conversation. She had to write to him, had to give evidence of their affection.

The time will soon pass, she wrote, *and then we'll have a marvellous talk. And by then perhaps Gillian will be with you again. I'm sure the police have made a mistake—that's the only possible explanation. It has to be.* She paused again, wondering if she had written those words just to be comforting. She didn't know anything about the police inquiries. But how could Gillian have anything to do with the theft? No, she was only saying what she believed. Then she penned the last sentence. *Please have faith in me, Hammond.*

She looked at it, not sure what it meant. It had come on the paper as automatically as the word Rostock. Faith that she was doing the right thing? If he knew what it was, would he have faith? She smiled. No, he would tell her in the most gentle way—not like her father who would be utterly con-demnatory—not to be so silly, because she could not possibly do any good. Well, for once Hammond would be wrong. He didn't know Karl, didn't know what he was capable of. She would do good all right. It was useless sitting on your backside and moaning. You had to do something, and something a sight more effective than demonstrations and petitions. Oh, if only she could tell him.

She signed the letter and sealed it. She would post it in the morning on the way to Heathrow. She and Karl were meeting there.

Lying in bed alone that night she felt nervous for the first time.

★

144

It had been a disappointing week. That was partly the reason why Superintendent Whitaker and Sergeant Cawston were in the office together on Saturday. But it was also because Whitaker had one of his hunches—not a remarkable hunch; in fact nothing more than the feeling that he would be unsettled and irritable at home, and so it would be better for Edie, as well as for himself, if he returned to his office in the tower of New Scotland Yard.

Gillian Ward still refused to make a statement, and so she had been detained on a charge of being concerned in the theft of electronic equipment from the premises of Digitalia Plc. The routine had been meticulous, and he was satisfied that there was little more to be gained from inquiries at Andover. In short, the ball was in his court, and the next point, if not the set and match, was expected to be his.

There were two distinct crimes—the killing of von Erbacher, and the theft. Or were they part of one design? He couldn't be sure. There was nothing that could incontrovertibly connect them. The theft they couldn't prove, but circumstantial evidence could be built up without much difficulty to implicate Gillian Ward. But where was the guidance system itself? He only had Rackham's word that it was probably now in East Germany. To produce evidence to satisfy a court that Miss Ward was a spy was more difficult. As for the killing of von Erbacher, he knew the assassin, had his photograph. But where the hell was he? Police constables from every force in Greater London had checked the hotels in their patch without producing any sign of Karl Heinze.

The only brief gleam of light had come yesterday from a particularly observant waiter at the Savoy Grill. He was sure that the man in the photograph had lunched there the previous day, and had ordered a half-bottle of Bollinger. He had especially remembered it because the man had sent for a red rosebud for his buttonhole. Assuming the reliability of the waiter's evidence, Whitaker was fairly sure that Heinze, or Argus, was still in London. Why? When the obvious thing would have been to get out of the country?

When he had told Rackham about the Savoy incident, the MI6 man had replied, 'Did he now? Quite characteristic, I'd say. Not your typical terrorist, Arthur. Quite a lad, eh?'

Whitaker found Rackham's whole approach irritating and superficial. But the fact remained, the Savoy incident was only yesterday. Heinze was still around. Somewhere in the streets down there, proud and immaculately dressed, walked Europe's most professional killer. Whitaker began to feel something of the burning hatred that he had for the Provisional I R A. He'd get the bastard, somehow he'd get the bastard. But where did the East German business fit in? If it did, he was sure that Rackham could tell him, but all he would say was, 'The blighters have got the guidance system, Arthur, and that girl's been helping them.'

The superintendent sought comfort and inspiration in his pipe. He leant back in his chair, heard the swivel squeak with his weight, and puffed a spiral of smoke towards the ceiling. At least every constable on the beat had the Heinze photograph in his breast pocket and was searching the faces of every passerby. You couldn't beat routine.

There was a tap at the door, and Sergeant Cawston entered. He looked stern.

'There's been a bit of a balls-up, sir. Nobody's fault, really.'

Biting on his pipe, Whitaker muttered, 'All balls-ups are somebody's fault. Tell me.'

'Well, sir, there are three hotels in Knightsbridge unchecked.'

Whitaker removed the pipe from his mouth, held it away from his face, and stared back through a gauze of smoke. 'Go on,' he said.

'The chap detailed had an accident and was whipped off to hospital, unconscious.'

'So?'

'That was—' Cawston paused, wondering how to put it. 'Several days ago,' he added. 'I suppose someone assumed the place had been—'

'Get on with it, Snap.'

'The constable regained consciousness this morning. One of the first things he said was that Argus was at the Bromsgrove under the name of Karl Heinze.'

Whitaker jumped up from his desk at a surprising speed for his size, pressed out the burning tobacco and stuffed the

146

pipe in his pocket all in one movement, and shouted, 'A car, quickly! Come on Cawston!'

As they entered the lift and Whitaker impatiently banged the ground button, he asked, 'Who's in charge of that section? I'll have his guts for garters.'

Cawston didn't bother to reply. They hurried to the car, he took the wheel and, with the headlights on full beam, blue light flashing and siren shrilling, quickly threaded the car through Petty France and Buckingham Gate, past Buckingham Palace to Constitution Hill. Cars and taxis edged rapidly towards the side of the road as the white police Rover surged past them. Whitaker took the radio microphone from its rest.

'Central Nine O to M P,' he called.

'M P to Central,' came the response.

'Can I have car-to-car, please?'

'M P to Central OK. Change to channel ten, car-to-car.'

In the next few seconds Superintendent Whitaker called nearby police cars to rendezvous at the Bromsgrove Hotel, Knightsbridge.

Cawston had scarcely braked the car to a standstill before Whitaker launched his bulk at the swing doors of the hotel. Even as he slammed the photograph of Heinze on the reception desk, he could hear above the sound of Knightsbridge traffic the sirens of other converging police cars.

'This man,' he said, 'Karl Heinze—what room is he in?' In his other hand he held aloft his warrant card, bearing his photograph and name as a superintendent of the CID, Metropolitan Police. His unique position in the Special Branch was not something disclosed on warrant cards.

Cawston was now close behind him.

The girl looked up with an automatic smile. 'Just a moment, sir,' she said, running her finger down a print-out. 'Oh, he checked out this morning, sir.'

'How long ago?'

The porter she had beckoned over was already alongside. 'Must have been at least two hours, sir,' he said.

'Does anyone know where he was going?' Whitaker addressed his question to anyone who might be listening, and that now included another porter and a lounge-suited young man who was presumably the assistant manager.

There was a shaking of heads, and muttered 'Noes', and then the first porter said, 'He had a couple of suitcases, sir. They were labelled with flight numbers and—' He paused, furrowed his brow. 'Yes, it was a word that was *Shone* something.'

'S-H-O-N-E-F-E-L-D?' Whitaker asked, spelling the word out letter by letter.

'That's it, sir.'

Other policemen thronged into the lobby.

'Has anyone else occupied Heinze's room?' Whitaker asked.

'No, sir.'

'I want it searched, please.'

The assistant manager led a couple of police officers out of the lobby and along the corridor. Cawston had disappeared immediately he had heard the name of the East Berlin airport. Now he rushed through the swing doors back to Whitaker's side. 'There are no direct flights to Shonefeld,' he said. 'K L M go via Amsterdam. Airport police are checking whether Heinze is at the airport or booked on any Western flight. There's also a connection via Prague. Czechoslovak Airlines, flight O K 755, was airborne five minutes ago.'

'Shit!' Whitaker breathed the word through his teeth. 'That'll be his flight. The bastard's got away.'

The pretty receptionist looked up, surprised. But Whitaker was looking beyond her, thinking.

'Manager's office,' he said. 'Quickly!'

As the girl came round to lead him to the far corner of the lobby, Whitaker turned to Cawston. 'Get me David Rackham on the phone,' he said. 'Stay by the switchboard, sergeant. There must be no other calls, either incoming or outgoing, while I'm speaking.' He then followed the girl into the manager's empty office, and stood by the corner of the desk, waiting.

The phone rang. 'Hello, Arthur, what's the panic?'

'Heinze has almost certainly taken off from London Heathrow for Prague, flight number O K 755.' He paused, looked at his watch. 'Just eight minutes ago.'

'Blast!' said Rackham in a tone that Whitaker thought was not wholly convincing. 'Bad luck, Arthur. Where are you?'

'Bromsgrove Hotel, Knightsbridge. He's been staying here. Look, David, we're after an international killer. That aircraft is still in British airspace. We've got—what? Twenty minutes? I don't know. It can be instructed to turn back. If needs be, RAF aircraft can be sent up to force it back.'

Except for an unusually long 'Yes', there was silence at the other end of the line.

'It would need C's authority, that's all,' said Whitaker.

'I don't know. Czechoslovak Airlines? The Defence Secretary might need to be consulted.'

'Don't believe it,' said Whitaker brusquely. 'But there's even time for that.'

'I suppose so.'

'For god's sake, David, get cracking. The whole of Western Europe wants the bastard.'

'That's right.' This time the tone was brisker. 'Leave it to me,' Rackham said.

Whitaker put down the receiver, and rejoined Cawston in the lobby. He had an uneasy feeling of anti-climax and dissatisfaction. They could have got the bugger but for some incompetent bloody cop—The indignation broke off as he recalled Rackham's tone of voice. It somehow hadn't carried one hundred per cent conviction. He had never understood these MI6 types. 'Come on,' he muttered to Cawston, 'we'd better take our own look at the fellow's room.'

An hour later he was back in the lobby, feeling even more frustrated. The room had yielded nothing of significance. Although it was still being checked, it even looked as though there were no fingerprints. Surfaces had either been wiped, or the chambermaid had been thorough with the dusting. He drove back in silence to New Scotland Yard. Cawston knew better than to interrupt.

Back in his own office, the superintendent punched out Rackham's number.

'Did you get him?'

'He was booked on that flight, with Mrs Heinze,' said Rackham. 'But like you, we just missed him, Arthur. Out of

149

British airspace before we could get it together. Too bloody bad, eh?'

Whitaker slammed down the receiver. He looked up at a startled Cawston, and repeated angrily, 'Too bloody bad.'

David Rackham always cooked himself a good breakfast —bacon and eggs, followed by wholewheat toast and marmalade, and coffee. He worked on the principle that he couldn't be sure when and where the next meal would be. In recent times, that was seldom true, but it had proved a good principle in the past, and he stuck to it. Moreover, it seemed to make no difference to his weight. He was contemplating *The Times*'s headline, MINERS CALL FOR PIT BALLOT, when he was interrupted by the telephone.

It was Hammond Acton, a sufficiently agitated Hammond Acton to dissuade Rackham from early-morning banter.

'She's gone to Rostock, David. Rostock!'

'Who's gone to Rostock?'

'Sandra.'

Rackham considered.

'Did you hear me?'

'Sorry, Hammond. Yes, I heard you. You're sure it's Rostock, not East Berlin?'

'Not in the mood for riddles, David.'

'No, I'm serious. She did say Rostock?'

'Yes, it's in a letter from her this morning. Of course, I phoned her immediately. No reply. I suppose she's gone.'

'With someone?'

'Yes, with some fellow she met recently—called—'

'Karl Heinze?'

'Yes, yes, that's it? How'd you know?'

'Never mind, old—not now. Look, you're quite sure she will have gone?'

'Yes—I know her. You'd better see the letter.'

'Then bring it up to town straight away. Meanwhile, have you got an East German visa?'

'Yes, I was planning a trip. Oh, I only export stuff the Department of Trade allows, but it's worth it. I should have been there now, but for all the business of the factory, and Gillian, and—'

'Don't suppose your man's in Rostock, is he?'

'No, East Berlin.'

'That'll do. There's a good train service to Rostock. I've just joined your company, Hammond. I'm a fellow director. We're leaving for East Berlin at once—just as soon as you can get up to town. O K?'

'But can you get a visa that quickly?'

Rackham chuckled. 'They're my stock in trade. No problem. You can fill me in on the journey—the technical stuff, I mean. Just so that I know the company I'm working for. Genitalia, isn't it?'

Hammond thought his friend's humour singularly inappropriate, but all he said was, 'Do you know what the hell she's doing there?'

'Haven't a clue, old chap.'

'Then why the urgency?'

'Instinct. There's a curious ship I don't understand on its way to Rostock. And because of Heinze.'

'What about him?'

'He killed that German minister, Martin Lange, in his flat in Bonn.'

There was a horrified silence at Hammond's end. Then, with sudden realization, he snapped, 'If that was known about him, why wasn't he arrested?'

'Ah, well, he very nearly was. We'd just run him to earth on Saturday, when he flew out from under our noses.' Rackham paused, and then added, 'It's all a rather complicated story.'

'I'm not sure I understand what the hell you're talking about. Is Sandra safe with him?'

'Yes, I think so—at the moment. But that's why we need to go there. He disposes of people when he's finished with them.'

'You mean he's using her for something?'

'Yes—certainly for sex. That's an obsession with him. But I guess there's something else we don't know. Perhaps her letter will help us. But I've got to find out. You haven't met him, I suppose?'

'No, she hasn't brought him down to Hampshire.'

'I'm not surprised. But he's been there.'

151

Hammond was puzzled. 'You mean—' he began, but was interrupted.

'He killed von Erbacher.'

15

In Rostock Heinze had booked into the only hotel worth staying at—the Interhotel Warnow—a modern building of one vertical block with glass horizontals, and boasting that many of its 558 rooms had 'private facilities'. Heinze had made sure that their room was so equipped, and had a television set as well. It was furnished in what could only be called sparse comfort, but it was quite luxurious by East German standards. Sandra held his hand tightly as she looked out of the window on to lawns and shrubberies and a pool with fountains. She'd held his hand for most of the flight and for the train journey too. She was nervous, perhaps a little afraid. He, by contrast, exuded confidence. He seemed to be at home wherever he was, whereas she was acutely aware of the strangeness of her surroundings.

It wasn't until after their evening meal, and they were back in their room, that she put something of her feeling into words. 'I'm behind the Iron Curtain,' she said.

Heinze felt a momentary impatience. Of course the damn woman was behind the Iron Curtain. What did she expect? But he smiled reassuringly. 'So what?' he said. 'You've got a passport, you've got a visa. You can go back again—now, if you want.'

She looked at him, perplexed. 'Oh, no. I must be with you. But—' She struggled to find the right words. 'I can't believe it—that it's really going to happen.'

Again he smiled, this time confidently, arrogantly. 'When I decide to do something, it's done,' he said.

Earlier in the day he'd made one phone call. He'd spoken in German, and she hadn't understood a word of it. But afterwards he said, 'The *Argus Viktor* hasn't berthed yet. There is nothing we can do for the moment.'

She just wanted to be in bed with him again, to feel the

safety of him. She hadn't realized that she would feel so insecure.

Sunday was a dull day. The sky was overcast and it was slightly humid; and the town seemed empty of people and looked grey and dead. About half of the old town, which had its roots in the fourteenth century, had been destroyed by Allied bombs during the war, and although a lot of the old buildings had been tastefully restored, there were also streets of boring modern blocks. It was depressing. The whole atmosphere contributed to her sense of disbelief, her feeling of uncertainty. Her reaction was to feel an even greater need for Karl. She could no longer imagine being without him.

So it was a shock when he said, during their evening meal, 'I shall have to go back to Berlin tomorrow.'

She looked stunned. 'But—'

'I'll be back Tuesday night—at worst Wednesday morning. We'll probably sail on Wednesday.'

He sounded so casual she could hardly believe it. 'Can't I come?' she said.

'No.' His tone was final.

She was hurt, astonished. 'What for? Why do you have to go there? And why can't I come?'

Heinze found it difficult to conceal his impatience, but he managed to subjugate it to his charm. 'Because, darling Sandra,' he said, 'I'll be able to get back here quicker if I go alone. I've got to go there to make some final arrangements about Operation Argus that can't be made here in Rostock. You trust me, don't you?'

Large brown eyes were looking meltingly at her. Of course she trusted him. She nodded, disappointed nevertheless. 'I shall feel afraid,' she said softly.

'There's no need to be. It won't be for long. Then we shall be together again.'

The soothing tone went against the grain, but he couldn't afford to upset her now. After all, he'd decided to have her with him for his own purposes. He had to tolerate her anxiety, her feeling of dependence. It had its advantages in other ways.

'All right. God knows what I'll do.'

154

'You can be a tourist. Have a look at the town.'

'Haven't I seen it? Anyway, they don't look as though they know much about tourists. Oh, Karl, it's so depressing.'

He squeezed her hand. 'Think of the voyage,' he said. 'Think of Operation Argus.'

She nodded, lifted her glass of wine and said, 'Here's to us then.'

On Monday morning Karl left early for Berlin. It was another day of overcast skies, which gave her the lonely feeling of looking on to a grey landscape. The hotel wasn't full, but there were plenty of people moving about the spacious lobby. They looked grey too—hurrying about their unfathomable ways. Sandra searched for an English newspaper. There were none. Her isolation was complete. She tried to comfort herself with thoughts of Operation Argus. It only made her more acutely aware of her dependence upon Karl. Even her passport and her visa described her as Sandra Heinze.

She spent much of the day walking about the town. She went the whole length of the Lange Strasse to the Ernst-Thalmann Platz with its strange mixture of neo-renaissance and neo-baroque houses with stepped gables. She wandered beneath the arches of the bright buff-and-white Rathaus, with the uneasy feeling that she was being watched. Then all the way back to Kropeliner Strasse, to stroll aimlessly round its chequered pedestrian area, wondering about its huddled mixture of architectural styles and the shops beneath that were striving to be bright, but offered her nothing that she wanted to buy.

She went to bed unusually early, feeling that her day had been wasted. This decision ensured that she met neither Rackham nor her brother until the following day.

It was late on Monday evening before the pair of them booked in. Since the Warnow was the only hotel that pretended to anything like an international standard, Rackham was confident that was the place Heinze would choose to stay. An inquiry at the reception desk confirmed a booking in the names of Mr and Mrs Karl Heinze. Their plan was to remain unobserved, and somehow they—or at any rate,

Hammond—had to see Sandra alone. At least Heinze had never met Hammond, so there was no real need for him to be surreptitious.

On Tuesday morning the sun was shining, and that made Sandra feel a great deal better and restored something of the excitement of what she was doing. Moreover, that night, or the next morning at the very latest, Karl would be back. After breakfast, she wandered out on to the lawn, sat down by the hedge and watched a couple of children playing in the fountain pool. She thought of the children in the primary school in Bayswater. They would be starting another day without her. She felt no guilt. After all, what she was doing, she told herself, was for them, for their future.

The children were lifting the water in their hands, and shouting with glee as it splashed through their fingers. For one brief moment she dared to think that she and Karl might have children too. There would be a better future for them. She suddenly felt proud, and she sat watching, half smiling to herself. Then, unexpectedly, she was aware—with a sensation like the one she had briefly experienced when walking by the Rathaus the previous day—that she was being observed. Slowly, she looked round.

She didn't believe it. Her mouth dropped open. She stared. Someone exactly like Hammond. Another man beside him. She was sure she'd met him once before. It couldn't be true.

'Sandra.'

She jumped up. 'Hammond! It *is* you. What on earth—?'

'Am I doing here?' He smiled. 'You know I do a bit of exporting to East Germany.' He paused. 'Oh, I think you've met David Rackham.'

She rushed over to them, briefly hugged her brother.

'What I really wanted to know,' he said, as he let go of her, 'is what *you're* doing here. How did you get a visa?'

Rackham interrupted. 'Our friend Karl Heinze arranged that, I shouldn't wonder.'

'Yes, but—' She broke off, sighed. 'You've come here especially to see me. Oh, Hammond, I told you to have faith in your sister. Why don't you?'

'Is Heinze here?' Rackham asked.

'No. He'll be here tonight, or tomorrow morning.'

Rackham nodded, as though he suspected as much. 'I think,' he said, 'I'll leave you two alone for a bit.'

Brother and sister stood looking at each other. 'Come along,' he said, 'let's see if we can find a couple of garden chairs.'

He led her away, and they settled into two chairs near the corner of a hedge, well away from any other guests.

'Hammond, dear Hammond,' she said, 'you've come to fetch me home. I'm sorry, but I can't—not yet.'

'Not necessarily,' he said. 'Anyway, it might not be so easy. You see, you're here with permission, Sandra. The authorities know about you. D'you have your own passport?'

She hesitated, and then said quietly, 'It's in the name of Sandra Heinze.'

'Oh god. All right, why *are* you here? What are you doing? What's Heinze doing?'

She didn't answer immediately. She wanted so much to tell him. He wouldn't approve, but she believed he would understand, because he always had understood her.

'When I come back, I'll be able to tell you. Even then it must be our secret.' She was appealing to the intimacy of their old relationship, but there was something uncharacteristically intractable about him.

He looked at her seriously, almost sternly. 'You said in your letter that you were excited and happy, and that it was a wonderful story, but that I might not agree. Come on, for god's sake, Sandra, nothing can be so secret that you can't tell me.'

She struggled with herself. Of course she wanted to tell him, but the whole thing was so important, there mustn't be the least risk of it going wrong. And he would want to stop her. That's why he'd come. It was obvious. But not now, not after she'd got this far.

'It's all right,' she said softly. 'You don't have to worry. It's quite all right. What about Gillian?'

Hammond wasn't going to be distracted. The mention of Gillian had been painful. That was something he would have wanted to share with his sister, but not now. He ignored her question; he'd got to know about her.

'It's not quite all right, Sandra. It could be dangerous, very dangerous.'

She twisted in her chair and looked straight at him. She could see his anxiety. Well, if everything went wrong, she supposed it could be dangerous. But not how Karl had planned it. No one was going to get hurt, only threatened, but the threat would be so imperative that it couldn't be resisted. And no one would know who was responsible. She and Karl would be safely lifted off the ship and, once back in Germany, would be able to return to Britain. It was really all so simple, nothing to worry about at all.

She said gently, 'If you don't know what I'm doing here, I don't see how you can say it's dangerous. I can tell you it isn't, Hammond—honestly.'

'I wasn't talking about what you're doing, whatever it is. I was talking about Heinze. It could be dangerous just being with him.'

Sandra laughed. 'Oh, honestly,' she exclaimed. 'That's nonsense. Whatever made you say that?'

'You remember that German minister—Martin Lange was his name—assassinated in his flat in Bonn?—Heinze killed him.'

She stared at him, horrified. 'You're—' she began, and then stuttered, 'That's ridiculous. It's just not possible.'

'Why do you think I've come all this way to find you?'

'But you don't know Karl. I do. I really do. He's not like that.'

Hammond said, deadly earnest, 'He killed von Erbacher.'

'That's absurd. What are you talking about, Hammond? It's mad.'

Hammond shrugged. 'I didn't think you'd believe me. Told David you wouldn't. It's true, my dear. It's true.'

'I suppose he stole your guidance system too?' she said crossly.

'No, he didn't. But he did kill von Erbacher.'

Sandra was angry and confused, and yet upset at being angry with her own brother. They argued, but never quarrelled, and they had always trusted each other. She tried to control herself.

158

'Look, Hammond, I don't know what all this is about —but I'm sure what you say is not true.'

Hammond stood up, looked round at the grounds, muttering at the same time, 'You'd better talk to David.'

'Why? How would he know?'

'Because it's his job to know.' He saw Rackham in the distance, watching the children in the pool, and beckoned him over.

Sandra said no more until Rackham joined them. She thought that his freckled face and cheerful manner made him look so good-humoured that he might have invented the whole thing as some kind of awful joke.

Hammond said, 'Tell her.'

Rackham raised his eyebrows. 'I thought you might not believe it,' he said directly to Sandra, as the three of them remained standing by the two chairs in the corner of the hedge. 'Here—look!' He took a photograph from his pocket of Heinze wearing a beard. 'That's issued by the West German authorities. You can recognize him, even with the beard, can't you?'

Sandra nodded. 'What's that prove? It's a photograph of Karl—so what?'

'Martin Lange,' Rackham said, 'was only one of a number of assassinations and acts of terrorism. Von Erbacher is the latest. Heinze is the most professional terrorist operating in Europe. Code name, Argus.'

She shivered with alarm, involuntarily. That single word suddenly and unexpectedly filled her mind with doubt. *Argus Viktor*. Operation Argus.

Rackham saw her apprehension. 'So what's he doing?' he asked.

'No—no,' she said. 'No, it can't be true. That's not Karl.'

Rackham took from his pocket Sergeant Cawston's photograph. 'Do you recognize him as a plumber? He's coming out of the Soviet Embassy. Heinze,' Rackham continued, unemotionally, 'is only one of many names. Oddly enough, it might be his real name. But in Andover he was Andrew Lane. So—what's he up to?'

Sandra stared at the second photograph. She had no doubt that it was Karl. She was confused. She believed Hammond;

159

between them was the trust of their life since childhood. But she loved Karl. He was necessary to her. They were bound together—as one. It was no good, she couldn't believe any of these allegations. Some dreadful mistake had been made—a double—something. It was the only possible explanation. Yet he had organized Operation Argus more easily than she could manage her school rota. She didn't know what to think—except, in her heart, she was sure of Karl.

She stared angrily at Rackham. She could afford to be hostile to him. 'It's got nothing to do with you,' she said.

'It has if he's about to kill somebody else.'

'Karl isn't killing anybody. He never has. I don't believe you. You're telling me these things just to get me to come back. They're not true. I know they're not.'

'I'm not trying to get you to shop him,' said Rackham, surprisingly. 'I'm just telling you the truth so that you can assess the danger for yourself. Heinze is a ruthless killer. It's best that you leave him while you can.'

She was blazing with anger. 'I'm not leaving him. He needs me.'

Rackham smiled.

She felt like hitting his silly freckled face. 'He's not what you say. I know he's not. For Christ's sake, I know him. You don't. You don't know a bloody thing. You can't.'

Rackham sighed despairingly, and turned to Hammond.

He looked anxiously at his sister. 'At least trust me,' he said. 'Whatever Heinze may or may not have done, I believe that you're in danger. Come back with us. The immigration people know you're here for a reason. They might try to hold on to you, but it is still a British passport. Come on, Sandra, please.'

There was no doubt of his anxiety, she saw that. But she couldn't go. Not now. They didn't realize, and even if she could tell them everything, they still wouldn't understand. They'd try to stop her. But Operation Argus was for mankind. It was going to start something—she was sure of it.

Slowly she shook her head. 'I can't,' she said softly.

Hammond pleaded with her. 'But, Sandra, it's dangerous.'

'No it isn't—not for me.'

Rackham was about to interrupt, but thought better of it. He made instead a gesture of hopelessness with his hands.

Hammond tried again. 'You can't stay. You mustn't. For god's sake, Sandra—please, I beg of you—be sensible.'

She looked at him sorrowfully. She hated hurting him, but she had to go through with it now.

'Don't worry,' she said soothingly. 'There's no need to, I promise you. You've just got to believe me. I know what I'm doing.'

'Which is what?' Rackham broke in.

'I told you—it's not your concern.'

'But it *is* mine, Sandra,' Hammond said urgently.

'I wish it could be—that would be marvellous. But you're just going to have to trust me.'

'Look, you've got to come back with us—you must.' Hammond sounded desperate. 'Please!'

She took his hands and held them close to her. 'It's all right,' she murmured softly. 'I'm quite safe. I've told you, you don't have to worry. Now forget it. I'm staying.' Then brightening suddenly at the thought, she added, 'Why don't you stay and meet Karl?'

'Yes,' said Rackham. 'I might just do that. I had it in mind.'

Hammond turned to him despairingly. 'Isn't there anything we can do with the authorities here about Heinze?'

'No,' said Rackham firmly.

For the moment that ended the conversation, but the three of them stayed together for the rest of the morning. Sandra tried to chat about other things, but the atmosphere was false. Hammond's anxiety upset her. But every time he returned to the subject of Heinze, she had to tell him firmly that she was staying. Only once, before lunch, did she leave them, and then only for a few moments while she returned to her room to fetch her handbag. When she asked for her key Rackham noted her room number. Then after the three of them had had lunch together and were drinking coffee, he excused himself for a few moments.

Rackham collected her key and hurried to her room. Quickly, with the skill of a professional, he went through the drawers and the wardrobe. There was an expensive grey suit belonging to Heinze hanging inside, but the pockets were empty. The whole operation took no more than five or six minutes, but that was long enough to convince him that there was nothing to be found—not a document, not a single piece of paper, nothing to connect Heinze with any activity at all. Rackham wasn't surprised. He returned to brother and sister with an innocent smile.

Shortly, Rackham made another excuse that he and Hammond had a little work to do concerning an export order that Hammond was negotiating. Sandra didn't know whether it was true or not, but accepted the explanation when she saw how readily her brother agreed.

Rackham had hardly shut the door of his room before Hammond exploded, 'For god's sake, David, what the hell can we do?'

'She's determined to stay,' Rackham muttered as though thinking aloud.

'Can't we force her to come back?'

'How?'

'Well, she's a British citizen—'

'With a dubious passport,' Rackham interrupted.

'And can't we say,' Hammond continued, 'that we have authority to take her back to England?'

'Against her will—at her age?'

Hammond was despairing. 'There must be some way.'

'Like tying her up and putting her in a suitcase?'

'It's not funny, David.'

'Sorry, Hammond. But if she's determined not to come back, there's damn all we can do, is there?'

'She not your sister. She's with a bloody killer.'

'I know, I know. But she can't be forced against her will,' said Rackham with the barest touch of impatience.

'Can't you arrest her?'

'No. I'm not a policeman, and even if I were, it wouldn't help in this country.'

Hammond threw up his hands in despair. Rackham went and stood by the net-curtained window that looked out on to part of the old wall of the city. He said, almost to himself, 'It's worrying, of course it's worrying, but you know there's just a chance she might not be in any personal danger.'

'Just a bloody chance is not good enough.'

'Well, whatever he's up to, is probably not going to involve Sandra. I mean she's not a potential terrorist, Hammond.'

'Look, he'll be back tonight. We don't leave until the morning. Why don't we deal with the bastard ourselves?'

Rackham, with surprising firmness, said, 'No,' and then continued mysteriously, 'But we might have a contact tomorrow. But to *deal* with him, as you put it, wouldn't suit our purposes.'

'For god's sake we've only one purpose—getting Sandra away.'

'H'm. In any event, Hammond, we wouldn't stand a chance of getting away with anything in this place. It wouldn't help anyone for us to land up in jail.'

'Too bloody gentlemanly, aren't we? Why don't *we* have ricin-tipped umbrellas?'

'That's not my scene. We've got to face it, she's determined to stay. You're going to have to do what she says —trust her.'

'Bloody defeatist. Didn't expect that from you, David.'

'Not defeatist. Realist.'

Hammond made no reply, largely because he recognized the truth of what his friend had said.

'Assuming Heinze does return here before we leave in the morning,' Rackham continued, 'you've got to promise not to try anything, Hammond. You could mess everything up. We may be able to make contact—usefully. But it's best if we keep out of his way.'

Hammond looked disbelieving, astonished. 'Let him do whatever he's going to do?'

'We haven't an alternative in this country. We might as well let him complete it, whatever it is, and then presumably Sandra will be free to come home.'

'If she doesn't get caught—involved with him.'

'You're forgetting that he's in friendly territory. They're not going to harm him here. Another reason for thinking Sandra's not in any great danger.'

Hammond wasn't convinced, but tried to assuage his anxiety by telling himself that Rackham knew his job— whatever it was.

They made one final attempt to persuade Sandra to leave with them in the morning, but failed. She was adamant. She had no alternative. But she couldn't understand about Karl. She couldn't believe what they had told her. It didn't fit her understanding of the man she loved and had come to depend upon.

It was a painful conversation, with Sandra attempting to laugh away her brother's fears. Of course, she would take care, and hadn't she said that she would almost certainly be home again within a fortnight.

Hammond dared to ask, 'With Karl?'

'Of course,' she said.

'Will you promise me that you'll come back anyway, even if he doesn't?'

'But he will.'

'Promise!'

'All right, Hammond, I promise. Don't worry.'

Before they parted to go to their respective rooms, Rackham said suddenly to Sandra, 'By the way, it would be better if you didn't mention this meeting to Heinze.'

'Why?'

'Let's say, safer.'

Sandra looked annoyed. 'I'll please myself,' she said.

Rackham shrugged, and the three parted.

Sandra bathed and went to bed, looked at television, but found it boring and incomprehensible. So she left the light on with the curtains drawn, and lay still, hoping that Karl would return, and thinking of the things that Rackham and her brother had said. The most professional terrorist operating in Europe. Code name, Argus. He had killed von Erbacher.

Now that she was alone the anger of her disbelief gave way to a questioning worry. She started to search for explanations. Of course, the most obvious of all was that they were dealing with a double—someone that looked exactly like Karl. In which case, he might be in danger himself. That photograph of him coming out of the Soviet Embassy—well, that was him all right. So what was he doing there? Presumably making some arrangements about Operation Argus. Wasn't the missile Russian? So they mixed with strange bedfellows, but if it was for the common good—? And it was going to benefit Russia too. It would benefit the whole world. So that could be explained. And obviously he would disguise himself just in case someone like—well, like Rackham, if that's what he did—should see him. She was still troubled by the use of the code name Argus. Was she going to talk to Karl about it? She didn't know. She both wanted to and was afraid to.

In the stillness of the strange room, with only the murmured noises of the indifferent city beyond, she began to feel lonely and afraid. It would be all right when Karl returned. But would it? What had they done to her? For the first time, she began to wonder if he *would* return. Supposing he'd gone to do—? The most professional terrorist—Supposing? And then he didn't return? Just left her? God, what had they done? Why was she thinking like this? It didn't make sense. Of course he hadn't gone to—The thought fractured. He wasn't a terrorist, she knew he wasn't. That was absurd —mad. And of course he was coming back. Why shouldn't he? He loved her. God, she wished he was there. She wanted him desperately.

It was midnight when she heard the key in the door. He entered softly, surprised, it seemed, to find the light on, and there he stood, looking calm and immaculate in a perfectly cut blue suit. She jumped out of bed and ran to him, holding him close, clinging. He kissed her, then looked at her and smiled. He eased away the shoulder straps and let the flimsy nightdress slip to the floor. He held her away from him and looked at her slim, well-made body appreciatively.

But she had to be close to him. She pulled him towards her, and her hands began to move over his body, peeling away his jacket, unbuttoning his shirt.

'Don't speak, don't say anything,' she murmured. 'I just want you inside me, part of me.'

He quickly removed the rest of his clothes and, in one desperate embrace, moved them both back to the bed.

It was a long time afterwards that, out of the drowsiness of her satisfaction, she asked, 'What have you been doing, darling?'

'Oh, just making the final arrangements. I'll check in the

morning. But it is morning, isn't it?' He laughed. 'Anyway, I'll check later, but the *Argus Viktor* should be berthed and, I guess, unloaded. We'll probably sail on the afternoon tide.'

All they had said was preposterous. Sandra didn't need any more convincing. So why was there this persistent anxiety? Why didn't she tell him about Hammond? Twice she thought she was going to, and then didn't. Instead, she said, 'How long will it take, then?'

'Oh, we should be on station in about three days.'

'And then it'll all be over.'

She thought he was about to reply, 'Yes,' immediately, but then he seemed to check himself, and said, 'Well, not quite. It'll be a few days before they give in, won't it?'

'Karl, they will give in, won't they?'

'If you were the government, wouldn't you? With a damn great missile threatening to blow open a nuclear power station?'

She nodded. 'H'm. How shall we know?'

'The radio, of course.'

'Yes.'

She looked thoughtful, preoccupied. He ran his hand through her hair. 'Shouldn't this pretty head be getting some sleep?'

She smiled, snuggled close to him, gratefully feeling the hardness of his body. She moved sinuously against him, and began to arouse him again. It was the only way she felt safe.

After he had gone to sleep, she was still awake, wondering why it was that the act of love alone reassured her. So now she *needed* reassurance. No, she wasn't going to accept that. Yet, as the night hours lengthened, she couldn't ignore it. At last she drifted into an uneasy sleep.

When she awoke it was daylight. She could see a patch of blue sky. Sunlight searched over the far wall. She could hear Karl in the bathroom. She lay staring up at the ceiling, and immediately wondered if Hammond and Rackham were still there. She didn't feel sure of herself. And that made her resent her own uneasiness. She decided, almost without knowing it, that she must somehow do something, if not to allay Hammond's anxiety—she doubted if she could do that—at least to keep him in touch. She couldn't tell him what they were doing. That was impossible. But perhaps a hint—just something. Of course it wouldn't stop him worrying, but it might relieve her own anxiety. A note. She could scribble him a note.

She got out of bed and was standing by the small table, her hand on the drawer that held the envelopes and notepaper, when the bathroom door opened and Karl was there. Even standing in his briefs and vest he looked full of confidence and authority. She felt guilty. But she wasn't going to tell him about Rackham and Hammond, and what they had said.

'You look startled,' he said.

'You surprised me.'

'Now you're awake, I can check.'

As she went into the bathroom, she heard him speaking German into the telephone. She ran water in the bath, and was lying full length in it when Karl came in.

He looked at her with undisguised pleasure. 'It's ready,' he said. 'The *Argus Viktor* is there. She's still off-loading, but will be ready to sail on the afternoon tide. We'll have breakfast and go.'

He returned to the bedroom, and again she heard him using the telephone, ordering breakfast. Now she was preoccupied with the task of acquiring paper and envelope, and finding the opportunity to write a note.

Karl noticed. 'What is it?' he asked. 'You're quiet.'

'Nothing. Perhaps I'm a bit nervous,' she smiled.

He looked at her sharply. 'No need to be.'

'I know.' She stretched out and took his hand. She was glad when breakfast arrived, and she had something to do. She gulped down the coffee gratefully. She saw Karl watching her, an amused look on his face. She smiled back apprehensively.

Immediately they'd finished Karl began putting their things together in their three suitcases. He was very careful about folding his spare suit and his shirts. Today he'd dressed himself in sharply creased trousers, open-necked shirt, and a very smart slipover. He went into the bathroom to collect his razor, toothbrush and toiletries. Just as quickly, Sandra rushed to the drawer, slid it silently open, and snatched an envelope and single sheet of paper which she

167

crushed into her shoulder bag. As he came back she said, 'Oh, I wanted to clean my teeth again.'

He held out her brush and the toothpaste. This might be her only chance. With the bag still over her shoulder, she kicked the bathroom door shut, casually, as though it didn't really matter, put the envelope and her ballpoint alongside the basin and then ran the water. She cleaned her teeth noisily with her left hand, writing Hammond's name on the envelope with her right. She just had time to shove it into her shoulder bag when Karl pushed open the door.

'I've packed some of your things,' he said, 'but I think you'd better do the rest.'

She followed him into the bedroom, wondering how she was ever going to write anything meaningful and coherent to her brother. She finished putting the clothes into her suitcase, and then looked up as brightly as she could and said, 'I'm ready.'

With the smaller case under his arm, he carried the three cases along the corridor to the lift. She walked just behind him. At the reception desk, she waited until he was paying the bill and then said, 'Sorry, darling, I must spend a penny. It's that's strong coffee, I guess,' and before he could look up she had slipped away.

In the lavatory she realized that she had no idea what she was going to write. She couldn't explain everything to Hammond. And yet supposing what they had said was true? It was the first time she had really allowed the thought to emerge explicitly. She was shocked at herself. So what was she trying to tell Hammond? She was muddled in her mind. They had distorted things. She couldn't think clearly. And that was because of her own anxiety. She knew it was, and resented it. There was no need for anxiety, she told herself. So what was she going to write? 'We're going to threaten to blow up Sizewell nuclear power station'? She couldn't do that—obviously. 'I'm safe with Karl, you need not worry'? But that was useless. He didn't believe it, and he was already worried. There was nothing—nothing. She felt desperate, even began to look round the small cubicle, as though somewhere on the tiled walls she would see the answer. If only she could meet Hammond going into the gents. It was possible—if he was still there. But she still wouldn't know what to say. She'd got to go. Hastily, all thought abandoned, she scribbled one word on to the paper, folded it, and sealed it in the envelope.

In the lobby, she looked round anxiously. She couldn't see Karl. But she was almost sure it was Rackham's back disappearing into the lift. There was no sign of Karl. She rushed past the reception desk, and slid the envelope along it at the same time. The girl looked at her strangely. She picked it up, read the name on it, and nodded. Then Sandra saw Karl.

'I've got a taxi,' he called.

She ran to the door and joined him.

Fifteen minutes later Rackham inquired at reception whether Mr and Mrs Heinze were still in the hotel, and was told that they had just checked out. The porter helpfully added that they had left in a taxi. When Rackham asked, 'Where to?' he looked suspicious and said he didn't know. But when Hammond came up the porter produced the envelope that Sandra had left.

Hammond tore it open. The single sheet of hotel note-paper inside bore one word. It was scribbled erratically in capital letters. 'SIZEWELL'.

Rackham stared at it. All he said was, 'We can't talk here,' and immediately led the way unerringly to the room Heinze and Sandra had occupied.

Hammond showed his surprise, and was answered by Rackham muttering, 'One of the first things I made a point of finding out.' As he expected, the room had been left un-locked. Hammond watched as Rackham skilfully searched the place. 'Blast! Nothing here,' he said.

'What did you expect?'

Rackham ignored the question, and hurried back to his own room, where he instantly began slinging belongings into his suitcase.

'Whatever it is they're going to do,' he muttered, 'they obviously can't do it from here. And we can't make phone calls from Rostock. We've got to get to the British embassy in East Berlin as quickly as possible.'

Hammond was still clutching the slip of paper. 'What do

you think it means?' he asked, as they hurried into his room and he began to pack, equally quickly.

'God knows. Bombs planted?'

Just over three hours later, anyone going into the Vulcan Arms for a lunchtime pint of bitter might have seen vehicles of the Bomb Disposal Squad turn left into the private road lined with trees and shrubs that led to Sizewell nuclear power station.

16

Sandra sat clutching Karl's hand as the taxi sped the thirteen kilometres from Rostock to Warnemunde, the Baltic coastal port at the head of the Warnow river. She had a tense feeling in the pit of her stomach, and her mind was in a turmoil. She wasn't sure what she felt or thought. The strength of his hand was the only assurance she had.

Karl had warned her that security at Warnemunde was tight, but she had her passport, her visa, and a special pass to the docks. That should be enough, but if it didn't satisfy the men on the gate, he had a telephone number they could ring that would give them both complete clearance.

'Who is it?' she asked.

'Doesn't matter. I fixed it when I went to Berlin.'

For the last half of the journey, the taxi was overtaking an increasing number of large container lorries, and then, as they neared the overseas harbour, Sandra could see the huge skeletal shapes of overhead cranes fretworking the clouded sky. The road narrowed into channels blocked with barrier arms that stuck out from the glassed huts standing on the central islands. The taxi stopped. Karl handed their passports and other documents to the guard. He gave them a glance and took them away. He returned in a few minutes and said something to Karl, pointing suspiciously at Sandra. Karl explained, patiently but with authority. The man went away again. He returned with their papers duly stamped, and they passed through.

'He thought it funny that I should be taking my wife,' Karl said. 'I had to explain that I had married you in England. At first I thought he was going to want proof. But he accepted it.'

They now threaded their way between large storage sheds, cranes and piled container boxes. Dominating the whole

171

landscape, much taller than anything else, was a huge structure which Karl told her was the cable crane at the VEB Warnowwerft, East Germany's largest shipyard.

The taxi drove them to Pier II. There were ships of one kind or another in every one of its thirteen berths. They stopped alongside a stack of container boxes and, to their left, sheering above them in a curving V, were the bows of the *Argus Viktor*.

Karl paid off the taxi. Sandra stood on the quayside, staring up at the brick-coloured bows. She hadn't known what to expect, but this seemed very large. Karl interpreted her look.

'Fully loaded,' he said, 'she's twenty-eight and a half thousand tonnes, and she's about two hundred metres long. Quite safe.' He smiled. 'Come on.' He led her towards the gangway.

A man with the three gold stripes of a chief officer on his shoulders was waiting for them on the main deck at the top of the gangway. Karl shook hands with him. Sandra had the feeling that they knew each other. He turned towards her. 'Sandra,' he said, 'this is Chief Officer Walther.'

The man didn't smile. He only nodded, and said he would take them to meet the master. He would have their cases stowed in his own quarters. 'That's where you are for the trip,' he said, in brisk clipped tones.

She followed without paying attention as they went down a companionway into the heart of the vessel. She had only an impression of narrow corridors and steep stairs and artificial strip lighting. But when Walther threw open a highly varnished wooden door to the master's cabin, she was suddenly surprised at the evidence of comfort. The room was large, the walls pine-panelled with a few well-framed prints of old merchantment. There were brightly coloured curtains that appeared to hide nothing, for the room was lit only by electricity. The chairs were deep and comfortable. There was one small desk, built out from the wall, holding a silver-framed photograph of a woman. Behind it was a stocky, square-faced man with short grey-bristled hair.

The Chief Officer said, 'Captain Zendermann.'

Karl shook hands, introduced Sandra, and this time she

felt the two men had not met before. They eyed each other as though each were coming to his own judgement. They spoke in German, and Sandra felt isolated. Neither man took the slightest notice of her, not even when she turned about and settled into one of the easy chairs. For the first time she noticed a humming sound, and she was aware of noises from outside. Some containers were still being loaded. The conversation of the two men became more intense. They were not arguing; it sounded more as though they were discussing details, and occasionally she heard the word 'Styx'. Ultimately, each seemed satisfied. She was surprised to see the captain extend his hand. Then they shook hands again, as though they were sealing a contract. The straight line of Zendermann's lips cracked into a smile. At last he turned towards Sandra.

'You must go about the ship,' he said, 'as you like. She is a nice ship, eh?' His eyes were unmoving, as he stared at her. 'Karl is a lucky man, eh?'

Sandra thanked him. She felt embarrassed. Perhaps she was imagining it, but she thought his stare was lecherous.

The Chief Officer took them to their quarters. It was on a different deck, reached by a steep companionway. She was only just beginning to realize that all the living quarters were in this white-painted superstructure, which was aft of midships, and that each level of it was described as a deck. She had always thought of decks as large open expanses of a ship.

Their own quarters were only a little less luxurious than the captain's. Again the living area was pine-panelled, and there were comfortable chairs and a divan. A room off also contained two divans—their sleeping quarters. There was another desk, looking more like a working desk. On a ledge alongside was a computer keyboard and a visual display. Walther saw her interest.

'It gives a reading of zer draught at zee bows and zee stern,' he said. 'So ve see—theese graph—that tell zer stress on zee ship.' He pressed a few keys, and what had been graphically displayed was printed out for him. He tore it off and handed it to Sandra. It meant nothing to her, and she smiled. 'But it tell me,' he said proudly.

Then he left them alone. Sandra put the print-out down, and looked up at Karl. Even in his casual slacks and slipover he looked well dressed, confident, strong. She was troubled, because she was no longer sure what she felt.

'What is going to happen?' she asked, subdued.

'I told you. We sail on the afternoon tide.'

'But what were you talking to the captain about?'

'The plan. Timing. Things that have to be done.'

'What has to be done, Karl?'

He thought he saw apprehension in her eyes. He smiled. 'Stop worrying. Everything's under control.'

'But you haven't told me what has to be done.'

'We were talking about the crew that know, and those that don't; when we shall move into the North Sea, what radio reports have to be made, when we shall be off Sizewell. That kind of thing.'

He was convincing. She shook her head gently.

'What is it?' he asked.

'When do we issue the threat?'

'When we're at sea.'

'But when?'

'About a day before we're on station.'

'How do I get—?' She realized she didn't know what deck she wanted. 'Up there,' she said, pointing.

'Just follow the companionways until you come out on the main deck—where the containers are. Why?'

'I'd just like to see them loading,' she said.

He shrugged, said he would unpack and let her go.

At one level, below the main deck, Sandra found that there was a narrow way that virtually led round the whole ship. After she had explored this and found her way back to the main block of living quarters and offices, she went up to the main deck. With the superstructure behind her, she leant over a rail and watched the loading of containers into the stern. The overhead crane positioned them exactly on to the cones at each corner of the previous container, and twist-locked them into position. And so they were stacked, one above the other—brown boxes, grey boxes, green, red and yellow. She was fascinated by the accuracy achieved by the crane driver, as his overhead cabin slid backwards and forwards.

But what was she doing here? The mere fact that the question had framed itself in her mind was disconcerting. She had never questioned the purpose or importance of what they were doing. She believed in it. Of course she believed in it, but her brother and Rackham had unsettled her. Now she was questioning her own judgement.

Karl found her staring abstractedly at the crane manoeuvring the containers each into their separate and numbered berth one upon the other.

'They've almost finished,' he said. 'Then we shall only be waiting for the tide.' He took her hand. 'Come, I'll show you something,' he said.

He led her along the outer edge of the main deck to midships. There, in the centre of a great circular plate, and standing free from all other containers, was one much larger box. He looked at her, and then looked at it, and smiled his satisfaction.

'It's much bigger than the others,' she said.

'It's twice the size. All container ships,' he said, 'are loaded with boxes known as T E Us—twenty-foot equivalent units. So they're either twenty feet long or forty feet long. This one's forty feet. Inside it,' he added with a distinct note of pride, 'is the missile—the S S-N-2C Styx. Only this one is rather special. It's capable of—'

'But why do we have to have it,' she interrupted, 'if we're only going to threaten?'

'You keep making the same point,' he said with a suggestion of irritation. 'I've told you—to be credible. Do you think, with satellites and patrolling aircraft, they're not going to know whether we've got a missile on board? They're going to see it. Then they'll believe us.'

'Yes,' she said. 'Yes, Karl, of course.'

Later in the afternoon, when they were at sea, he took her on the bridge to show her something else. Zendermann and Walther were both there.

She was surprised at the very small wheel, no bigger than that in a Mini, and nobody was steering the ship by it.

'How is the ship being steered?' she asked.

175

Zendermann looked at her just as he had done in his cabin. 'Auto-pilot,' he answered. 'Iron Mike, we call it.' He showed her the radar screens and radio direction finder. 'And over there—see,' he said proudly, 'is the satellite navigator. That gives our exact position in latitude and longitude at regular intervals as we pass from the surveillance of one satellite to another.'

The entire fore part of the bridge was made up of huge glass windows, each with enormous windscreen wipers. The glass panels continued round port and starboard sides of the wheelhouse. Towards the after part of the bridge was the chart table, where the second mate undertook the ship's navigation. Looking ahead, she had a clear view above all the containers to the bows of the ship. They seemed a very long way off. She could even see, isolated, the forty-foot container that held the Styx missile.

'There it is,' said Karl, excited. He pointed to a contraption not much bigger than a shoe box mounted on a tripod to the right of the ship's wheel. 'That's the laser target designation.'

'What does it do then?'

'It transmits an almost invisible laser beam. Now we know the exact position to minutes and seconds of one of the two reactors at Sizewell. This device is set precisely to those co-ordinates, and locks the laser beam on to the target. In the cone of the missile is a laser-seeking mechanism. That follows exactly the path of the beam transmitted from here.'

'What happens if the ship pitches or rolls?'

'Doesn't matter. Look, this is gyroscopically mounted. As long as the gyroscope's in position it's deadly accurate.'

'Can't anything interfere with the laser beam?'

'Yes, rain or fog. Operation Argus,' he smiled, 'is for a clear day.'

'Satellites or patrolling aircraft won't see this,' she said.

'So?'

'We don't need it, do we?'

He stared at her, said nothing, merely smiled.

Radio sound broke noisily into the humming quietness of the bridge. Zendermann picked up the microphone and gave his call sign. There followed a radio conversation in German. Sandra looked inquiringly at Karl.

'We're being shadowed,' he said, 'by an East German naval vessel.'

'Why?'

'It's carrying a helicopter. We've got to be lifted off at some time, haven't we?'

'Sorry,' she said, with a weak smile, 'I'd forgotten.'

'Its presence,' he added, 'will also stop anyone interfering.'

She was troubled. All this sounded too much like real action.

He sensed her anxiety. 'Even a threatening ultimatum,' he added, 'might make the British Government consider some kind of action.'

'I thought you said they wouldn't go for an East German ship in international waters.'

'No, I don't think they will, but the frigate makes it certain that they won't. You haven't got cold feet, have you? I thought you really wanted to do something practical to get rid of nuclear weapons? Well, this is it.'

'I know. I'm sorry.'

'And when you get back to your school no one will know it was you. After all, no one knows you're here.'

'No.' But she thought of her brother and David Rackham. They didn't know she was on the ship. But they knew she was with Karl. And if Rackham knew, the British Government could know. For the first time she wondered if she would ever go back to her school. She shivered involuntarily. Karl appeared not to notice.

Throughout the evening she was preoccupied. They had a meal with Zendermann and Walther and the second mate. Perhaps they didn't notice her silence, because they occasionally tended to forget her and break into German. There was an unreality about the conversation, starting, as it did, with something of Zendermann's career at sea, the countries he'd been to, the cargoes he'd carried, and then, and more tentatively, the current news. Sandra felt a falseness, and was even relieved when they continued the conversation in German.

In her little flat off the Bayswater Road and in Karl's suite at the Bromsgrove Hotel she had been sustained by her own enthusiasm. Everything had seemed possible. The rallies, the mass demonstrations and the peace camps had none of them—in spite of her commitment and the devotion of countless others like her—been able to achieve what was, thanks to Karl, now within her power. Yet on this ship, the distant hum and throb of the engines urging it steadily towards the North Sea, she had lost that sustaining enthusiasm. Only when they had gone to bed, and Karl was making love to her, did she feel secure again, and the nagging doubts cease altogether.

The next day was clear with a blue sky and a calm sea. She put on a bikini, spread a towel on the one large area of open space near the missile container, and sun-bathed. Once Zendermann came to have a chat with her. She felt his eyes moving over her like slugs on her skin. Then Karl came, and for a while he lay with her, and she could close her eyes and imagine that they were on a cruise ship in the Caribbean.

On the bridge in the afternoon Karl told Zendermann he would like a rehearsal of what he called 'the missile deployment'. The master jerked his square, short-cropped head in acknowledgement. He picked up the nearby microphone and barked an order in German. Sandra looked inquiringly at Karl.

'The crew have been told to stay clear of midships,' he said.

She looked ahead to where the huge container sat on its turntable. Karl had a brief exchange in German with Zendermann, and then he pressed buttons on a small control panel in front of him. First she saw all four sides of the forty-foot container collapse. She'd expected to see the missile itself. Instead all she saw was a long ribbed barrel facing towards the bows of the ship.

'That's the container-launcher,' Karl told her. Then he pressed another button, and the turntable slowly swung the missile and its launcher through ninety degrees until it pointed starboard. The touch of another button and the launcher elevated to about forty-five degrees.

Karl and Zendermann looked at each other with obvious

satisfaction. Then Karl turned to Sandra. 'It works,' he said. 'Wasn't that beautiful? That's the beast,' he added, 'that's going to call the tune.'

Sandra felt she should be happy and excited. She wasn't. That worried her. But she watched, fascinated, as Karl repeated the process in reverse, and the missile, ensconced in its launcher, was once more a forty-foot container isolated in the middle of the ship.

Sandra noticed that Karl spent what remained of the afternoon talking to Zendermann and Walther and going about the ship. Some members of the crew seemed to know him; others didn't. All the conversations he had were in German and, after a while, Sandra stopped following him, and stood alone on the deck, letting the lightest of breezes ruffle her hair. Everything should have been perfect. Perhaps she might just have persuaded herself that it was but for what happened that evening.

She had put on the radio in their cabin to listen to the BBC World Service news. After the first item Karl looked up and said, 'You don't really want that, do you?'

She nodded, but he ignored her, got up and switched it off.

'I wanted it,' she said. 'I want to know what's going on.'

'What's it matter? It's no concern of ours here, is it? We're free of it. We're going to make our own news, darling.'

She smiled faintly. 'I'd still like to hear it.'

'Oh, all right—if it's so important to you.'

For the first time, he sounded and looked irritable, as she turned the set on again. She muttered a soft, 'Thanks,' and they listened in silence.

After some minutes she looked at Karl, suddenly startled. The news reader was saying, 'According to the East German government, one of the GDR's merchant ships, the *Argus Viktor*, has been seized by what the statement calls "Western terrorists". The vessel is said to be in the North Sea *en route* for Angola with a mixed cargo. The statement says it is assumed the terrorists boarded the ship at Rostock, its last port of call, and have been in hiding until today. No details are given of how many terrorists are involved or what demands they are making. It does, however, say that the master of the ship is being held at gun point and that the vessel is under the complete control of the terrorist group. An East German naval vessel, complete with helicopter, is in the vicinity, and is shadowing the *Argus Viktor*. The statement says the German Democratic Republic will not tolerate this kind of piracy on the high seas. The nationality of the terrorists is not mentioned.'

This time it was Sandra who leant across and switched off the set. She stared at Karl, open-mouthed in utter disbelief.

'Rather good, wasn't it?' he said.

'Good? For heaven's sake, what was it about? Karl, what's happening? What's it mean?'

'It's part of the plan.'

She sighed, despairingly. 'I don't understand.'

'You don't think the East German Government could admit to attacking—to threatening to attack a British nuclear power station, do you? It's got to be done by terrorists, hasn't it? Then the GDR navy launches an attack with a helicopter, and captures the terrorists. That's you and me. No one knows it's us. Once we're back in East Germany we can return to Britain whenever we want to.'

She looked and felt bewildered. 'Was this your plan?'

'Yes.'

'Why didn't you tell me?'

He shrugged. 'I told you the important bit—that we'd be rescued.'

'I—I didn't know it would be like this.'

'Like what, for god's sake? Look, Sandra, it's been carefully planned. It's going to work. Don't be so bloody silly. Face the facts. We've got a job to do. You wanted to do it. Don't forget, you wanted to do it. Well, we're going to bloody do it. And it'll work. It'll work because I planned it. Now shut up!'

Sandra covered her face with her hands. She wasn't crying. She was trying to control herself and to think clearly. She had never seen him angry before.

He got up, stood opposite her. Her face was still covered. The stupid little bitch. What did she think this was—a sea cruise? He might have known she would be like this. Greenham Common was about all she was capable of—a useless, pathetic demonstration by a lot of other silly bitches. He shouldn't have brought her. But then why should he deprive himself? For a moment, he wanted to beat her, take her by force. He hoped Zendermann would appreciate her when he'd gone. After all, he'd done the groundwork.

It was the slight chuckle to himself that caused Sandra to withdraw her hands. She saw his expression—a mixture of anger and amusement. She didn't know what to think. He was right, of course. She had wanted to do this—passionately. Why was she questioning it now? Hammond and Rackham on the lawn, in the corner by the hedgerow, at the hotel. But they couldn't be right. She mustn't believe they were right.

Karl's manner changed. He laughed self-confidently.

'Well, what's it feel like, my love, to be a terrorist?'

He took her face in his hands, kissed her on the forehead. 'Don't look so serious, so worried. It's all right. After all, the British government would call us terrorists, if they knew, wouldn't they?'

She tried to smile. She'd had such unquestioning faith in him. Hadn't she still? Perhaps. She got up and hugged him. 'I'm sorry,' she said. Then drawing away, and looking at him, 'You were angry.'

'H'm. I'm sorry, too. I guess I didn't understand when you'd been so keen all along.'

'So when are the "terrorists" captured?' She tried to sound light-hearted.

'After however long it takes for the British Government to respond.'

'How will they respond?'

He shrugged.

'Suppose they don't agree to our terms? What are they going to be? We threaten a missile attack on Sizewell unless they agree to withdraw cruise weapons from British soil? Well, what if they don't agree?'

Again he shrugged. 'They will, eventually. They wouldn't dare risk it.'

'But if they don't?'

'We have to fire the missile.'

'People will be killed—by radiation. That's horrible.'

'Some will—yes. It's worth it—isn't it?—if you get rid of the weapons. They'd kill far more.'

Sandra tried to remain calm. She hadn't thought it through before. Why not? Because she'd been carried along by her own enthusiasm and by his self-confidence and his authority. And—and because she loved him. Well, this was the reality. People being killed. But if it was to mean the end of Britain's nuclear weapons—if? She was somewhere in the North Sea. She was committed now. There was no alternative.

'Shouldn't we be issuing the ultimatum? Have you got it ready?'

He looked at her. He didn't want a row now. It would spoil the night.

'Yes,' he said. 'We'd better tell the bastards, hadn't we? I'm going to the radio room.'

17

Sir Dick Randle (he didn't like Richard, and had even expunged it from *Who's Who*), the Director-General of the Secret Intelligence Service—M16—stood by the window of his office on the top floor of Century House, staring unseeing but thoughtfully towards Big Ben. He was a tall, thin man with a triangle of a face, so wide was the forehead. His hair receded from it thinly. This morning, by the window, he was stroking his aquiline nose with his forefinger. He invariably did when he was thinking. He wasn't a man who wasted time on anger; otherwise he would be angry now.

David Rackham was standing several feet behind him, his shoes cushioned by the thick pile of the carpet.

'The damned Special Branch would have to slip that report in to the Prime Minister,' Sir Dick muttered. 'We could have done without that, David. Whitaker, I suppose. It's his reputation as the terrorist expert. Not the first time the PM has put him in charge. So how much does the Old Man know?'

'Only what's in the report—the identity of Argus, such as it is, and the fact that he killed Martin Lange and von Erbacher, and has escaped to East Berlin.'

'Does he know about the girl?'

'Yes. There was no way we could keep that from him, with pictures coming on the data link from the patrolling Nimrod.'

'But the other matter?' Sir Dick asked with a thin smile.

'No, sir. And Whitaker knows about the girl, of course. But not the other.'

'Thank god the Old Man doesn't know. We can't have politicians interfering, David.' He paused, stroking his nose again. 'You're sure it's properly tied up?'

'There's no money if it isn't.'

'I suppose we can't do better than that. As long as the PM isn't—er, well, troubled.' He turned back to face Rackham. 'Anyway, you wanted to see me?'

'We've only had the one word SIZEWELL to go on and, as you know, the bomb squad turned up nothing. The place is as clean as a whistle. And we had no idea where Argus and the girl had gone. Until now.'

He withdrew three large photographs from the folder he was carrying. The first merely showed the *Argus Viktor* at sea. One of the others was of Sandra in a bikini with Heinze lying beside her. The third pictured the container-launcher of the Styx missile pointing starboard from the deck of the ship.

'It was those reports we had about the *Argus Viktor*. I didn't honestly see that they had any significance, except the word Argus seemed too much of a coincidence. A Nimrod has had the vessel under surveillance since it came out of the Kiel Canal.'

'So they're in the North Sea?'

'*En route* for Angola with a mixed cargo. But we know there's a consignment of arms.'

'And what's this thing?' Sir Dick pointed to the container-launcher.

'According to the experts it's the latest mark of the Soviet Styx missile. It's mounted on a special turntable that enables it to swing to starboard.'

'Which,' Sir Dick interrupted, 'is the side of the vessel that will be facing Sizewell, as it comes down the North Sea to the English Channel.'

Even in these circumstances Rackham couldn't restrain a grin as he murmured, 'Western terrorists. That's what the GDR calls them. World Service reported it last night—the vessel taken over by Western terrorists.'

'Yes, I've got a note of it.' The tone was short. 'Blast, the PM will have to be told this. It's a full emergency, David. They'll want to evacuate Sizewell. I mean, we can only assume that they're going to hit it with a bloody missile, can't we?'

'Looks like it, sir. I thought I'd ask Whitaker to pull in young Strang for questioning. He might know something.

He's close enough to the Russkies, and we've got that picture of him with Shokolov.'

'A KGB operation, using a GDR ship. And the bloody thing will be outside territorial waters, bound to be. At least those are problems for the politicos. You'd better get cracking, David.'

Superintendent Whitaker looked at the gangling figure in front of him with distaste. Philip Strang's finger tips were stained with nicotine, and did he have to leave that mop of fair hair unbrushed and uncombed? The superintendent had taken Sergeant Cawston's place, sitting opposite Strang at a small table in an interview room at New Scotland Yard.

'Ah, the brass! Do I have to go through it all again now?' Strang whined.

'I haven't noticed that you've gone through anything yet,' Whitaker replied curtly, and then deliberately sat in silence for a minute or so. Only when Strang fidgeted slightly did the superintendent slowly extract from his pocket the photograph of Strang and Shokolov taken in Queen Mary's rose garden in Regent's Park. 'What was that all about?' he asked.

Strang stared at the picture, surprised. 'Fucking Gestapo, aren't you? Bloody invasion of privacy, that's what it is.'

'The cultural attaché at the Soviet Embassy?'

'I'm interested in Russian art.'

'H'm, proper little socialist realist, aren't you?'

'Perhaps you'll tell me, Superintendent, what I'm doing here. What right have you to question me?'

'I'm holding you on suspicion of conspiracy.'

'Conspiracy of what?'

'I might even charge you under the Prevention of Terrorism Act.'

'Ha ha! There's no law against talking to a Russian diplomat.'

'But there is against conspiring with a Russian diplomat in an act of terrorism.'

Strang's eyes shifted nervously. 'Pigs,' he snapped. 'Bloody pigs, you are.'

'Perhaps we'd better take you to Sizewell, so you can watch the operation.'

185

This time Strang was unable to hide his startled expression. 'What do you mean?'

The superintendent turned to Cawston, who opened a folder and handed him a much larger photograph. Whitaker put it on the table between them, facing Strang. It was the one received from the Nimrod showing the container-launcher holding the Styx missile. 'Do you know what that is, Strang?' Whitaker had already noted the surprise in the man's eyes.

Strang shrugged.

'It's a Russian missile, known as Styx,' said the superintendent.

'So what? It's a Russian missile.'

'Which is going to be targeted on Sizewell. When, Strang —when?'

'Huh! You're talking balls.'

Whitaker drummed his fingers on the table. 'I asked you a question, Strang. When?'

'You must think I'm fucking stupid. You produce a bloody picture of a Russian missile—could have been taken anywhere—and you tell me it's going to be fired at Sizewell. You're round the effing twist, Superintendent.'

'Look, Strang, I don't like doing a deal with crap like you. But you might improve your chances a whisker. I'm not promising, but you might. When is it planned to launch the thing?'

Strang's narrow eyes darted glances between the photograph and the stern, ample figure of the police officer. He grinned. 'I don't get what the hell you're talking about. Just the picture of a Russian missile, and you tell me it's going to hit Sizewell. It doesn't make sense. Where is it? Where's it coming from? Who's firing it? It's a bloody fairy tale.'

'You can take it we know the answers to those questions, Strang. We also know,' he deliberately lied, 'that you're involved in the plan—'

'What, just because your bleedin' spies have got a snap of me talking to the Russian cultural attaché? Do me a favour!'

'I'm surprised you trust your Russian friends,' Whitaker remarked with apparent indifference.

Strang sat staring at the photograph, his lips clamped together.

The superintendent let the silence continue. Then he said quietly, 'Karl Heinze, code-named Argus. He's a friend of yours, too, isn't he?'

It was a long shot, but the superintendent noticed the brief nervous flicker in Strang's eyes.

'Never heard of him.'

Whitaker produced another photograph—Heinze and Sandra lying on the deck of the container ship. 'That's Argus,' he said. 'Not the one in the bikini.'

'Very droll, Superintendent. Looks as though he's having a good time, whoever he is. What am I—some bloody travel agent?'

Whitaker drummed his fingers, as his dislike increased for the tense, nervous creature facing him. 'It's better,' he said distastefully, 'if you co-operate. Are you going to tell me what the pair of you planned, or am I going to have to rely on the Russian and East German versions?'

'Your photographer had the day off, did he? Haven't you got one of me and this Argus chap setting land-mines round the perimeter of Sizewell? You're slipping, Superintendent.'

Whitaker felt like taking Strang by the throat and shaking him. Instead, he said, in as benevolent a tone as he could manage, 'I'm going to give you one more chance. That ship is the *Argus Viktor*. It is *en route* from Rostock to Angola. It's now in the North Sea. We've reason to believe it's going to launch a missile attack on Sizewell nuclear power station. I ask you again, Strang—when?'

'"We have reason to believe",' Strang mocked. 'Piss off, you sodding pig.'

'Nice types they breed for social security these days,' Whitaker muttered as he rose from the table and left the room.

Back in his office, he stretched in his chair, filled his pipe, and puffed little spurts of smoke thoughtfully into the air. He buzzed for Cawston.

'Nothing fresh?' he asked.

'No, sir.'

'Strang knows—I'm bloody sure he does. We can't make

the link though—can we? We haven't a damn thing to connect him with Heinze. Just a suspicious picture. He and Shokolov were probably talking about something altogether different. The bastard is close enough to them.'

The telephone interrupted them. Whitaker picked it up with one hand, and removed the pipe from his mouth with the other. He listened, said only, 'Yes, sir. Yes. I'll be there.'

He looked up at Cawston. 'I'm summoned to No. 10, Snap. Emergency meeting, in an hour's time.'

Britain and most of northern Europe were enjoying a spell of settled summer weather. The only clouds were like small white powder-puffs. The North Sea was merely crinkled.

About three miles above it, and flashing silver in the brilliant sunlight, the Nimrod of Coastal Command cruised in close circles above the *Argus Viktor*. Its cameras, even from that height capable of zooming in to show whether Sandra had used eyebrow pencil or not, were periodically transmitting pictures, via its base, back to London. Most of them were destined for 10 Downing Street.

The aircraft's radar showed, some three miles off, the shape of the GDR's naval vessel, and its cameras confirmed that it was one of the Soviet Union's 'Koni' class frigates —the *Leipzig*. Like its two predecessors, *Rostock* and *Berlin*, it had been built in Leningrad, had a full-load displacement of 2,000 tonnes, and was equipped with SAM SA-N-4 missiles and guns. It differed from its sister ships in having a helicopter pad at the stern.

From the Nimrod, data-link computers processed all the relevant information back to base. This, too, was transmitted to Downing Street. The aircraft had orders to stay with the *Argus Viktor*.

In 10 Downing Street itself, the Prime Minister, Mr Lionel Bryce, was gratified to see that the very last transmission from the Nimrod, only a few minutes old, showed the Styx missile safely crated in its container.

Lionel Bryce was an experienced, pragmatic politician who liked to feel he could be calm in a crisis. He was justified; he invariably was. Such calm went with his appearance. He was a tall man, distinguished by a mane of well-brushed grey hair, but that was not the feature by which he was most known. Thanks largely to the attentions of the cartoonists, it was his strong jutting chin which, in the public eye, was his trade-mark. His astuteness had given him a flair for good publicity, which endeared him to his party. He dressed elegantly and expensively.

He sat alone in the Cabinet Room beneath Van Loo's famous portrait of the first Prime Minister, Sir Robert Walpole. The Cabinet Secretary was by the white doors that led to the small ante-room which was connected to the front door of No. 10 by a long straight corridor. In the red folder in front of him the Prime Minister had reduced the papers to a minimum, but they did include reports from the Director-General of the Secret Intelligence Service and from Superintendent Whitaker of the Special Branch. Both men were coming to the meeting; not all Cabinet ministers would, but only those with a specific interest. The remainder would be informed later at a special meeting of the full Cabinet. Today, the Prime Minister wanted around him the ministers who would have responsibility for the action that had to be taken, and experts who could assess the dangers and were qualified to give the best advice. He could hear them arriving in the ante-room. Through the tall windows he could see the garden beyond. At this time of the morning the sun didn't get in there, but Lionel Bryce knew it was a bright, sunny day, and calm. And that worried him. They might not have much time.

He nodded to the Cabinet Secretary, who opened the doors. The Foreign Secretary, the Home Secretary and the Lord Chancellor came in together, with the Defence Secretary close behind them. Each took his usual place at the boat-shaped Cabinet table. The Chief of the Defence Staff and the three defence chiefs were there, as was the government's Chief Scientific Adviser, a specialist in radiation sickness, and nuclear experts from the Central Electricity Generating Board. Sir Dick Randle was there, and so were the Metropolitan Commissioner and Superintendent Whitaker.

The Prime Minister's jaw was set. He opened his folder, leant across the table. He thanked them all for coming at such short notice, told them that they were facing a grave emergency and that, like any Cabinet meeting, the proceedings were secret. Then, quite succinctly, he told them about the *Argus Viktor*, and what appeared to be a threat to Sizewell nuclear power station.

'You may want to ask how we know this,' he said gravely. 'That is something I can't tell you at the moment. I will be honest and admit that many might consider the evidence flimsy. But in what evidence we have there is one positive indication: it is that Sizewell is the target.

'The East German authorities,' he continued, 'are making quite a fuss, and saying that this ship has been seized by Western terrorists. They have even sent protests to the British and American governments. The terrorist on board is, in fact, German-born, although he has a British passport, doubtless among many others. He has the code name Argus. He killed the German minister, Martin Lange, in Bonn, and he also murdered Hans von Erbacher at Andover. None of that need concern us, but he appears to be in charge. The vessel is equipped with a Russian missile—the S S-N-2C Styx. It appears that the whole operation is being monitored by an East German naval frigate, the *Leipzig*, standing three miles off. It's equipped with a helicopter.'

The Prime Minister paused to stroke his chin. 'What we have to decide,' he continued, 'is the nature of the threat. By which I mean the damage this missile could cause, the potential danger to the public, the way the public would react and, finally, what action it is feasible for us to take to prevent the missile being launched.'

He elaborated briefly on these points, added that they would also have to decide what action could be taken to protect local people, and then called on the Chief of the Defence Staff.

General Sir Frank Kendall had seen service in many parts of the world, and more recently had been Commander in Chief of the United Kingdom Land Forces. He had a weather-beaten appearance with features as crisp as his manner. He began by asking about the protection given to the reactor core, and was told by a representative of the Central Electricity Generating Board that the pressure vessel containing the reactor was made of steel just over four inches thick, and this was protected by a shield of concrete twelve feet thick.

The General looked directly at the Prime Minister. 'The missile,' he said, 'is six and a quarter metres long with a diameter of seventy-five centimetres, and it weighs at least two thousand three hundred kilograms. The warhead has four hundred and fifty kilograms of high explosive. We have to assume that they have the right information to target the missile accurately. It would do a lot of damage, but I doubt if it would penetrate the reactor core.'

The Prime Minister's eyebrows lifted in surprise. 'Then—?' He shook his head, mystified. 'Then we have no need to worry?'

'Even if that were so, Prime Minister, you would presumably want to evacuate people in the immediate neighbourhood. Perhaps the aim is just to create panic.'

'H'm.' The Prime Minister considered. No one moved or spoke. He looked up. 'Is that your view?' he asked.

'It's a possibility, Prime Minister, but I find it difficult to believe that they would go to all this trouble just for that. They will want to demand something of the government. The panic, the public reaction, public pressure upon the government, would be so much greater if the attack caused a leak of radiation. I think we must still consider that to be their aim.'

'But you've said that this Styx missile is unlikely to be able to achieve it.'

'Yes—unless, Prime Minister, it were fitted with a shape charge, a hollow charge as it's often called. That wouldn't demand any major modification of the weapon. A hollow space is created in the cone. The diameter determines the depth of it. Anyway, the ultimate effect is to cause the explosive force of the weapon to explode inwards instead of outwards. We call it implosion. In this case it would implode with great jets of white-hot metal and gas, and there would be no problem in penetrating the core of the reactor.'

'And you reckon that's what they've done?'

'I don't think we can assume anything less, sir.'

The Prime Minister made a note, had a brief word with the

Cabinet Secretary, and then called upon a nuclear engineer from the Central Electricity Generating Board, and put to him the single question, 'What would happen?'

The engineer, who had a slight academic stoop, replied, 'The reactor core weighs two thousand tons. At the bottom the temperature is 220 degrees centigrade; at the top it's 360 degrees centigrade. If the containment is breached, the gas coolant escapes until it's down to the atmospheric pressure, but the actual heat output of the fuel itself would be comparatively low. There would be a fire. How serious depends upon the extent of the damage. If it was severe it could be a big fire. The escape of radioactive fission products could only arise from the fire itself. There would not however be sufficient energy to carry a plume high enough to disperse radioactivity over a wide area—'

'But there would be a hazard?' the Prime Minister interjected.

'Oh, yes. People in the immediate neighbourhood of the power station would be at risk. If there was a strong onshore breeze the radioactivity would be dispersed over a wider area.'

'How wide?'

'A few miles. It might reach Leiston, two and a half miles away. Population, 5,000.'

'Any further?'

'Possibly. But in my judgement very unlikely.'

The Prime Minister considered. 'Even a minimum hazard,' he said, 'could cause a lot of panic. People are afraid of radiation.'

'A north wind, of course,' the CEGB expert continued, 'could disperse radioactivity the same distance south to Thorpeness, a compact community increased by holiday-makers. Aldeburgh is a further two and a half miles away with a resident population of about 3,000, but again swollen by holiday-makers. A north-west wind, which is commoner, would have little effect. The risk then would be confined to the few houses at Sizewell Gap and the immediate neighbourhood of the power station. A north-east wind would threaten Aldringham, but little else. South-west, and it's blowing offshore.'

From the Chief of the Naval Staff the meeting learned that the missile could be launched at any time, but if the attack was to be made from the sea off Sizewell, then the *Argus Viktor* was no more than twenty-four hours away. At the moment, the wind, such as it was, was coming from the north-east, and to do the maximum possible damage, Argus would need an east wind. If he was going to wait for that it would give them all that much more time.

Lionel Bryce listened carefully as the experts discussed the problems that would face the emergency services if the missile was launched, but after twenty minutes he held up a hand to interrupt the discussion.

'Gentlemen,' he said, 'before we go any further, we must start at once organizing for a full-scale emergency at Sizewell. Everyone living in the immediate area of the power station must be evacuated within the next few hours to places at least ten miles away. We may have to evacuate Leiston as well, but not for the moment. I don't want to precipitate panic. The Chief Constable of Suffolk must be taken into our confidence, but that's all.' He paused, thought for a moment, as he rubbed his chin. 'The reason for the evacuation—and the press can be told this immediately it is under way—is that some very large high-explosive bombs and mines have been washed up on the foreshore. Overflying by light aircraft or helicopters, except those belonging to the Services or to the police, must be forbidden. So I am releasing Superintendent Whitaker at once to put these arrangements in hand. It will be for him and the Chief Constable to decide how the area should be policed, and where an operational headquarters should be established. I suppose we shall have to say that the explosives pose no danger to the power station. We'd better have some bomb disposal chaps in the neighbourhood—to add conviction. Questions, Superintendent?'

Whitaker shifted in his chair. 'No, sir.'

'Good luck, then.'

Superintendent Whitaker left, and Cabinet ministers, Service chiefs, experts and officials began to discuss the more difficult issue: could the attack be prevented? It was the Secretary of State for Defence who crystallized the problem.

'The *Argus Viktor* can be attacked by a naval frigate, a

193

boarding party could be launched. It could be attacked from the air by helicopters with suitable escort. But for what reason do we attack a container ship of the German Democratic Republic's merchant fleet which, to all intents and purposes, is going about its lawful business in international waters? All right, the vessel has, we are told, been taken over by terrorists. But the East Germans say they are Western terrorists, and that they are dealing with the situation. They have a ship with helicopter standing by.'

'What would be the reaction of the GDR government?' the Foreign Secretary asked. 'More important, how would the Soviet Union respond?'

At the far end of the table, his long legs twisted round each other beneath his chair, Sir Dick Randle, Director-General of MI6, was deciding for himself that, somehow or other, the *Argus Viktor* would have to be boarded. There were certain things the Prime Minister, ostensibly responsible for the Secret Intelligence Service, did not know. He would eventually have to know if the operation was going to succeed; if it was going to fail, it was probably better that he didn't know. A risk, Sir Dick knew, as his finger ran the length of his aquiline nose, but that was something he alone had to calculate. Of course, if young Rackham had ballsed it up, it would be his head on the block.

For some moments the Servicemen and the experts left the discussion to the politicians. They had to take the policy decision. After that the specialists would devise ways of carrying it out.

The Prime Minister let his colleagues explore the possible courses of action and the likely consequences, and all the time he was listening he was also assessing the problem himself. His reputation was for decisiveness. As the reporters said from time to time, he led with his chin—determined. This time, however, there was more at stake than favourable publicity—But suddenly he had decided.

'Gentlemen,' he said, 'how we do it, I don't know. But I am certain that it is our responsibility to ensure that that missile is not launched.'

There was an immediate silence. All eyes were directed at the Prime Minister. At length he said, as though thinking aloud, 'Can we do it surreptitiously? Is there any way, for example, that we could sabotage it?'

Again there was a thoughtful silence, this time interrupted by the Chief of the Defence Staff. 'Lieutenant-Colonel Alex Graham,' he said.

The Prime Minister looked up inquiringly.

General Sir Frank Kendall added, 'He commands Comacchio Group of the Special Boat Squadron at Arbroath, Prime Minister. They're responsible for oil rigs and nuclear power stations. He's your man.'

'Let's get him here fast. Meanwhile, the meeting is adjourned until he arrives. I would like all of you to stand by—close at hand—so that you can be summoned back here within, say, half an hour.'

Sir Dick Randle waited until they had all left. Then he joined the Prime Minister, leaning against the marble mantelpiece. In the centre, beneath the portrait, a small clock ticked quietly.

'I suppose,' said Sir Dick, almost lethargically, 'if we use the SBS, they'll want to capture Argus.'

'Of course.'

'H'm. Thought so. He's on an East German vessel, you know. Prime Minister, I would want one of our chaps to go in with the SBS.'

The Prime Minister stared back suspiciously at the wide forehead and wary eyes of his intelligence chief. 'The marines won't like that,' he said.

Sir Dick shrugged. 'I don't want Argus killed,' he said.

'It mustn't impair the operation.'

'It would be an experienced man—one with equivalent training.'

'If it's necessary,' the Prime Minister conceded.

With his lanky figure poised against the edge of the mantelpiece, Sir Dick looked a bit like a heron about to strike. And strike he did.

'Prime Minister,' he said, 'I want my man to be in charge. Oh, no, the SBS commander will, of course, be responsible for the military operation. But my man must be in overall charge. He must be responsible for on-the-spot policy decisions. It is not just a military operation, Prime Minister.'

Lionel Bryce stroked his jaw thoughtfully. Argus was wanted by the West Germans. He had killed one of their ministers. The Prime Minister was a little surprised they had not made more fuss about the murder of von Erbacher. And Argus was wanted by the British police as well. Presumably Sir Dick thought he might be useful in uncovering foreign agents.

The MI6 chief interrupted the Prime Ministerial thoughts. 'It would be as well to make it clear from the beginning.'

'Very well. If we decide to send the SBS in, your man goes in with them. And he is in overall charge, and held personally responsible.'

Sir Dick smiled faintly. Poor Rackham—held personally responsible. Maybe. But he—Sir Dick Randle—would be the one who, perhaps in only a few days' time, would have to face the Prime Minister again. There was bound to be a bloody great row.

18

The *Standard* in London, and most provincial evening newspapers, ran down-page or inside-page mystery stories about the East German container ship 'seized by Western terrorists'. Early evening television bulletins also had the story well down the running order, especially as no one had been able to find library stills of a ship called *Argus Viktor*. But all the stories commented on the apparent inactivity of the GDR frigate, *Leipzig*, complete with helicopter, and noted that, apart from a formal protest to the British government, there had been no request for British assistance to deal with the terrorists. On the contrary, the government of the GDR had said emphatically that the East German navy was fully in control. The terrorists would be captured and dealt with. There had been no statement or comment from No. 10 but in the circumstances the media hardly expected it. Their mood was scepticism.

Meanwhile, a Royal Navy frigate had since appeared in the North Sea within a mile or so of both GDR ships. The weather was still clear, and nearly three miles above them all was the silver shape of the Nimrod, cameras locked on to both German ships, transmitting pictures to London and thence to 10 Downing Street.

The Nimrod had also reported that since leaving the Kiel Canal the *Argus Viktor* had maintained radio silence. In itself, however, that was not unusual. There was no reason for her to report until in the Channel approaches.

Superintendent Whitaker—Snap Cawston for once being left behind—was flown by helicopter to the headquarters of the Suffolk County Constabulary at Martlesham Heath. The aircraft dipped low over woodlands and, in a vast green clearing dotted with groups of silver birches, Whitaker saw a modern cube of dark red brick and glass. It was flanked by other low buildings and a large area of car-parking space. The helicopter settled on the expanse of green lawn in front of the building.

Whitaker walked briskly beneath the flailing rotors, but not so briskly that he didn't have time enviously to compare this sylvan setting for Suffolk's police headquarters with the tower block of New Scotland Yard. On each side of the front entrance was a moat with spattering fountains, all surrounded by small conifers and ground cover. In the spacious glass entrance hall, with its inevitable display cabinet of silver trophies, a police officer guided him to the lift and up to the third floor. The Chief Constable, Paul Grantham, had been warned of Whitaker's visit, and came forward from behind a modern curved teak desk to welcome him.

Grantham wore a grey lounge suit, was younger and slimmer, and looked as though he probably kept up the exercises which Whitaker had long since abandoned. He looked alert and had an amused expression creasing the corners of his eyes. Whitaker immediately thought he would like the man. He was confirmed in his view when he told the Suffolk chief all he knew of the impending operation.

After a ten-minute no-nonsense conversation about emergency procedures, the Chief Constable led Whitaker back to the ground floor, along a corridor and through a door on the right to the Force operations room. For security reasons this was right in the middle of the building, with no outside walls. Whitaker knew that Suffolk had been used as a guinea-pig before the nationwide introduction of computers in police forces, with the result that the county now had an advanced and efficient communications system. There were six consoles, each with its computer keyboard and visual display unit, with panels of buttons alongside for radio communication. By one wall was a large magnetic map of the county, and there were even instruments displaying wind speed and direction.

The superintendent in charge of communications was waiting for them at the inspector's console. The Chief Constable issued orders for channel two to be cleared and reserved for Operation Argus. He gave an amused twitch of his lips as he uttered the phrase. It clearly appealed to him that they were using the same code phrase as Argus himself.

Crisply the Chief gave instructions to the inspector and within seconds all available police cars were directed to Sizewell Gap to warn local inhabitants that, as soon as suitable accommodation was found, they were going to be asked temporarily to leave their homes. All other emergency services were also informed. Within half an hour a well-rehearsed plan for such a contingency was in full operation. Local authority services were called in, and the Women's Royal Voluntary Service was standing by to make any feeding arrangements that might be necessary.

The Chief Constable and Whitaker followed the Downing Street instructions that the public, and even the policemen engaged in the operation, should be told that high-explosive bombs had been washed up on to the shingle on the beach at Sizewell Gap, although Grantham pointed out that it was highly unlikely with such a calm sea. Nevertheless, policemen, soldiers and members of the bomb disposal squad fenced off an area of beach two and a half miles north and south of Sizewell power station, and all access was prohibited.

At Sizewell only the station manager and his deputy were informed of the real nature of Operation Argus, and they immediately activated their own communications unit which was permanently available in a training wing of the police headquarters, although Whitaker made it clear that the Chief Constable must remain in overall charge of the civil operation.

Grantham himself prepared a brief press release about the unexploded bombs. He added that no photographs would be allowed because the explosives were suspected of being too unstable, and he was not prepared to put photographers' lives at risk. Because of the construction of the building there was, however, not the slightest danger to the power station.

He looked up with a grin at Whitaker. 'I hope that sounds convincing. I must say I wouldn't believe it.'

The superintendent's first inclination had been to set up a mobile operations HQ as near to the site as possible, but since Martlesham itself was no more than about sixteen miles by road from Sizewell, both he and the Chief Constable decided that it would be more efficient to use their own headquarters with all its resources readily available, especially as the helicopter that had brought Whitaker was being retained for any necessary surveillance.

After a couple of hours the two men were able to pause. Whitaker had been enjoying their brisk co-operation. He had that satisfying feeling of having accomplished something, and he felt very much at home with his Suffolk superior.

'So what,' said Grantham, 'are they going to do?'

Whitaker fumbled in his pocket for his tobacco pouch and pipe. 'D'you mind?' he asked.

'I don't myself, but carry on by all means.'

Whitaker nodded his gratitude, filled the pipe, and held the match poised above the bowl. He felt he deserved this unhealthy luxury.

'I don't know what they're going to do,' he said. 'They hadn't decided when I left No. 10.'

'Are they sure about the missile?'

'I don't know that either. The Friends tell me they are. And if Argus is waiting for the most favourable launch time, we've got perhaps twenty-four hours.'

'Foreign ship. International waters. Not much justification for intervening, is there? They need pretty strong proof that the missile is going to be used.'

'Spoken like a policeman,' muttered Whitaker, as he lifted his head and sent a puff of smoke towards the ceiling. 'I think they're going to manage without proof. Circumstantial evidence.'

The Chief Constable's telephone buzzed. He picked it up, listened, and replied, 'We're coming now.'

As he led Superintendent Whitaker back to the operations room, he said over his shoulder, 'Some fool's aloft in a helicopter over the beach.'

The Special Boat Squadron had its beginnings in the Second World War. Volunteers from the 6th Commando quickly developed highly specialized and daring skills to carry out some of the most dangerous but secret operations of the war.

Since then, as part of the Royal Marines, the SBS has refined its skills and expertise to make it, with the SAS, one of the world's most efficient and formidable fighting units, capable of undertaking anything from sabotage, infiltration and kidnapping to sophisticated reconnaissance and intelligence gathering. Each member is a highly qualified swimmer-canoeist and parachutist, whose gruelling training keeps him at the peak of physical and mental fitness. They are equipped with some of the most advanced weapons, aids and communications systems, and no assignment is too difficult for their expertise.

All this the Prime Minister knew as he waited for yet another and much smaller meeting to assemble. In the interim there had been an emergency meeting of the full Cabinet, and this had confirmed the Prime Minister's decision that the government had a responsibility to ensure that the missile was not launched. That must be the primary aim of any operation. So this time Lionel Bryce had with him only those ministerial colleagues most closely involved and the necessary experts.

Principal among these was Lieutenant-Colonel Alex Graham. He was well built, muscular without an ounce of spare flesh, and with rugged features and clear blue eyes. His voice had the merest suggestion of his Scottish origins.

After he had explained the situation to the colonel, the Prime Minister said, 'The policy decision has been taken. So how do we stop the missile being fired? We have ruled out aerial attack, or torpedoing the ship; the likely international repercussions are unacceptable. So your task, Colonel, is to immobilize the weapon or prevent those responsible from launching it.'

'How many terrorists are there on board?' the colonel asked.

'There is Heinze, code-named Argus, who I am told is the most professional operator in Europe. But our aerial surveillance shows that neither the captain, nor anyone else, is being held under duress. There is no sign of terrorist activity on board. So the conclusion is that Argus is in charge of an operation that has had the full co-operation and support of the East German government and, therefore, undoubtedly of the KGB.'

The colonel's gaze was fixed on the Prime Minister. 'I suppose,' he said, 'there is no plan of the ship?'

'No. But we have as many photographs as you want, showing every detail of the main deck from bow to stern.'

'Splendid, Prime Minister. That will be sufficient.'

'You mean you can do it?'

'Yes. We shall use ten men. They will be under the command of Lieutenant Gerry West.'

For the first time the Prime Minister turned his attention to the junior officer sitting alongside the colonel. He was not as tall, but his stocky frame suggested enormous strength and toughness. He looked to be in his late twenties, and had that confident, self-assured look that can only come from experience.

The lieutenant said, 'The operation will be at night, Prime Minister. So, at the soonest, that means tomorrow night. Unfortunately there is still a bit of waning moon. Are there any British naval vessels in the area that could shelter us should we need it?'

'Yes, there's a frigate, appropriately called *Southwold*.'

'You want Argus captured?'

The Prime Minister nodded, and then half turning towards Colonel Graham, said, 'I'm sure, Colonel, you will appreciate that there is another dimension to this thing. Espionage. A man like Argus could yield valuable information. The West Germans, of course, want him, and I shall keep the West German Chancellor informed of our action. But for this reason, Colonel, it is necessary for a senior member of the Secret Intelligence Service to accompany your men on the operation.' The conscious effort of the colonel to hide his displeasure did not escape the Prime Minister. 'I'm sorry, Colonel, it is necessary, I assure you. Of course, Lieutenant West is in charge of the operation, and so far as the military action is concerned he must be totally obeyed. The MI6 man, I can tell you, while not having had quite your rigorous training, is highly trained in the way that you would understand. You won't find him an embarrassment. On any issue of policy, gentlemen, as distinct from your tactics and military action, his decision must override yours.'

Colonel Alex Graham and his tough young lieutenant exchanged glances. The Prime Minister looked directly at them, and said, 'Those are my orders, and I accept responsibility for them.'

At the far end of the table Sir Dick Randle stroked his aquiline nose with satisfaction.

'I presume,' said the colonel, 'that the firing mechanism for the missile will be on the bridge?'

'We believe so,' said the Prime Minister. 'The weapon itself is amidships, but we have a couple of quite remarkable photographs from the Nimrod that look straight through the bridge windscreen. We've got blow-ups for you. They show you the captain and Argus, but more important they show a device mounted on a tripod, which I'm advised is a gyroscopically controlled laser target-designation.'

Colonel Graham nodded, and turned to Lieutenant West.

The lieutenant considered a moment, and then addressed the Prime Minister. 'As it's the centre of the roped-off area and, by then, likely to be the nearest point to *Argus Viktor*, we shall leave from Sizewell Gap, with *Southwold* between us and the East German ship, but for the last mile probably we shall be in open water—'

With a slight cough, the Prime Minister interrupted. 'Won't you be spotted by *Argus Viktor*'s radar, or at least by the radar of the GDR naval ship?'

'Most unlikely, Prime Minister. We shall be too low in the water, and what metal we have with us will be stowed at the lowest level. It is my plan,' he said confidently, 'to get to the stern of the ship unobserved. Then it should be a matter of seconds, sir.'

'An operational control,' said the Prime Minister, 'has been set up at the Suffolk Police headquarters at Martlesham Heath, with the Chief Constable and Superintendent Whitaker, the Special Branch's terrorist expert, in charge.'

'Normally,' said Colonel Graham, without explaining what he meant by the word, 'I would want an assault force of about seventy men ashore, so that they could follow up and seize the ship, capture the crew and bring them to port. I don't think that would be appropriate in this case. It must be a quick in-and-out operation.'

The Prime Minister agreed. 'Any further questions?' he asked.

For the next fifteen minutes the meeting discussed a variety of details, and then the Prime Minister brought it to an end by wishing the operation luck.

Within half an hour of the end of the Downing Street meeting, David Rackham had a call into Andover.

'Hammond? May have a spot of good news. I've got a photograph of that sister of yours stretched out in a bikini on the deck of an East German ship called *Argus Viktor*. Guess what? It sailed from Rostock. Heinze is with her.'

There was a groan at the other end. 'Where are they?'

'In the North Sea.'

'So what's good about it?'

'Well, we know where they are.'

'That's a hell of a lot of good. What are we going to do? Call in for tea, and bring her home?'

Rackham understood the exasperation but there was nothing he could do about it at the moment.

Before he had time to reply Hammond added, 'How'd you get the photograph anyway?'

'Ah, that's a secret. But, in your trade, you might be able to guess.'

'The parents are worried stiff—or at least Mother is,' Hammond added. 'I don't know that this is going to help very much.'

'Oh, I wouldn't tell them anyway—not yet.'

Hammond sighed. 'I suppose there's nothing we can do? Do you know where they are going?'

'The ship's going to Angola—'

'Oh, my god.'

'Just the ship, Hammond.'

Hammond gasped, not sure that he understood, and before he could question his friend, Rackham continued, 'Oh, there I go again—far too indiscreet for my service, you know. Look, can't tell you more now. But get over to Suffolk tomorrow morning—County Police headquarters at Martlesham Heath. I'll make sure they're expecting you.'

'Yes, but can't you—? Martlesham Heath?'

'Yes, see you there.'

19

The engine room of the *Argus Viktor* looked as aseptic as a hospital ward. A single engineer, his ears protected by muffs from the throbbing roar of the nine huge cylinders below him producing nearly 30,000 horse power, faced a panel of dials and switches and video displays which, between them, contained about 150 separate alarms. Every aspect of the ship's progress and the minutest behaviour of those powerful engines was being monitored. Either he was in control on directions from the bridge, or the captain could control the engine room from the bridge automatically. Behind the engineer was a grey wall of cabinets. They were the generators that provided power to the whole ship. Patiently he shouted explanations in very broken English of what was happening and why to the young woman beside him.

Sandra had come down there merely for something to do. She was unsettled more than bored, and needed something to occupy her. She thought sadly how excited the eight-year-olds in her school would be if they were with her now.

The note of the engines changed. Slowly the ship's speed was cut until it sounded as though they were only idling. The engineer responded to a series of bells as he shouted something incomprehensible to her. Had she been able to translate, it would have been something like, 'What the hell does the old man want to stop here for?'

That morning in their cabin she had listened both to the BBC's World Service news, and also to the Home Service's Radio 4 news. There had been nothing about an ultimatum being issued to the British Government. She had expected it to be the main story. The British Government had been told that unless it undertook to remove cruise missiles from its soil, Sizewell nuclear power station would be the target for a missile attack that would scatter radioactive material over a wide area. Emergency plans were being made to evacuate all towns and villages in the immediate vicinity. It was a hell of a story—but not a word.

She had looked up at Karl, perplexed. 'They haven't mentioned it—the ultimatum,' she said.

He stretched, pondered, wondered if last night had been the last time; whether he ought to take her again now, before he left her to Zendermann. 'What?' he said, distracted.

'The threat—not a word.'

'They're keeping it from the people,' he said, with authority. 'Afraid of panic.'

'Do you think that's what it is?'

'What else? They must be out of their tiny minds wondering what to do.'

She was silent, puzzled. She supposed so. That could be their first reaction. Too dangerous to tell the public. Hoping they could deal with it. So?

'Then what's going to happen?'

Heinze shrugged. 'They'll try to communicate—secretly, by radio. Try to bargain.'

'When?'

'Almost any time.' His tone was confident and casual. 'Yes, the radio operator knows,' he added.

'What do we tell them? Do you speak to them?'

He nodded. 'There's no bargain. They agree, or we fire the missile.'

'H'm,' she sighed, full of misgiving, but no longer knowing what to say. Nothing was what she had expected. In her flat, in Karl's rooms, the whole project had excited her —idealism being given a practical push. Anything had seemed possible. Now she realized it had seemed exciting and possible just because at the back of her mind must have been the conviction that it was never likely to happen. But he had made it happen.

With sudden alarm, she said, 'They will agree, won't they?'

'Of course. There's no alternative. I've told you before.' There was a hint of impatience.

Her anxiety was plain to him. There was something appealing about it. A little frightened, she looked even more

207

desirable. But hell, why should he bother? There were probably only hours left. He must go up to the bridge and find out the wind direction.

So they'd had breakfast, and she'd wandered about the ship, and had ended up in the engine room. Then when the vessel had idled to a standstill, and the engineer had thrown up his hands inexplicably, she went back to the main deck. It was sunny and warm, but a slightly fresh breeze pressed her blouse against her body and ruffled through her hair. As she stood on the starboard side, she could see distantly the coast of Britain. She looked down at the water; it was still, barely crinkled by the breeze. For some time she just stood there, breathing the salty air, and wondering when they would hear news of the government's response.

She supposed that was the Suffolk coastline. Sizewell would be there somewhere. She wondered if they had been observed, and if the British knew exactly where they were. Karl had said he was sure they would know. The ship would almost certainly have been under constant surveillance. Indeed, there was another ship—it looked like a naval vessel of some kind—between her and the shore. Then, suddenly looking up, she saw the slow silent shape, the diminutive silver bird of the Nimrod. Oh, surely not that? Much too far away. Yet it stayed with them, almost floating, it seemed, in wide circles. She took several deep breaths until she felt faintly light-headed. When would she be back at school? When would she see Hammond again? She turned away and made towards the bridge.

There were Zendermann and Walther, and the second mate by the chart table. And there was Karl, standing alongside Zendermann. As she arrived the captain was giving orders to drop anchor.

He turned his square head of bristling grey hair towards her with a grin of satisfaction. She had felt uneasy with him when they first met; she felt more so now.

'The wind. It is still north-east,' he said. 'But it comes more round to east. Good, eh?'

'Yes,' she said, not knowing why she had replied, but anxious not to offend him. She looked appealingly at Heinze.

He smiled, his dark eyes glowing reassuringly. 'Well, we want the wind in the east, don't we?' he said. 'Should make them think a bit more quickly.' He beckoned her. She went and held his hand, looking forward through the screen at the containers that stretched towards the bow. Inevitably, her gaze lingered on the single forty-foot container that stood by itself. But Karl was saying something.

'Look,' he said, pointing to the tripod with its gyroscopic control. 'See over there—you can almost see it with the naked eye.' He handed her a pair of binoculars, however, and she peered in the direction he indicated. 'That's Sizewell,' she heard him saying. 'Remember, we have the exact position, in minutes and seconds, of one of the reactors in that building. This thing here is now sighted precisely on those co-ordinates. The gyroscope ensures that the movement of the ship makes no difference. It is locked on, and is transmitting a laser beam which will guide the missile accurately to the target. It's foolproof, unless Captain Zendermann goes and falls on it.'

The German gave another grin and a little chuckle. 'Clever, eh?'

She didn't know what to say. She looked at Karl. He was smiling reassuringly again.

He said with earnest enthusiasm, 'It's what you wanted, darling. What we planned. You never thought it was possible, did you? I told you it was; I told you it could be done. Well, here we are. In one stroke, we achieve what all your peace camps have failed to achieve. Even the wind is going to help us.'

Heinze wondered if she believed it. Certainly Strang had, and the KGB had considered the possibilities sufficiently attractive. He presumed it depended either on how many were likely to be killed, or the effectiveness of panic. As far as he was concerned, it didn't matter. He already had £125,000 in cash, and even if the bastards defaulted on the rest, he still had a very large sum coming from another quite trustworthy source. Pity, really, to leave her to Zendermann, but then did he really want to be bothered with her in East Berlin?

Sandra said nothing until they were later alone together in

their cabin. Only then did she say, 'What has the wind got to do with it? We're not firing the missile.'

Heinze was standing by the pine desk, and she was on the other side of it. He looked straight into her eyes, and for the first time she saw a hardness in his gaze. Determination she had seen before, but this was quite different.

He said coldly, 'Of course we're firing the missile. There was no ultimatum. There was never going to be any ultimatum. Do you think the people who're behind this bandy words?'

She shifted her eyes nervously, glanced down at the pale polished top of the desk. It divided him from her, seemed to symbolize a sudden, even frightening barrier between them. Perhaps she was imagining it, but as she met his eyes again, she knew it was real. She bit her lip to stop it quivering. She must control herself.

'You lied to me, Karl. I trusted you.'

He smiled. 'I didn't want to worry you.'

'People will get killed. Radiation. It's horrible. We can't do it—we can't.'

She rushed round the desk. She must break down whatever it was between them. She clung to him, pressed herself against him, stroked his face, but all she muttered was, 'Karl—Karl, please. Please, Karl.'

He sighed, gently pushed her away from him, and looked into her tear-filled eyes. 'It's worth it,' he said.

'To kill people? No, not to kill, Karl.'

'Look—you want Britain to get rid of cruise, don't you? Well, I don't guarantee they will. But think of the impetus this will give to the peace movement. Nuclear power killing people. It might not be many, but people will get killed. The outrage will be enormous. In the end, the demand from the people will be irresistible. At least that's what the Russians think, otherwise they wouldn't have been prepared to go ahead.'

'All the time,' she muttered desperately, 'you said we were only going to threaten—'

'You didn't seriously think—?'

'I believed you. I love you, Karl.' She held back the tears. 'What else were you lying about—what else?'

He was about to stroke her hair, try to soothe her, but he held back, his hand in mid-air. There was no need to bother; it would all be over in a few hours.

'Well,' he said, 'there's nothing we can do about it. The missile is being launched, and that's that. Stop sniffling. It's what you wanted—it's no good pretending.'

'I never wanted it—not that. You knew. You said it wouldn't be necessary. You lied, Karl. You lied.'

'Oh, for god's sake, what's it matter? It's going to work.'

She could feel herself trembling. She tensed her jaws, trying to hold back the emotions that threatened her. The German minister killed in his flat in Bonn. Hammond looking worried, deadly serious and saying, 'He killed von Erbacher.' Her anger, her confusion, her refusal to believe because, as she had said, 'You don't know Karl. I do. I really do.' And the freckled face of Rackham looking at her earnestly as he had said, 'Heinze is the most professional terrorist operating in Europe. Code name, Argus.' The words hammered into her brain. She stared at Heinze, unbelieving, and yet knowing. 'Heinze is a ruthless killer,' Rackham had said. 'It's better that you leave him while you can.' And she had refused, furiously. In her anger she had refused to believe anything. Even Hammond had said that he believed she was in danger. Why hadn't she believed her brother? They had always had such a close understanding. She looked up at Heinze. He was smiling. Suddenly she was frightened.

Perhaps he saw her fear because he said, 'There is nothing for you to worry about.'

She tried to answer but couldn't. She wanted to accuse him, to blaze at him angrily, 'You killed von Erbacher —didn't you? You killed him.' But the words wouldn't come. All the time he stood there, immaculate in perfectly creased slacks, open shirt and meticulously tied and fluffed cravat, looking calm and confident.

'According to the weather forecast,' he said, 'the wind —such as it is—is veering a little more to the east. It should be round as far as it will go by tonight. We'll launch the Styx then. It will be more effective in the dark, won't it?'

She still couldn't find words. She stared at him in horror.

At last she half screamed, half shouted, 'No! No! Oh god, no!' Then she sank to the floor and burst into tears.

Through the haze she saw him move, heard the door slam behind him. Slowly she got up from the floor, went into the bedroom and washed her face. She must control herself. Tears wouldn't help, but—it was the sudden loss of something, someone she had believed in. That was what was unbearable—the sudden destruction of faith. She looked at herself in the mirror, and slowly tried to repair the damage.

Then she lay on the bed and tried to think. What was to happen to her? Karl had said that they were going to be 'rescued' by an East German helicopter. Now she had no idea whether that was true or not. And if they were lifted off—did she go with him, or would that put her in greater danger? In East Berlin with Karl. Or supposing there was no helicopter, and they both stayed on the ship all the way to Angola? And back? But he had never been cruel to her. She tried to console herself. Perhaps she was different for him—just as long as she was aware of the danger. But the more she thought about the situation, the more frightened she became. At present there was nothing she could do. For one frantic moment she even considered diving off the side of the ship. The sea was calm, couldn't be better for swimming. But four miles? She could manage a mile, perhaps a mile and a half, but four? If he wanted to kill her, she would be a sitting target in the water. Suppose she tried to behave normally? Could she? After all, he had no idea what she knew about him. But was that only giving herself a false sense of security? Presumably he would get rid of her whenever he wanted to. She shuddered at the thought.

She got up, inspected herself again in the mirror. Just presentable, she decided. So she went out, down the companionway to the main deck. The blue sky had only a few skeins of cirrus cloud. She looked up. There was still a toy silver aircraft suspended high above them. And now, steaming between them and the coast was the grey line of a Royal Navy frigate. She was sure—although it was really too far away to be certain—that it was a British vessel. But then it was bound to be, wasn't it, so close to the coast? For a moment she even wondered again if swimming was so mad after all. Then she thought of Karl, leaning on the rail, rifle at his shoulder. The air was warm, but the breeze that brushed her cheeks did seem to have the merest edge to it. It was coming more from the east.

She walked beyond the last batch of containers, locked into their individual places, to the stern. There was the space, the pad where the helicopter could land. She was leaning against the rail, still staring at it when she was aware of someone beside her. She turned. It was Karl. She tried to smile, and felt how unconvincing it must have looked.

He put an arm round her shoulders. He said casually, 'Feeling better now?'

20

The morning after his visit to No. 10 Downing Street Lieutenant Gerry West was joined at Martlesham Heath by nine other men from his unit, flown from Arbroath by Sea King helicopter. The weather was still fine, and there was only the thinnest gauze of cloud in the blue sky. The wind was veering a little more to the east, and the forecast was set fair for at least another twenty-four hours. The sea was reported calm.

The Sea King was parked alongside the police Bell helicopter on the lawn in front of the headquarters, and West led his men into a briefing room specially set aside by the Chief Constable. He briskly outlined the task they had been assigned. Then he spread a full set of detailed photographs on the table. Some of them were enlargements of comparatively small areas of the *Argus Viktor*. They included the shot through the windows of the bridge, showing a close-up of the gyroscopically controlled laser target-designation. There were also pictures of the Styx missile housed in its forty-foot container, and with the container sides down, and the missile swung to starboard in its launcher.

'That's our target,' said West. 'We have to stop it being launched, and disable it. We also have to capture Karl Heinze, code name Argus.'

The group gave especial attention to the series of photographs that showed the area from the stern of the ship to the entrance to the superstructure. From another set, it was obvious where the companionways led upwards to the bridge.

'There is no reason,' said West, 'why any of the doors should be locked. In normal operation they will be undone, and there is no sign that the ship is not operating normally. The terrorist story is an obvious blind. Look at them.' He pointed to the picture of Heinze and Sandra sunbathing on the deck. 'There is no indication that the master is acting under duress.'

There was only one area that lacked cover, and that was the helicopter pad in the stern. That had to be crossed before reaching the protection of the containers on either the port or starboard side. If the weather remained clear, there would be some light from the waning moon and stars. But such a small area to negotiate would give them little difficulty.

They went on to work out the detail of the operation, from the moment when they left the escort shelter of *Southwold* to the moment that the bridge was taken. West and three other men would enter the bridge, two men would stay on the main deck. Three others would hold the main companionway leading from the bridge down to the officers' and crew's quarters. That left the coxswain, who would take the Gemini back to shore.

The object was to reach the bridge unobserved. If this was not possible because of encountering an officer or crew member in one of the companionways, then the person concerned must be dealt with noiselessly. Once the bridge had been secured, the three men holding the companionway would go down through the quarters until they found Heinze. No killing. Remember, they were on a foreign ship in international waters. Their only concern had to be the protection of British lives by preventing the launching of the missile. Once Heinze had been taken, three members of the force were assigned to disable the targeting of the missile.

'What about the girl, sir?' asked the sergeant.

'Ah. She's British. She is being held under duress. I presume we have orders to rescue her. That will be confirmed shortly. Which brings me,' he added sourly, 'to a slightly unfortunate matter. We shall have a passenger—fellow from the S I S. While I'm in charge of the operation, he has overall authority. He will be here this morning.'

Someone groaned, and West acknowledged it with an understanding if grim smile.

'Is Heinze a British subject, sir?'

'He has a British passport—among others. I'm told he's

German. He's a professional killer. Make sure you can recognize him.'

They discussed and decided on the equipment they would take, made repeated studies of the photographs, and went over the detailed routine again and again.

Ultimately the sergeant looked up, grinned and said, 'It should be a piece of cake, sir.'

The Chief Constable of Suffolk had the morning papers spread over his desk. For most of them it was still not a big story. After all, nobody knew about the *Argus Viktor* and the missile threat. It was just some unexploded bombs found on the beach, and for their own safety people in the immediate neighbourhood had been evacuated. In the local *East Anglian Daily Times* it was naturally a bigger story, and there was an aerial photograph of the foreshore at Sizewell Gap, clearly taken from the helicopter that had appeared the previous afternoon. It carried the embarrassing headline, WHERE ARE THE BOMBS? There was one other aspect of the story that both Whitaker and the Chief Constable had overlooked, and that concerned the staff at Sizewell power station. If there was no threat to the power station, why was only a volunteer skeleton staff remaining?

'We shall have some explaining to do,' mumbled Whitaker, as he tapped out his pipe in the ashtray that the non-smoking Chief Constable had thoughtfully provided, 'if that missile is fired.'

Late the previous evening they had been informed of the Prime Minister's decision to send in the SBS, and Philip Grantham had prepared for their arrival that morning. They had also been warned by David Rackham that he would shortly be with them, and that they were to expect Hammond Acton.

'Most grateful,' Rackham had said to the Chief Constable, 'if you can just make him comfortable. There's nothing for him to do except wait for the arrival of his sister. She's being held on the ship,' he added, to the police chief's surprise.

'How the hell did she get there?' Grantham asked Whitaker.

The superintendent shifted his bulk in the chair, sighed. 'Presumably by courtesy of Karl Heinze, but there are things the Friends never tell us—blast them.'

The Chief Constable looked sympathetic.

At that moment a staccato tap on the door announced Rackham himself. He breezed in with, 'Good morning, Chief Constable, glorious morning. Hello, Arthur. Thought you'd be jogging a lovely morning like this.' Then turning to Grantham, he added, 'I'm David Rackham. Sorry to be a nuisance. Should all be over in twenty-four hours. SBS arrived?'

Grantham politely shook hands, told Rackham where Lieutenant West could be found, and decided, as his eyes quickly assessed his visitor, that there was probably a great deal more to Rackham than the bright and breezy manner suggested.

Whitaker swivelled round, and with a touch of indignation asked, 'How did the Acton girl get aboard?'

Rackham grinned. 'Ah, love will find a way, Arthur. Or held against her will.' Then by way of diversion he added, 'Have you got that Ward girl all tied up yet?'

'Cawston's working on it.'

'Not just theft you have to pin on her, you know. It's espionage, Arthur. Can you really prove it?'

Whitaker nodded. 'I hope so.' He was irritated. 'There are still some things I'd like to know. For example, who blew up that poor bloody waiter?'

'He's getting on all right.'

'I know. But who tried to kill him?'

'You can write that off, Arthur. We shan't get him. Diplomatic immunity, I shouldn't wonder. The work of one Herr Stoebel.'

Whitaker sighed, fished for his tobacco pouch again. 'Yes, and who forced *him* off the road?'

Rackham shrugged, and grinned. 'Don't worry your head. More important things today. Well, if I'm going to be on the briny tonight, I guess I'd better find Lieutenant West and his boys in black.' With that, and the afterthought, 'Thanks for everything, Chief Constable,' Rackham briskly let himself out.

★

With the men of the S B S David Rackham adopted a slightly different manner from the moment he extended his hand to the lieutenant and announced who he was.

'Sorry to be a nuisance,' he said. 'It's not my idea, but I have to be there.'

West looked at him with steel-cold eyes. 'Can you get up a rope—fast?'

'Yes. I shan't hold you up.'

'No. You'll be the last one.'

'That's all right. You won't have to wait for me.' Rackham offered the faintest of smiles.

West outlined the plan, and went over some of the details twice.

'That's good. It'll work.'

West would have been annoyed if Rackham had sounded condescending, but he hadn't. The words had been uttered as a simple statement of fact, and West appreciated that.

After they had chatted a little more and Rackham felt they were on familiar terms, he said firmly, 'There must be no killing tonight—not even Argus. And the girl has to be rescued. I shall have to be with you on the bridge—and when you take Argus.'

'Understood,' was all West said. After a few moments, however, he asked, 'What is the plan if they launch the missile before we get there—like this afternoon?'

'It's bloody disaster.'

'Is the operation still on?'

'No. The Prime Minister says the purpose of the operation is to prevent the missile being fired. He doesn't think the government can justify boarding a foreign vessel in international waters for any other reason. But I'm told he's still thinking about it. Justification? They fired the missile. We're entitled to capture the "Western terrorist" who did it. We'll be getting instructions—I hope.'

West nodded with a touch of impatience.

Rackham smiled. 'I've other reasons for wanting to be on that ship,' he said. 'Which reminds me, the girl's brother is coming here. I'd better see if he's arrived.'

West announced the time of the final briefing, and when they were to get into their kit. They would go to Sizewell Gap in a police van. That would excite no interest, and they would enter the water from the beach in the Gemini inflatable.

'See you later then,' said Rackham, and was out of the room before the lieutenant could reply.

Rackham found Hammond Acton in the room belonging to the superintendent in charge of communications. It looked out on to a group of silver birches hung with nesting boxes, and beyond were playing fields and heathland. Acton had been supplied with a cup of coffee and a handful of magazines.

'What the hell's going on here?' he asked immediately Rackham put his face round the door. 'Everyone's been very kind, but no one seems to know what's happening.'

'You've read the papers, old man. Unexploded bombs on Sizewell beach.'

'I've also seen this.' Hammond dangled the front page of the *East Anglian Daily Times*. 'Where are the bombs?' he asked. 'And what's this you told me about Sandra stuck on a ship with that bastard Heinze?'

Rackham became suddenly serious. 'There are no bombs, Hammond. We believe Heinze is planning to fire a missile —Russian, incidentally—at Sizewell power station. That was the meaning of Sandra's scribbled note in Rostock.'

'So we're just sitting here waiting for it to happen?'

'Steady on. It's highly secret, Hammond. Only the Chief Constable knows. We intend to stop it.'

'How?'

'A raiding party. Tonight.'

'And if they fire it before then?'

'That's the second time someone has asked that question this morning. But the short answer—at least until the Prime Minister makes up his mind—is: too bloody bad. I think Heinze would go for a night launch. Causes more panic.'

'He'll have heard the radio about unexploded bombs on the beach. He'll guess we know.'

'Perhaps, perhaps not. It only went out on local radio. Anyway, I reckon he'd be counting on traditional British reluctance to attack in international waters a foreign vessel that, on the face of it, is offering no threat whatever. In that event, he'd probably still choose the night.'

Hammond considered. 'And Sandra?'

'If the raiding party is a success, we shall bring her back. That's why I wanted you here.'

'I suppose she'll go straight into the cells?'

'Ah, I've been thinking about that. If only she'll co-operate a little bit more than she did in Rostock, we might be able to keep her out of those. That's where you come in—persuading her.'

'Anything. Tell me.'

'Well, only you and I know about the letter she wrote to you. So it—er, doesn't exist. She was made to go with Heinze under the most awful threats. That wouldn't be difficult to accept. Heinze is a ruthless international terrorist. So he forced her to go with him. Just as he forced her to write that letter to her school. And he's held her on the ship under duress.'

'What, sunbathing on the deck? I'd like to see that picture.'

Rackham grinned. 'Well, what alternative had she—with a creature like Heinze? And in spite of being held against her will, she bravely manages to smuggle a note to you bearing the one-word warning, SIZEWELL. But for that infor-mation, we would never have known anything about a missile threat. O K, we had pictures of the damn thing on the deck. But that in itself doesn't mean anything. A ship carrying arms is entitled to have a missile aboard. But Sandra's warning, plus our aerial surveillance, and the know-ledge that Heinze was aboard, have led us to the conclusion that Sizewell is being threatened. So, you see, the girl has acted quite courageously, not to say patriotically.'

Acton sighed with relief.

'Well, it's up to you, Hammond,' Rackham told him. 'If she won't go along with that story, then she's an accomplice. And she'll go down for quite a stretch.'

'But the police will want to question her first, won't they?'

'They know nothing about her relationship with Heinze. They have no idea that she hasn't been under duress. They're not unreasonable, Hammond. After her experience, I'm quite sure they're going to allow her to be comforted by her brother just as long as necessary, before they get down to any interrogation.'

Hammond gave his friend a worried but grateful smile. 'Thanks. I hope by tonight she'll have become disillusioned with that bastard. Is there anything else I can do here?'

'Don't think so. I'll introduce you to the Chief Constable, Philip Grantham—nice man. Come to think of it, a police version of you. Successful.' Rackham grinned. 'Good to make your number with him.'

Hammond nodded. 'What about Gillian, David?'

'I hope you weren't really thinking of marrying her.'

Hammond looked surprised and hurt. 'I just can't believe—'

'Sorry. Of course, she's still refusing to co-operate, but—'

'You mean it's all circumstantial? You might not be able to prove it?'

Rackham sighed. He would have liked to be able to save the girl. He wished she had got away in time. But it was his evidence that could easily convict her. It would make him feel a little less of a swine if he didn't have to use it, if the police could manage on their own.

'The circumstantial evidence, Hammond, is pretty convincing. She's been working for the Eastern bloc—either the East Germans or the Russians—for years. Since you began employing her, I should think. Until she starts to help it's hard to know how much she's given them. Of course she wasn't actually seen handing a package to Stoebel. But, at that stage, on the assumption that she had, the CIA tried to intervene—not very successfully.'

Hammond shook his head despairingly. 'The bloke in her flat?'

Rackham nodded.

'So thanks to her we've lost our beat on the Russians?'

'Perhaps. Perhaps not. We shall see.'

'Well, if we can save Sandra—David, we've got to, we've got to.'

'Sandra possibly. Gillian—no.'

★

In the middle of the afternoon a journalist listening to East German radio programmes at the B B C's monitoring station at Caversham heard the announcement that ruthless Western terrorists on board a G D R container ship, *Argus Viktor*, had forced the captain, at gun point, to drop anchor in the southern half of the North Sea. The report said that the ship was now under the total control of the terrorists, who were threatening to kill the captain and the entire crew unless their demands were met. The report, however, gave no indication of what those demands were supposed to be. It said that, at this stage, the nationality of the terrorists was not known, only that they came from one of the 'so-called Western democracies, probably America or Britain'. With naval forces of the German Democratic Republic close by, the report continued, there was no chance of the terrorists succeeding in their arms. Their triumph would be temporary.

The story was immediately flashed to the Foreign and Commonwealth Office, and within minutes the Prime Minister had it before him in the Cabinet Room at No. 10. It was also in the hands of David Rackham, Superintendent Whitaker and the Chief Constable of Suffolk.

After a suitable interval, the captain of *Southwold* signalled the captain of the East German *Leipzig* and offered any assistance in dealing with the terrorists who had taken over the *Argus Viktor*, adding, tongue in cheek, that it was in their mutual interest to prevent piracy of this kind.

Ultimately, from the German frigate came the curt response that no assistance was needed. They had the situation under control.

Rackham handed transcripts of the exchange to the Chief Constable. 'Very droll,' he remarked.

'How do you suppose the Germans plan to end it all anyway?'

'Oh, once the missile is fired, they'll take control of the ship, capture the "terrorists". In other words, they'll lift our friend Argus off to freedom in East Berlin.'

The Chief Constable looked up with sudden determination. 'I'm glad they won't get the chance,' he said.

★

Pictures transmitted to base, then to London and on to Suffolk, from the Coastal Command Nimrod still circling almost three miles above the North Sea, again confirmed that there was no sign of terrorist activity aboard the *Argus Viktor*. Indeed, through the windows of the bridge, the captain was seen in friendly conversation with Heinze.

In the early evening the Nimrod sent back pictures showing the sides of the forty-foot container collapsing to the deck. This was followed by pictures of the Styx missile in its container-launcher being swung to starboard and elevated to about forty-five degrees. There it remained, facing the Suffolk coast.

Lieutenant Gerry West still saw no point in starting his operation until darkness had fallen. If they were seen, he contended, it might precipitate the launching of the missile. Rackham agreed with him. The dials in the operations room at Martlesham Heath showed that the north-east wind was still veering to the east. Both men were gambling that Heinze would wait until it had moved as far east as was likely. According to the weather forecast that would be at least three hours after dark. They dared to hope that the advantage would lie with them.

The Prime Minister, the Foreign and Home Secretaries, the Defence Minister and the Lord Chancellor, were in the Cabinet Room together, when pictures of the readied missile came through. They exchanged anxious glances, and the Prime Minister said decisively, 'That decides it, don't you agree? Even if they launch the damn thing, we go in. There's still Argus, there's still the girl.'

His colleagues mumbled their assent.

The decision was received in Suffolk by Lieutenant West and David Rackham with relief.

When the Prime Minister reported on his scrambler telephone to the West German Chancellor, the latter said, 'Good, Lionel. We want Argus dealt with. We don't care who does it. Good luck.'

In Suffolk no traffic was being allowed to move within a three-mile radius of Sizewell power station. The standard plan for any Sizewell emergency allowed for the evacuation of everyone living in a mile-and-a-half radius of the power plant, but the Chief Constable was worried about the possibility of radioactive substances being carried on the wind to Leiston. It was only two and a half miles away. In spite of the standard plan, had the decision been his, he told Whitaker, he would have faced up to the wholesale evacuation of the town, but the Home Office had decided that 'evacuation was unlikely to be necessary'. CEGB experts advised that radiation would not be carried that far. The Chief Constable was not convinced. It was true that the dials in the operations room showed a windspeed of only a few miles an hour, but it was veering further to the east. He could envisage an almighty catastrophe with hundreds, perhaps thousands, dead. He had, of his own initiative, taken the precaution of alerting all doctors in the area and all hospitals to stand by for a severe emergency. He could not, however, warn them that what they might have to deal with were the effects of radiation. And that, he asserted to Whitaker, was a grossly irresponsible decision for the government to have taken.

In the circumstances, he did all he could. He made sure that the ambulance service was on full alert throughout the whole of East Suffolk. Moreover, with warnings of top secrecy, he spoke privately to a personal friend who was a leading consultant at Ipswich Hospital, and just hoped that he might be able to do something to ensure that the medical services were not taken completely unawares.

Finally, he telephoned his wife and told her to take the children with her to visit her sister in Bury St Edmunds. No, he couldn't tell her why, but it was important that she should.

Then he said to Whitaker with a grim smile, 'After the civil servants, there's just one more neck I'd like to wring. That little bastard, Argus.'

21

Half an hour before darkness Lieutenant Gerry West and the other nine members of the SBS, accompanied by David Rackham, loaded themselves into a dark blue police van. All the equipment had been carefully checked, the Gemini inflated. Rackham, like the rest of them, was garbed in a black rubber wet-suit, and his face was blacked. The lieutenant was armed with an Ingram MAC II, a light, short-barrelled weapon that can fire twenty rounds of 9mm bullets a second. The other two men detailed to take the bridge with him carried Heckler and Koch MP5s. Apart from the sergeant, who had an Ingram, so did the rest of the unit. Rackham, of course, was unarmed. Since it was very unlikely that any doors or hatches would be locked, West had decided it wasn't necessary to bring any pump-action shotguns, the favoured weapon for blowing hinges off doors.

The van was accompanied by one police car. For the last three miles the roads were deserted. One car, driven by a journalist, attempted to follow them, but within four miles of their destination it was stopped by the escorting police car and headed in the opposite direction.

The journey was made in silence. All the arrangements were completed. Every man, including Rackham, knew, minute by minute, what he had to do. There had been a discussion about whether, for the last part of the journey, kayaks should be used, or even whether the last mile should be swum, but West decided that the risk of them being spotted was so slight that this was unnecessary. For the final mile they would paddle the Gemini; until then, they would be within the shelter of *Southwold*. There would be no radio communication, because that might be detected. With the help of the circling Nimrod, *Southwold* would monitor the operation and decide when to call in the Sea King to lift them back to shore.

The police car stopped on the short cul-de-sac of Gap Road, behind the beach at Sizewell. The Vulcan Arms, which they had passed a few yards back, was quiet and in darkness. So were the few houses by the road. The only glimmer of light came from the great cube of Sizewell power station.

Between the road and the sea was a stretch of sand-scarred grass, followed by a slope of shingle, and then a narrow strip of wet sand. The equipment was unloaded and stowed, and the Gemini carried to the top of the shingle ridge, occupying a gap between two beached inshore fishing boats, each bearing an L T registration number. In the dim light Rackham could see the low shapes of a number of other boats. The sea shuffled on to the sand with a regular seething sound and the warm air had the tangy smell of weed and salt.

The stocky figure of Lieutenant West sat down beside him. 'Could be darker,' the marine said, 'but it'll have to do. We'll give it another ten minutes. If he's waiting for the most favourable launch time, we've still got the best part of three hours. That's luxury.'

It was twelve minutes later that West consulted his luminous watch, looked up at the thinnest sliver of moon, and said, 'All right, we'll go.'

The Gemini was manhandled to the water's edge, pushed into the ruffling sea, and then the eighteen-horse-power outboard motor jerked into life. The smaller-powered engine had been chosen because it made less noise and provided enough speed for their purpose, but Rackham was surprised how it seemed to roar into the stillness of the night.

West must have guessed his thoughts—he certainly couldn't see Rackham's expression—because he said, 'We've got *Southwold* between us. Even if they hear us, they won't see us. We're too low for their radar, and they would probably assume it was some activity connected with *Southwold*. Anyway, for the last mile we shall be completely silent and in this light well nigh invisible.'

He spoke with such authority that Rackham didn't for a moment doubt him.

The coxswain was taking his time, letting the inflatable surge forward slowly so that it scarcely made a white ripple of bow wave. Even so, the sleek grey shape of *Southwold* seemed rapidly to be getting closer.

For Sandra it had been a worrying day. From the moment that Heinze had found her by the rail he had been especially attentive, full of the assured charm that had first captivated her. For the first time she was aware of it more objectively. He didn't again mention the missile or his decision to launch it. She began to hope, as the day passed—the ship totally motionless as it sat anchored in the calm sea—that perhaps he would not do it after all. But if he hadn't issued the ultimatum—and she was sure he hadn't, or it would have been mentioned in the news on the radio—then he hadn't changed his mind either.

He smiled at her, told her that the light breeze brought roses to her cheeks and made her look even lovelier. She stared at him, trying to understand, but said nothing. She hadn't the emotional energy left to retaliate. He remained close to her all day, suggested that they sunbathe on the deck, even that they dive over the side for a swim. It was a pity not to on such a gorgeous day. She replied quietly that she didn't want to, and he said considerately, 'All right then, anything you like, darling.'

She stood by him in the bow of the ship, the stacked containers behind her, and the unmasked missile swung on its turntable and facing the distant Suffolk coast. And behind that the white superstructure of the bridge. He took her hand. It remained limp in his. He looked at her, puzzled. She looked back into his eyes, and could see nothing but her own reflection.

It was in that moment that, at last, she decided she hated him. She didn't feel afraid, though she knew she had every reason to be, at least not there in the sunlight on such a normal day. She might later, but she must not show it. She couldn't respond to him warmly any longer, but she could be polite, perhaps even manage to act naturally. That would help. She had no idea what she could do. Probably nothing. But she felt that something was demanded of her.

'When do we weigh anchor?' she asked. 'Is that what it's called?'

He even laughed. 'Yes. Later tonight.'

After the missile has been fired, she thought to herself, but she said only, 'And then?'

'I've told you the plan before.' Heinze wasn't going to be trapped into making promises that he hadn't the least intention of keeping. He had made his decision. He was leaving her on board. He didn't give a damn what happened to her. Through binoculars he could see the helicopter on the pad of the German frigate. That was for him.

Sandra looked at him, wondering what he was thinking, not daring to think about what on earth she was going to do in East Berlin. Perhaps, she thought desperately, Hammond and Rackham would be able to do something, if only they had guessed what 'Sizewell' meant.

By the time the pair of them sat down to an evening meal with Zendermann and Walther, Sandra was weary of the effort of making conversation. She sat in silence, picking at her food.

Zendermann grinned at her. 'What is the matter with Mrs Heinze tonight, eh? It can't be the sea. It is what they call a millpond.' He laughed.

'Perhaps I am tired,' she said.

'Ho—that is not a good sign,' he chortled, looking at Heinze.

Sandra ignored him. Karl said something to him in German, and the three men talked among themselves. She was unable even to catch the occasional word. She felt isolated.

For some time after the meal they remained in the captain's cabin, the three men drinking a German brandy. Sandra declined it, which gave Zendermann another opportunity for a ribald comment. It was dark by the time he got to his feet. Sandra thought he looked like a small bull with a grin.

'We go to the bridge now,' he said. 'To see the fun, eh? We get away soon.'

Sandra thought she would rather go to her cabin, but Karl took her firmly by the hand and she followed, having no alternative.

The bridge was spacious and light. The great expanse of glass in front and to port and starboard enclosed them in a blanket of darkness. Zendermann went over to the radar. Sandra, behind him, watched the scanning arm sweeping across the sea and, in the immediate neighbourhood, bleeping into existence only the German frigate and the British naval vessel that was between them and the shore.

Heinze looked at his watch, consulted the wind direction. 'It's not likely to get better than this,' he said.

The Gemini outboard was cut, and the inflatable glided close in the shelter of the grey side of the frigate *Southwold*. As they came round the stern, two men lifted stumpy paddles, and with scarcely a ripple sent the craft smoothly and silently towards the *Argus Viktor*. The rest of them, including Rackham, crouched as low as possible.

West had no real anxiety about being spotted by the container ship. There had been every sign that the master, officers and crew were behaving in a thoroughly relaxed way, and that the watch was not especially alert. Moreover, West knew that they were almost invisible on the water. The East German frigate, however, could be expected to have more sophisticated surveillance, and West was relying a good deal on the protection offered by the bulk of the container ship, which he was careful to keep between them.

Rackham saw West consulting his compass. An order was whispered to the coxswain. The Gemini veered direction slightly, and much sooner than Rackham had imagined, the hulk of the *Argus Viktor* loomed ahead of them. He breathed the salty air deeply. The breeze was blowing onshore and had freshened slightly, but not enough to roughen the water. It moved like the humped shapes of seals.

The coxswain brought the inflatable just under the starboard side of the stern, so they were completely hidden from the German frigate. For a few moments they remained still, hard in to the stationary ship. It was quiet but for the lap of water on the steel sides. Satisfied that they were unobserved, Lieutenant West gave the prearranged signal. Then everything that had been planned happened precisely in order, swiftly and silently.

The first man, clutching two magnetic grabs, rubber-fringed for silence, fastened the first one as high as he could reach on the stern of the ship, and hauled himself up. Then he reached over with the second grab. When that was firmly fastened his thumb flicked a switch on the first grab to release the magnetism that came from a powerful nickel-cadmium battery. In this way, positioning one grab above the other, he was flat on the deck in seconds. The rope that he had trailed from his waist was fastened securely to a hand-hold. In a few more seconds the rest of the team were also lying flat on the deck, and the rope was swinging in Rackham's hands as he hauled himself up the stern. As he clambered aboard, he was alone and briefly exposed. The two men who were to remain on the main deck were already crouched within the shelter of a container on the starboard side. They beckoned, and he crossed the space at a stooped run as fast as he could.

West and the two men who were going for the bridge were already huddled between the last group of containers and the white superstructure, waiting for him. The lieutenant, however, showed no sign of impatience as he joined them, merely giving him a nod.

West moved across the yard of space that separated him from the white steel door leading into the superstructure. As he had anticipated, it was unlocked. He pushed it open, indicating to Rackham something that it was quite unnecessary to point out to his colleagues—the raised sill of the door. He couldn't afford to have Rackham making even a rubberized clatter as he tripped over the entrance.

The eight of them were now in the passageway at the back of the superstructure. A companionway on the starboard side led upwards to other decks and the bridge; one on the port side led down to the engine room.

In no more than eight seconds they were all on B deck, and with something that looked like a stethoscope, West listened quickly at each door. Then, just as swiftly, they were up the next companionway to C deck. The same process was repeated.

On D deck where the captain and the first officer had their quarters, the sergeant and three other men were to remain to control the companionways to the decks below. Their role was quickly to silence anyone who came up to this level, and to prevent any access to the bridge. Thanks to his 'stethoscope', West had been able to determine electronically the exact position of everyone occupying quarters above the main deck.

It was time now to make his electronic surveillance of the bridge.

There were only the four of them on the bridge. Zendermann stood looking out into the dark distance, seeing nothing. Close by him, but with his back to the windows, was the first officer, Walther. Sandra stood near them, separated from Heinze by the tripod with its gyroscope, and the small ship's wheel. In front of them all was a control panel with various dials, visual displays, switches and buttons.

The only sound was the hum of the ship's electrics. Heinze half turned towards her with a faint smile. Her eyes were focusing on the row of buttons in front of him. This was it. He was really going to do it. Press one of those buttons and fire the thing—launch it with an almighty explosion into the core of the nuclear reactor. People were going to get killed. Some would die horribly. Hundreds, perhaps thousands, might die of radiation sickness. She felt weak, desperate.

Heinze examined the gyroscopically controlled laser target-designation, checked the reading. He looked up at her. 'Accurate to the second,' he said. 'It'll rip out the heart of that bloody reactor.'

She thought she was going to faint, gripped the edge of the panel in front of her and breathed deeply.

'Haven't you the stomach for it?' Heinze laughed, and moved back to his original position, a row of red buttons in front of him.

Sandra was staring at him, hypnotized by his hands as they seemed to hover over the small red discs on the control panel. She was no longer aware of either Zendermann or Walther, only Heinze, and the power of death in one finger.

'So this is it,' he said.

She gaped, her eyes staring, fixed. His right hand moved. A couple of phrases floated into her mind. 'As long as the gyroscope's in position it's deadly accurate' and 'It's fool-proof unless Captain Zendermann goes and falls on it'.

Sandra screamed as Heinze's finger pressed the button. She hurled her body at the tripod holding the gyroscope.

There was a sudden blast like rushing wind. The ship rocked.

'Bitch! You bloody fucking bitch!'

Sandra heard his shout, saw the gun drawn from his pocket, and then—there was a vivid flash, an ear-splitting explosion, hardly separated from the sound of automatic fire. Bullets were whining and tearing into the fabric of the ship.

It was all noise, confusion. Yet she had no time to wonder if she had been hit. Still with the sound of bullets snapping out of a machine-pistol, she was grabbed by the legs and dragged away.

Suddenly, she wasn't hearing any more. She was on the opposite side—the starboard side of the bridge—being held firmly by a man all in black with a blackened face. Then she saw Karl. He was also being held by a 'black' man, but far more securely, one arm twisted painfully up his back, and the barrel of a sub-machine gun stuffed into his ribs. A third similar figure was close by, sub-machine gun at his hip, covering the stunned and bemused Zendermann and Walther, who were cautiously picking themselves up from the floor. Standing slightly in front of her was the man who was obviously in charge. Like the others he was wearing a black rubber wet-suit, and held a gun in his hand.

She looked round nervously. Behind them all, unarmed, was another man. He grinned at her. She stared. He was still grinning. It was Rackham, she was sure it was. She could almost imagine his freckles beneath the blacking.

The man in charge was speaking. She could only hear him distantly.

'Do you understand English?' West asked, looking at the two men picking themselves up from the floor.

Zendermann nodded.

'No harm will come to you,' said West in a crisp tone that perhaps suggested disappointment. 'We are only interested in these two.' He jerked his head sideways at Heinze and Sandra.

The fourth man moved briskly across the bridge and checked that the captain and his chief officer were unarmed.

'Are any of your men armed?' West shouted.

Zendermann shook his head, and Walther muttered, 'No.'

'Good. But if they are and we have any trouble, we shall shoot to kill. Now, you'll stay here, Captain, until we've quit the ship. Understand?' Zendermann's eyes wandered towards the radio microphone. West nodded. The fourth man ripped it from the control panel. 'We don't want to hurt you, Captain,' West added.

Zendermann nodded again.

Sandra glanced sideways at Heinze. His face was fixed, expressionless, until he saw her looking at him. Then he turned his face towards her, his eyes, she thought, bright with hatred. But the missile—had she been too late, or could she have knocked it off course and, if so, what had happened?

Lieutenant West tilted his head, and they all preceded him down the companionway to D deck. There Rackham spoke for the first time. He touched Sandra's arm, and whispered light-heartedly, 'Your worries are over, darling.' Then he turned to Heinze. 'Argus!'

Heinze looked at him for the first time. He smiled, as though in recognition, and then quite deliberately nodded.

Rackham turned to Lieutenant West. 'Sorry, Lieutenant, we have to make a short visit to this bloke's cabin. Shan't be a moment. Where were you, Argus?'

'Here. Chief officer's billet.'

Still with the Heckler and Koch threatening his rib cage, Heinze led Rackham into the cabin. The rest of them remained outside.

Two minutes later Rackham returned carrying a package. The three men who had held D deck went ahead. There was the sound of shouts, threats and running. When they were all together again, the sergeant turned to West and said, 'Second mate and a couple of ratings, sir. They've been seen on their way. No harm done.'

On the main deck were three more wide-eyed ratings, who were gestured away by a threatening Heckler and Koch, and readily disappeared. They all moved towards the stern.

233

Rackham saw the sergeant looking skywards in the direction of *Southwold*, clearly privately cursing the delay. Then he moved over to Sandra again.

'Hammond's ashore,' he said quietly.

'Oh. What happened to the missile?'

'Don't know. Didn't hit the power station though.'

'How do you know?'

'Well, look. There'd be a bloody great fire if it had. No sign of anything.'

'Oh—thank God,' she breathed. Rackham looked at her, surprised. 'I threw myself on the gyro,' she said.

'Clever girl. That'll hold you in a lot of good stead.'

There at last was the sound of the whirling rotor blades of a helicopter. A searchlight snapped on to the rear landing pad.

'Jesus,' muttered the sergeant, 'that's no Sea King.'

Of the raiding party only Rackham and West did not seem surprised. The vortex of air swirled in Sandra's hair and sent flushes of cooler air on to their faces. The helicopter settled, its rotor blades still turning. It bore the markings of the German Democratic Republic. The Heckler and Kochs rose immediately to the hips of the S B S men as they took up firing positions, ready to fight their way out.

'No,' snapped Lieutenant West. 'Hold fire. Don't fire, unless I order it.'

He turned inquiringly towards Rackham. The S I S man nodded. West said between his teeth, 'This really goes against the grain.' Then he turned to his men and snapped, 'Release Argus.'

For a moment nothing happened. The man who had the sub-machine gun pressed into Heinze's ribs stayed like that.

'Sorry,' shouted West. 'I ordered, release Argus.'

The gun was lowered. Heinze walked erect, almost debonair, into the pool of brilliant light that surrounded the aircraft. As he got close to the open door, the sergeant could restrain himself no longer.

'We're not letting that bastard escape, sir?' He lifted his gun so that it covered the departing figure.

Rackham could almost feel the *frisson*, that ran through the squad. He wouldn't have been surprised to hear a sudden burst of fire rip into the side of the helicopter as Heinze stepped aboard. They were uneasy. It went against all their training.

The sergeant shouted again, 'Not that bastard, sir?'

'Yes, Sergeant. That's the order. He goes. I don't understand it either. But orders are orders. Understand?'

Heinze was already stepping into the aircraft. He paused in the open doorway, turned directly towards Rackham, and waved.

'Jesus!' groaned the sergeant.

They had all been so preoccupied with Heinze that none had noticed the sound of the wide-circling Sea King. Once the German machine had lifted off, the larger Sea King roared in towards the stern of the ship. Leaving nothing to chance, it switched on its own bright landing lights.

Again draughts of air swirled about them as the aircraft shuffled itself down on to the landing pad. Training took over, and in seconds the whole squad were aboard, Sandra and Rackham preceding them. As a precaution, two men crouched near the open door, their sub-machine guns in a firing position. Nothing happened. The *Argus Viktor*'s own searchlight went out, the Sea King veered away and headed for the Suffolk coast. Sandra reached out and clasped Rackham's hand.

22

The Sea King crossed the coast at Aldeburgh, headed inland over Tunstall Forest and Rendlesham Forest and then, as it came in low towards Martlesham, Rackham glimpsed the grey flickering shape of the River Deben beneath them. Soon after, he saw the cube of light that was the headquarters of the Suffolk Constabulary. The helicopter swung round, hovered, and settled on the front lawn. Sandra was still holding on to him as they ran, bent double, towards the projecting canopy of the police HQ.

The Chief Constable, in spite of his lack of sleep as alert as ever, led them briskly to the debriefing room. This was his territory, and he was in charge. Beside him stood the bulky figure of Superintendent Whitaker. He was looking impatiently at the group as it assembled. Philip Grantham sensed his impatience, and then, almost simultaneously they asked, 'Argus—where is he?'

The Chief Constable's eyes flicked from face to face. West and Rackham turned and looked at each other silently, and then Rackham, with an embarrassed cough, said, 'I'm afraid he—er, got away.'

There was a momentary, disbelieving silence, and then Whitaker exploded.

'He—*what?* Bloody impossible. You—god almighty!'

'There was no alternative.' Rackham's voice was quiet, and he tried to sound authoritative. It was difficult, garbed from head to foot in black, and his face all smudged.

'Of course,' he continued, 'Lieutenant West and the boys could have had him in the bag in seconds, but it would have meant firing on an East German helicopter. We had no authority for that. In fact, we had the Prime Minister's specific instructions not to.'

The marine sergeant shifted and made a quiet, grumbling

sound, but West, who obviously saw no reason why when they had Heinze in their hands they could not have kept him, nevertheless added loyally, and yet with unmistakable disapproval, 'There was, unfortunately, no alternative, sir.'

Both senior policemen looked stunned, and totally unconvinced. Whitaker muttered accusingly, 'Armed to the bloody teeth, and you couldn't—it's unbelievable.' His tone changed to scorn. 'Oh, the Prime Minister is going to be pleased, isn't he? His crack men letting that bugger go. I don't envy you having to tell him. And how's he going to tell the West German Chancellor?'

Rackham found it a little difficult not to succumb to the humour of the situation, but managed to maintain a quietly serious air.

'I think Sir Dick Randle will be able to explain it satisfactorily,' he said. Later, and privately, he would give the two police officers a full explanation. Lieutenant West, however, would have to be content with the inexplicable decisions of the wretched politicians. Rackham added, further to exonerate West and his men, 'Argus was picked up by an East German helicopter. We could have shot at the helicopter and prevented the pick-up, but that was strictly against orders. We could have shot Argus himself. That was also against orders. He's wanted alive.'

'Or,' said Whitaker irritably, 'you could have simply held on to him, and told the Jerries to bugger off.'

It was obvious that Rackham should have known Whitaker would jump on that one. And there wasn't an answer. He was forced to resort to, 'Well, it wasn't quite like that. I'll be able to explain it to you, Superintendent, later.'

Whitaker shrugged impatiently, but had recognized the significance of Rackham's remark. The Chief Constable thought he had, too, and immediately resumed charge.

'The missile was launched,' he said, 'but it was fortunately a long way off target. It came down about two miles south of Sizewell, and went slap into the middle of an area known as The Fens, just behind Thorpeness. It threw up a lot of water, mud and stuff, and made a damn great crater. Apart from that it did no damage.'

Before anyone could say anything, Rackham cut in, 'Ah,

we have to thank this young lady for that. Miss Acton, who was abducted and held against her will by Heinze, did a very brave thing. The missile was targeted by a laser beam, and the targeting, which could have been completely accurate, was controlled gyroscopically, so that any movement of the ship would not affect it. The only way of upsetting it was to upset the gyroscope itself. Miss Acton did this by simply hurling herself at it. That threw the targeting designation awry, and explains why the missile fell where it did. As Lieutenant West and his men burst on to the bridge, Heinze was about to shoot Miss Acton. She behaved very courageously.' Rackham suddenly realized that she was still holding his hand, and he looked down at it slightly self-consciously.

Sandra said nothing. She was still too stunned to speak.

The debriefing continued briskly with an account of the boarding of the ship, the entry to the bridge with stun grenades and automatic fire above the heads of Heinze and the rest of them, and the rescue of Sandra Acton.

Finally, the Chief Constable announced that he had prepared a press statement which said that unexploded bombs on the beach had been defused and removed. He proposed that they should take up the East German story about the *Argus Viktor* being held by terrorists as a completely different and unrelated story. Somehow or other—presumably during a struggle between the G D R authorities and the terrorists on board—a missile had been accidentally fired. Fortunately it had done no damage—and so on.

Rackham doubted if they would get away with it, but agreed it was worth a try. But not yet. The press could be kept waiting long enough to miss the last editions. Give the police, and the government, a little more time to think. In any event, the press release would also have to be agreed with 10 Downing Street.

Taking advantage of a pause in the proceedings, Rackham suggested that, before they began their interrogation of Miss Acton, perhaps she could be allowed to see her brother.

'Of course,' said the Chief Constable. 'There's no desperate hurry to begin our questioning. The important thing is that she's safely released.'

Rackham nodded, thanked him and led Sandra away.

Hammond was sitting in an armchair, drinking coffee and looking drowsy. He almost spilt it as he jumped to his feet when she preceded Rackham into the room.

Sandra ran to him, and for several seconds clung to him. Her main feeling was of relief, compounded by exhaustion. She could, perhaps, have cried, but somehow didn't want to. She was grateful—to her brother, to Rackham. She wanted to show that gratitude with a certain personal strength. She had, after all, been incredibly stupid. As she broke away from him and they looked at each other, she muttered, only just audibly, 'Sorry. I'm sorry, Hammond.'

He patted her arm. 'It's over,' he said. Then he looked up, saw Rackham, and burst into laughter. 'Good grief, you only need a forked tail to be the devil himself.'

Rackham grinned. 'Yes, it's time I got out of this gear.'

'What happened?

Briefly Rackham gave an account of the whole operation.

'And you mean to say Argus got away? I can't believe it.'

'Nor can Superintendent Whitaker.'

Before Rackham could continue, Sandra interrupted. 'What's going to happen?' she asked. 'I mean—' She looked blank, suddenly miserable. 'Oh god, I suppose I'm a terrorist. I expect—'

'Not so fast,' Rackham interrupted. 'Don't start supposing anything yet. I'm going to leave you with Hammond, and get out of this black skin. Perhaps if you listen to him, this time—' Rackham uttered the words gently, trying to keep any suggestion of accusation out of his voice. 'Well, remember, too, the Chief Constable knows how courageously you have behaved—under threat, liable to be shot, throwing the missile off course, and preventing what might have been a hell of a disaster. Hardly the act of a terrorist, is it? As I say, you listen to your brother Hammond, hey?'

Rackham turned to go. 'Oh, I nearly forgot,' he added with mock seriousness. 'I've got this for you.' He held out the package that he had been clutching to his side ever since he returned from the *Argus Viktor*.

'What—?' Hammond took it. 'My god, it's—'

'Yes, it's your guidance system.'

Both Hammond and his sister looked incredulous. 'But,' Hammond stuttered, 'I don't understand. Where did you—? I mean, how'd you get it?'

Rackham grinned. 'From Argus,' he said. 'That's why he was allowed to escape. It was part of the deal. He would retrieve the guidance system from East Germany and, in return, we'd let him go. I hoped I might collect it in Rostock. That's why I searched his room. When I discovered it wasn't there I admit I didn't know how he was going to get it back to me. I had no idea, of course, that he was planning a missile attack on Sizewell. Still, I guessed that somehow he would manage to deliver the package. That was his problem. But that was the deal. No payment unless it was returned. And the payment, Hammond, was a big one.'

'You—you trusted him?'

Rackham nodded. 'He was a double agent. Double double, for that matter. Work for anyone if the money was right. But—a deal is a deal.'

Both Sandra and Hammond were staring at him in astonishment.

'Mind you,' he smiled, 'I'm glad I'm not the one who has to tell the Prime Minister.'